NEW PLANET
NEW WORLD

A Novel

Always Maggie,

Ian

November, 2016

Ian Prattis

Manor House

Library and Archives Canada Cataloguing in Publication

Prattis, J. Ian, 1942-, author
   New planet, new world : a novel / Ian Prattis.

ISBN 978-1-988058-16-0 (hardback).

--ISBN 978-1-988058-15-3 (paperback)

   I. Title.

PS8631.R39N48 2016
   C813'.6   C2016-904810-1

Printed and bound in Canada / First Edition.
Cover design-layout / Interior layout: Michael Davie
288 pages. All rights reserved.
Published Oct. 1, 2016
Manor House Publishing Inc.
452 Cottingham Crescent, Ancaster, ON, L9G 3V6
www.manor-house.biz (905) 648-2193

"This project has been made possible [in part] by the Government of Canada. «
Ce projet a été rendu possible [en partie] grâce au gouvernement du Canada."

Funded by the Government of Canada
Financé par le gouvernement du Canada

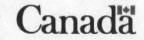

For Those Who Dare To Dream

PUBLICATIONS BY DR. IAN PRATTIS

- New Directions in Economic Anthropology. Special Edition of the Canadian Review of Sociology and Anthropology, August 1973

- Leadership and Ethics

- Reflections: The Anthropological Muse

- Anthropology at the Edge: Essays on Culture, Symbol and Consciousness

- The Essential Spiral: Ecology and Consciousness After 9/11

- Failsafe: Saving The Earth From Ourselves

- Earth My Body, Water My Blood

- Song of Silence

- Redemption

- Trailing Sky Six Feathers

- Eight eBooks on Amazon Kindle

- 2 CD's

- 2 DVD's

- 4 films

- 8 Professional Honors

- 20 Consulting projects

- 10 Scientific and technical reports

- 100 professional articles/chapters/book reviews published

- 26 Electronic publications of television courses broadcast at Carleton University and by TVO

- 50 articles in Pine Gate – Online Buddhist Journal

- 200 articles in newspapers, community magazines

- 25 Working Papers

PRAISE FOR NEW PLANET, NEW WORLD

- **Virginia Minchkin**, poet:

  "This work is exquisite. Colours, movement, confusion, overlap, confrontation, visceral interpretation of connectedness – these are the words *'New Planet, New World'* bring up for me. ...the last book in a trilogy, bringing the vibrancy, violence, cataclysms, and expansive growth of the characters' experiences on different planets, back full circle to share in the humanity of hope for us all!"

- **Julia Ann Charpentier**, Literary Critic:

  "Ian Prattis' admirable command of language brings to every scene a striking visual clarity."

- **Joslyn Wolfe,** Editor: *Focus on Women Magazine*:

  "Ian Prattis has been gifted with the ability to move, encourage and inspire others through his books. He writes about ethics, religion, personal experiences, spirituality, transformation and excels at the task. It is time to celebrate his many accomplishments with this recent literary masterpiece."

- **Maggie McLeod,** Artist:

  "I am deeply honoured to see part of this journey...What Ian Prattis has already done for this world and what he continues to do with this book provides a sense of relief and gratitude not only to me but for anyone who turns the pages of this epic work."

- **Camila Reimers,** Chilean-Canadian author:

  "Ian Prattis is a master storyteller. His writing style reminds me of Magical Realism used in Latino American literature, where there is magic in the rational world and there is no lineal time, the characters live in a circle where past, present and future happen simultaneously. At this time of turmoil the message of hope that Ian has to offer is very much needed by new and old generations."

- **John Lundin,** author of The New Mandala - Eastern Wisdom for Western Living, written with the Dalai Lama, and Journey to the Heart of the World, written with the indigenous elders of la Sierra Nevada in Colombia:

  "In his new book, *New Planet, New World*, author Ian Prattis shares a compelling futuristic Hero's Journey of hope for humanity. And he offers an age-old prescription for bringing about the realization of that hope: the cultivation of love, the mainspring for authentic and responsible living, as taught by the elders of all spiritual cultures throughout history. This book is a wisdom teaching of its own, with the past informing a hope for the future."

- **Rabia Wilcox,** Counsellor:

  "Ian Prattis has created a magnificent journey through time and space - dimensions too - in sacred ways of honouring all peoples, their ancestors, future generations and the kindly power of Nature. The acts of generosity, the authentic responsibility explored and experienced throughout this book nourishes my body, mind and spirit."

- **Anita Rizvi,** Therapist:

"New Planet, New World" is a powerful novel which explores an alternative to the destructive path civilisation is presently on. The intricacy of many themes keeps the reader engaged with brilliant writing that is exciting, tender, engaging and thoughtful. The underlying message is the fostering of love as the basic philosophy for the future. Most arresting is the fiery rant by Dr. Tom Hagen at the UN in 2080 addressing the stubborn refusal of governments and corporations immersed in the oil/carbon complex to take heed. The relationship between Catriona and Rising Moon is particularly moving. We observe two young women from different worlds coming together to create a haven for young people, placing their safety above ego fostering. Through these characters, we consider how any two nations can apply similar principles while civilisation still has the chance. The battle with jihadists is riveting and difficult to bear, but even here compassion prevails.

This futuristic novel combines science with Pope Francis' Encyclical and strong warnings regarding the disregard by carbon cabal leaders. Tolstoy's assertion of love as the basis for proper living pulsates as an undercurrent throughout each chapter. Dr. Prattis succeeds in offering us a gift of hope in troubled times via the presentation of a new way of living based on ecology, respect and compassion. "New Planet, New World" not only is one of the most important books of 2016; it is a wake-up call for all of humanity. Ian Prattis' writing moves me... a visionary sent from God to our troubled world."

- **Lynn Ross Adamson-Malelli,** photographer:

"In this original and surprising plot twist, the final book of this trilogy leaps into the near future. This future does not exist as a separate chronological entity, it is simply part of the eternal 'now', the 'now' that requires mindfulness. We learn through the twists and turns of the individual stories that the spirit of this Mother Earth is in all of us, at all times, wherever we are in the universe. The trilogy as a whole guides us from one man's macrocosm, through the connectedness of spirit throughout time and out into the expanse of the universal macrocosm."

- **Eleanor Aronoff,** Reiki Master:

"The stories in the trilogy are diverse and very human tales that touch deeply into the emotional heart. The beautiful and evocative writing brilliantly weaves the stories together, carrying us along as we evolve with the author, learning what it truly means to be human. This final book completes the journey that has taken us across great distances of time and space while also keeping us rooted firmly in our hearts. I highly recommend *New Planet, New World*. Not only is it an inspirational and heartfelt story, it is a magnificent adventure to savour and enjoy."

TABLE OF CONTENTS

Acknowledgements

New Planet, New World owes a huge debt to characters drawn from my last two books. Rising Moon, daughter of *Trailing Sky Six Feathers*, arrives from the eighteenth century to a new earth-like planet in a nearby galaxy. From my book *Redemption,* Dr. Tom Hagen, his wife Sian and daughter Catriona arrive from the twenty first century to the same planet. They are on board a failing spaceship in the near future, yet escape safely. In the prior two books these four characters played minor roles in the narrative. In this final book of the trilogy they stand front and center, almost as though they are demanding to stand in the light. They seem to open up by their own volition to an adventure forward in time from the present.

Critical eyes on earlier drafts were generously offered by Carolyn Hill, Terri Letemplier, Lee Grigas and Lynn Adamson-Malelli. I appreciated the Testimonials from poet Virginia Minchkin, literary critic Julia Charpentier, Joslyn Wolfe editor, artist Maggie McLeod, counsellor Rabia Wilcox, therapist Anita Rizvi, photographer Lynn Adamson-Malelli, and authors Camila Reimers and John Lundin. The extensive research required for this work was enhanced by the expertise of Dr. Kimberley Brayman, Professor Koozma Tarasoff, Ute Webb, Camila Reimers and Nerys Parry. I also wish to thank my editors Lisa Fugard and the publisher's Michael Davie. Their critical editing eyes enhanced the work beyond measure.

PROLOGUE: Chronicles of Awakening

Book One: Redemption

Book Two: Trailing Sky Six Feathers

Book Three: New Planet, New World

New Planet, New World is the final book of a trilogy. The first book *Redemption* was a lost manuscript, first written in 1975. I rediscovered this heartfelt book in 2011. The narrative was vivified with hindsight from my writer's eye forty years later. The story is an allegory for life difficulties I experienced at that time. I was a real mess, yet despite my desperate state of mind this novel about Awakening emerged.

Redemption is set in The Hebrides, islands off the northwest coast of Scotland, with startling cycles of maturing and downfall of the epic character, Callum Mor. He was a gifted child, master mariner and derelict drunk, who eventually gains wisdom from a hard life's journey. He enters the dark zone of alcoholism and withdraws from society. With only his animals keeping him this side of sanity, he survives in a bleak solitude. Laced with grim humor, the novel has nature's harsh and beautiful rhapsody as the background for tragic human failings; violence, power, murder, rape and madness.

The failings are ultimately topped by the triumph of the human spirit. A family with a young girl seeks refuge from a storm at his house and slowly Callum Mor steps away from self-destruction to an astonishing awareness that triumphs over his tragedies. He saves the girl's life in a blizzard and the glimmer of awakening dawns in him to set the stage for the final drama that illustrates the resilience of the human spirit.

Redemption is a deeply moving tale of desolation, love, loss, transformation and hope. It reads like an extended prose poem reflecting the primal forces of nature and of human nature. Its starkly gorgeous and remote island setting creates and reinforces the central themes of struggle, family, community and wonder at the beauty of the world. The rich cast of characters offers numerous gripping interludes that brim with interpersonal drama. The story centres on and is always connected to Callum Mor, but he is surrounded and influenced by a fantastic cast of family and fellow islanders. They provide a deep well of material as their conflicts and intrigues move the plot forward and offer a vast array of powerfully emotional moments. The story arcs of other characters in the novel offer intriguing counterpoints to one another and to Callum Mor. Their hopes, desires and difficulties intermingle in a tumultuous tapestry of human existence.

The narrative tone, generally quiet and introspective, is often punctuated by storms both literal and metaphorical. Loaded with the symbolism often found in parables, *Redemption* alludes to more than what is openly stated. Every scene provides a striking visual clarity that mystically slips into the realm of timeless storytelling. All of this provokes the tapestry for deeper, more subtle messages of compassion and faith to carefully unfold. From the rhapsody of an idyllic childhood through traumatic tragedies to the derelict zone of alcoholism and then a state of awakening, I depict the stations of a personal Calvary that ultimately leads to *Redemption*.

Dr. Tom Hagen, his wife Sian and daughter Catriona comprise the family taking refuge at Callum Mor's house. They are writ large in the final book. I place them in *New*

Planet, New World in the near future of 2080. Dr. Hagen becomes the chef-de-mission of the International Space Agency mission to settle on a planet in a nearby galaxy. Tom, Sian and Catriona move from a minor key in Book One to a massive symphony in Book Three, as their characters fill *New Planet, New World* to the brim.

Book Two of the trilogy, *Trailing Sky Six Feathers,* is a Hero's Journey as if Indiana Jones meets the Buddha with a dash of Celestine Prophecy. Shamanic healing of childhood sexual abuse, guru training and near death experience in an Indian ashram has this author stumbling through the first part of life, then standing strong in his own sovereignty in the latter part. Past life memories collide head on with the present, all thanks to the persistence of Trailing Sky, the Muse who refused to give up on me. Karma is reversed, the internal battles are over as the author begins to live life as a Meditation for Gaia. The relentless shadowing by this engaging Muse brings understanding not only to me, but to anyone engaged in overcoming the darkness of their past.

With a voice steeped in authentic experience, I navigate past and present lives over four centuries; from brutal raids on Indian settlements in 18th century Arizona, insane sea voyages off the Scottish Hebrides in the 20th century, to a decisive life moment of surrender to the Muse in the 21st century. These screenplay-worthy epic tales weave seamlessly to create inspiration for a wide range of fellow spiritual seekers. The genre is legend mixed with autobiography. Trailing Sky initiates a dream vision in 2008 that caps my slow process of remembering a clear mosaic of experiences stretching back in time over four centuries. Over a period of thirty years (1980 - 2010) four extraordinary mentors enhance this process of remembering for me, while Trailing Sky waits patiently from the distant

13

past. I learn how to reconfigure my understanding of time, place, consciousness and Carl Jung's psychology.

When I talk to folk about Book Two, the first question is usually, "Why did you write this book?" I reply, "Global Citizens are staring into the abyss yet instead of being eaten up by it all I say to you 'Awaken Spiritually.' That changes everything. We have made our world an unpredictable beast because we fail to work with it intelligently. Rumi's wise words are cogent, 'Sit down and be quiet. You are drunk and standing on the edge of the roof.' We have to take back control of ourselves and this is a spiritual matter. Turning on the switch of awakening seems to be a good idea right now. We just need to touch the sacred in ordinary experiences of life to find the courage, skill and determination to transform. I wrote *Trailing Sky Six Feathers* to shed light on issues that will affect our world for generations to come. The example of my own challenging journey and personal transformation illuminates one path to inspire others to choose their way to expand consciousness and chart the course for a future beyond the abyss. The human race does not need to be stuck with maladaptive options and patterns. We can and must transform. The key to change this deep freeze is Awakening, a spiritual relationship with self and Mother Earth."

Our industrial growth civilization is a system devouring itself, dislocating the organic structures of Mother Earth to the point that all species, not just our own, are at risk. It has taken us to a dangerous precipice. From there we stare into the abyss of climate change, ecosystem and financial collapse, ISIL, resource wars, cyberbullying, terrorism and anarchy. The two main characters that open the book in 18th century Arizona are Trailing Sky Six Feathers and Eagle Speaker. When the reader encounters Trailing Sky Six Feathers, my Muse from the past, they encounter a powerful, relentless woman who transforms my life in reality in the 21st century, not in historical fiction. She has been described as one of the most powerful woman in modern Canadian literature. Eagle Speaker is her husband and also my transformation vehicle. He dies cradled in her arms in a medicine wheel in the year 1777. As he takes his last breath Trailing Sky whispers to him, "I will find you. I will find you." She assures her daughter, Rising Moon, that she too will find him. Rising Moon has a minor role in Book Two, yet by transferring her to the new planet in the final book, *New Planet, New World,* I bring the 18th century to collide with the 21st century. Time, culture, space and consciousness are fused across centuries to create the final book of the trilogy.

New Planet, New World provides a counterpoint to the demise of modern civilization. I chart a Beginning Anew for humanity, a communal Hero's Journey to reconstruct society based on ecology, caring and sharing, as power elites ignore their complicity in the destruction of life on Planet Earth. This adventure is not without risk or cost. The clash of centuries opens Chapter One with a lyrical and dangerous meeting on a distant planet later this century. The protagonists are from different centuries and cultures. From the 18th century Rising Moon is hurled by shamanic means to Planet Horizon in a nearby galaxy. From the 21st century Catriona gets there from a failing spaceship in an escape craft. Catriona is taken prisoner but fights back screaming, "I am not your enemy." Instead of killing one another the two young women choose to be blood sisters and embrace survival, accepting nature as their Matriarch. This fragile thread is challenged by the brutal abduction and rape of a main character, Sian the Celtic seer. Her inner strength, of being more than a violated body, inspires the community of pioneers who escape safely from the damaged spaceship. They create a

15

communal structure of living and carve out a home and presence on the new planet.

Four Hopi Sacred Keepers offer their lives in a ceremony to enable renewal on a distant planet that none of them will experience. Mysticism combines with hi-tech to enable a Transfer Particle to seed the new planet and establish settlements. The expansion of communities is interrupted by a jihadist attempt to take over. A terrorist cell on Earth hijacks a spaceship and imperils the lives of the pioneers, who respond with tactical violence to kill them. The stark violence of survival prepares a backcloth for three distinct love stories to emerge. Ethical settlements grow as a mirror for Tolstoy's vision of "people of the twenty fifth century" – ahead of their time. The dark episodes and lyrical passages move the story along with action, fear, resolution, death, execution, rape, bravery and exile in a futuristic opportunity for humanity.

This action packed book of intertwining plotlines arc into the epiphany of the final chapter (Thirteen), which muses about human survival anywhere. This end game is a philosophy for the future. The inclusiveness of science combines with Tolstoy's vision, Pope Francis' Climate Change Encyclical and not repeating the mistakes of the carbon cabal. The underlying message is from Tolstoy, the 'Conscience of Humanity.' He described humanity's bottom line as the cultivation of love, the mainspring for authentic and responsible living. I do not present this as idealism, rather as down to earth wisdom. That is why I wrote this futuristic novel that takes place in the near future. It is the final book of "Chronicles of Awakening."

The reader now begins to anticipate and harkens to the rip tides of this futuristic novel.

1: Catriona and Rising Moon

In the minutes before the spaceship blew up, Catriona tried to resist her father's entreaties to leave him and her mother on spaceship PRIME 3.

The spaceship was disintegrating in the dense stratosphere of the new planet they were heading towards.

Catriona's father, Tom Hagen, had carefully strapped her into the sleek escape craft, well equipped for survival. Her mother Sian Hagen adjusted the oxygen mask on her daughter's face and placed Catriona's precious violin case in her arms.

Her father put a slim metal box next to her body and murmured that this was a new tool for her lonely journey.

"Catriona, you must live," he said firmly.

Just before they authorized the ejection protocol she heard her mother's tremulous voice whisper: "Remember everything we taught you. Live my child."

Then, her escape craft sped away from the failing spaceship. Through the small window she saw the explosion of the spaceship that had been home for her three-month journey from Planet Earth. She closed her eyes tightly shut after seeing the destruction of the spaceship.

Her heart was breaking as her escape craft sped through the stratosphere before descent parachutes opened to slow it down. She felt the splash down and rocking motion of waves. She scanned her tense body, concentrating on her breathing as she uncurled her clenched fists, stretched her fingers and opened her closed eyelids. She flexed her muscles up and down her body several times.

She whispered to herself: "If only my parents are still living is this worthwhile." Her voice resonated with deep sadness.

As instructed in training for this emergency, she opened the hatch above her chest and pulled in the two large white parachutes, stowing them in the empty compartment below her feet.

Like a robot she muttered, "I must live. I must live," echoing the last words from her parents.

She had a moment of hesitation before removing the oxygen mask from her face and gulped in fresh morning air. Doubting the atmosphere, she discovered that it was similar to that of Planet Earth – just as she had been told.

Catriona unstrapped herself and started the motor. The escape craft also functioned as a small enclosed boat. She sat up and looked out through the open hatch for signs of land, navigating to the nearest point she could see. She set course for a quiet, tree fringed bay with soaring rock bluffs at one end and forested sloping hills at the other. She noticed birds flying from the rocks at her intrusion, as she guided her small craft to settle on a sandy beach. Catriona stepped ashore and pulled her craft up onto the sand so it was safe.

She looked around for combustible material to build a fire, while her mind deeply grieved the loss of her parents. There was an abundance of dry, weathered wood on the sandy beach. Catriona quickly gathered a clumsy pile and ignited it with her small hand laser. Then she consumed the emergency landing rations – protein, liquid and sedative. She followed all the necessary protocols as the wood caught fire. Then the shock hit her. She was shaking uncontrollably, frightened and at a total loss. Catriona sat weeping next to the bonfire. Tears splashed on her delicate hands, leaving wet blotches on her grey space tunic. Her sobs were accompanied by the gentle lapping of the lake, as it washed ashore driven by wind.

She felt a presence close by and turned around.

A young woman wearing an embroidered buckskin dress and calf length laced moccasins was standing there with her bow pulled back, an arrow pointed right at the middle of her chest. She gasped at the stern yet beautiful face, noticing a cut on the woman's forehead and a long braid of black hair hanging loosely at the front. She took everything in about this fierce apparition who clearly meant her harm. She watched the woman carefully approach closer, one silent foot after the other, the arrow unwavering from its destination. The woman had a long knife in a sheath at her embroidered belt. Her deep dark eyes pierced right into Catriona. She had not been on the spaceship.

Catriona summoned all her courage, abandoning her shock and grief. Her voice quivered, "Who are you? Where did you come from? How are you here?" Her cry echoed through the deadly silence.

In halting English the strange woman replied tersely, "Why you need to know?"

There was a fierce edge to her words. The stranger's eyes glared steadily at the young red-haired, blue-eyed woman dressed in a body tunic from neck to feet. She noticed the tear-streaked face and the strange craft pulled up on the shore.

Catriona bravely stood her ground though her hands were shaking. She stepped forward and in an instant the intruder lowered her bow and swiftly threw a lariat so the noose settled around Catriona's neck. With a sharp jerk Catriona went face first into the sand. Her assailant quickly bound her hands behind her back with a leather strap from her belt. She then jerked Catriona upright and they were face to face.

Catriona's deep blue eyes blazed with anger. She was suddenly alert and yelled into the woman's face, "I am not your enemy. We may be the only two people on this planet and you choose stupidity."

Then Catriona head-butted the dark eyed woman on the bridge of her nose, just as she had learned in martial arts training aboard the spaceship. As the woman stumbled back, Catriona with her hands still tied behind her back, pivoted on her left foot and landed a perfect round house kick to the side of her assailant's head with her right foot, followed by a swift side kick into her ribs.

Catriona's onslaught briefly caught the woman by surprise yet once again she faced an arrow aimed right at her heart. Catriona saw the woman pull the bowstring back and stared into dark angry eyes.

Time stood still, then the woman's eyes suddenly changed and her mouth fell open. She had heard her mother's voice speaking inside her mind to put the bow down. She felt the weight of her mother's hand lower the bow. The two young women were both breathing heavily. The fire leaped in flames as it caught the adjacent logs. There was only a ripple of air across the lake. Both women were indifferent to the morning's layered colors spreading across the lake and into the sky.

Out of the mouth of the intruder came the words, harshly spoken, "My mother's spirit does not permit me to kill you. She tells me that I am not your enemy." She had also been told by her mother's inner voice that this woman was a blood sister for her, yet made no reference to that intense guidance. She dropped her bow on the sand, released the lariat around Catriona's throat and untied her bound hands. They looked deeply into the eyes of the other, searching for violence and harm. Neither could find any. They stood by that gentle lake, starkly silent until their breathing calmed.

Catriona was the first to speak: "I thank the spirit of your mother for saving my life." She trembled at still being alive. Overwhelmed at that moment by the loss of her mother and father, she started to cry. Deep sobs surfaced as she dropped to her knees. The woman awkwardly raised her up yet held her gently as Catriona's grief came pouring out. They stood like that for a long time, allowing their bodies and the softness of their surrounds to provide comfort and solace. Catriona did not move from the surprising embrace and said, "I was in a spaceship that exploded in the sky – and you were not on it. Do you come from this planet?"

"What is a spaceship?"

"It is a huge vehicle that flies through space bringing people to this planet. Our Planet Earth was about to blow up from volcanoes exploding everywhere. My mother and father put me in an escape craft – over there." Catriona pointed to the sleek craft and spoke nervously, "My parents wanted me to live and not die with them on the spaceship that was doomed. They were leading a mission to find this new planet." Catriona stopped and bit back the sobs that arose when she mentioned her mother and father. She turned away to hide her emotions.

"Your mother and father are dead?" asked the once dangerous stranger.

"Yes. They died when the spaceship exploded after I escaped."

The dark haired woman slowly stepped back and said, "I am not from here, just far away from my tribe. My father died when I was young. His spirit went into the future and my mother's spirit followed him."

She once again stepped closer to Catriona, who noticed intricate embroidery on the neck and hem of her buckskin dress. It rang a memory deep in Catriona's mind as she remembered her father researching Native American lore.

She asked the sloe eyed beauty who no longer posed a threat, "Tell me about your tribe and where you come from."

"My mother was a medicine woman from the Hualapai tribe who lived in the sacred mountains near the great canyon. My father was Sinagua who in his lifetime united many tribes that had been at war. She was named Trailing Sky Six Feathers. He had the name Eagle Speaker."

"You said Trailing Sky Six Feathers?" Catriona asked incredulously. She dug into her satchel left on a log close to the fire and pulled out her Earth History console. The dark haired woman immediately placed her hand on her knife.

22

"No, No," exclaimed Catriona "This is not a weapon. It shows memories of Earth History. Look, see here, the images of people who might be yours."

She showed sketches and photos of aboriginal peoples of the Americas to the dark stranger. When she got to eighteenth century South West tribes, she showed sketches of women with buckskin dresses bearing the same embroidery at the neck and hem as on the stranger's garment.

The woman gasped audibly, as Catriona's swift fingers cross referenced the sketches with literature about that era.

Catriona frowned with concentration as her computer device, powered by daylight, took her to startling evidence once she found the book she was looking for. She took a deep breath and turned to the stranger who no longer felt like one.

"I know who you are. Your name is Rising Moon." Catriona observed the woman give out a small shrill cry and saw the eyes of her assailant open wide with wonder at being recognized.

Catriona continued, "This book on my Earth History module tells the story of how your father named you."

Rising Moon now reached out tentatively and touched the machine, "How does it know?"

Catriona said, "Would you like me to read out the passage of your naming?" Rising Moon nodded her head vigorously, wondering how her history could be known in the machine held by this red-haired woman. She was overwhelmed and confused, yet affirmed that she would listen.

Catriona said, "Look, here is the front cover of the book. There is a woman, your mother perhaps, standing in the middle of a medicine wheel with her right arm raised to the sky. And here is the passage about your naming in Chapter Two."

Rising Moon examined the cover intensely, running her fingers over the image and said, "That could be her. I can scarcely believe it. I remember the story handed down to me about my naming – can you read what the machine has to say. I am ready to hear it."

Catriona began to read in a clear voice:

"Eagle Speaker waited outside his home as the birth of his child took place, with some anxiety and much patience. He looked into the sky for a sign. The full moon was shrouded by drifting clouds. The movement of clouds by a westerly wind made it appear as though the moon was continually rising. On the first cry of the baby girl, he drew in a deep breath of relief and joy. Long Willow chanted the midwife's song of a new birth. The mother's voice joined in weakly. He smiled to hear Trailing Sky's voice. Then it was carried along by the medicine women chanting in unison. He listened and bathed in this glorious sound of birth and renewal. Eagle Speaker offered prayers of thanksgiving to the Creator for blessing him with so much richness. Later, Long Willow stepped through the doorway with the girl child wrapped in a soft antelope skin with a newly woven blanket around it. Long Willow gently placed the daughter in her father's arms. He held this new life close to his heart, breathing her in to his core and said: "Her name is to be Rising Moon. She is the beginning of our renewal."

There was a lingering silence between the two women. Catriona could see how deeply impacted Rising Moon was, with tears gathering in the corner of her eyes.

She remained silent as deep emotions stirred in her new companion. Rising Moon glanced at her and dried her eyes.

Catriona continued, "I remember the book. My father read it to me when I was a small child. He was fascinated by your era and cultures. The author is a Canadian man and he writes about how the past from the eighteenth century caught up with him in the twenty first century. It was a story about the relentless shadowing of his life by a medicine woman from the American South West in Arizona. The book was named after your mother – *Trailing Sky Six Feathers*. The writer's name is there too on the book cover – do you see Ian Prattis at the bottom?"

Rising Moon was sitting forward, rocking back and forth on her heels, resting her chin in her hands, almost in a trance. She looked more like a child than the deadly warrior who first encountered Catriona.

Rising Moon stopped rocking and quietly spoke, "I have memories of this. My mother, after she died, would come to me in dreamtime. She found where my father had travelled to in the future. But the man his spirit entered was a bit dumb – for the longest time refusing to accept who my mother was."

She paused and asked Catriona directly, "Do you know if this writer, Ian Prattis, was worthy of my mother?

Catriona pursed her lips and thought deeply before answering, "What I remember is that the energy of your mother transformed the writer. He eventually surrendered to her wisdom. But it was not a love story, just a combination of energies from your time in the eighteenth century to my time in the twenty first century."

Then she stopped, startled by insight and suddenly yelled out to Rising Moon, "Just look at the two of us, right

25

here, right now. We are doing what they did – finding ourselves together on this new planet from different centuries. Only we have done it in physical form, not just energy. Do you not think that is totally amazing?" She gave Rising Moon a spontaneous smile, as was her nature.

There was no resistance from Rising Moon, who was surprised yet strangely relieved. How swiftly everything had changed with this young woman she had intended to kill only moments ago.

Catriona asked, "Tell me how you came to be here on this new planet from your place in the eighteenth century? You know how I got here, what about you?"

Rising Moon was completely drawn to this red haired woman who had found her history. She revealed that after her mother's death, soldiers had raided her village with the intent of raping her. She killed one of them with her knife then was pinned down by one soldier while the remaining soldier readied to rape her. She screamed out in desperation to her mother and the Sky People to save her. A furious whirlwind of deadly energy raced in, killing the two soldiers and hurled her through time and space to the high bluff overlooking the bay where a fire was burning with a woman next to it. She knew that she was travelling through space, as her mother had taught her beforehand. She was aware that this planet was different to the earth she had left behind and knew she would not be going back. Her bow, arrows and knife travelled with her.

Rising Moon said, "I believe that the whirlwind was my mother and the Sky People. I just know it was them. There is no other explanation."

They sat with one another for a while before Rising Moon turned to the young woman she had almost killed,

26

"You have discovered so much about me. What is your name, what do you do, what did your mother do?"

"My name is Catriona. My father was a scientist. My mother was a teacher of music and a counsellor, that's a person who listens to people and helps them to become whole. I am so afraid they may be dead in the spaceship explosion, but something gives me hope."

A pang of loss seared through her. She gulped on some air at the tightening in her chest, as deep emotions of grief swept over her. Rising Moon reached out and comforted her in her arms.

The welcome embrace enabled Catriona to slowly recover her composure then state in a matter of fact way, "As for me, I would describe myself as a prodigy."

"What is prodigy?" asked Rising Moon.

Catriona smiled, "Let me show you - that will explain it better." She picked up her violin case and opened it, taking out the violin and the hair string bow. The moment Rising Moon saw the bow she thought it was a weapon and once again aimed an arrow at Catriona's chest.

Catriona confidently waved her bow in a gentle arc, "Put your arrow down, this is harmless. Please Rising Moon, just listen."

She quickly tuned her violin, drew a deep breath and closed her eyes for several minutes, then drew the bow across the strings as Mendelssohn's violin concerto soared into the evening sky.

The music resonated right through Rising Moon's body and mind. She exulted at the extraordinary sound of Catriona's playing. She had never heard such soaring, luminous tones as these. Catriona played the last few notes and held her bow in the air with her eyes still closed.

Rising Moon broke the silence and whispered in awe, "That was the Creator singing to me through your music." She paused for a moment, "I understand what prodigy means."

Catriona clapped her hands together in delight. She said, "The person who created this music was also a prodigy. His name was Mendelssohn and he lived a bit later in your time, only he was across the ocean in Europe in a place called Hamburg. Of all the music I play this piece is my favourite."

"Would you show me how to play that thing?"

"Of course I will. It is called a violin. In return would you show me how you and your mother spoke to plants and the Sky People? I remember that from the book. Speaking of that book, there is still plenty of daylight, so I can read the first three chapters to you. It has the story of your mother and father. Shall I go ahead?"

They stared at one another for a long time. They were profoundly at ease, sensing something extraordinary emerging between them that both allowed.

They sat beside one another by the fire. Catriona's clear voice read aloud the first three chapters. Rising Moon listened to the rapture of her parent's first meeting and early adventures with a feeling of great comfort. She loved hearing again the passage about her father naming her and both young women cried tears at the description of her father's death.

Catriona stopped reading and put her arm around Rising Moon's shoulders. "Do you want me to finish?" she asked. She knew that Trailing Sky's haunting last words to Eagle Speaker would be difficult but Rising Moon wanted her to continue reading.

"Yes, I was there when he died."

In a very soft and respectful voice Catriona continued to read: *"I am Trailing Sky Six Feathers. I ask you all to witness my last words to my husband, Eagle Speaker, before he died in this medicine wheel on the high bluff above the river."* It was as though every one of The People took a deep breath at the same time, waiting for Trailing Sky's next words.

"As he smiled to me and took his last breath, I said to Eagle Speaker, I will find you my husband, I will find you." The ensuing silence cut through everyone's tension, fear and grief. The words that had been heard by Eagle Speaker, now voiced by Trailing Sky for The People, was taken by a whisper of wind into every heart. The trees heard her words and told the animals and birds. The clouds heard her words and extended them to the Sky People. Across the forests, grasslands and mountains, her words echoed, growing stronger and more penetrating so that the universe itself paused to listen. Such was the power emanating from Trailing Sky.

On hearing her mother's words Rising Moon gasped out loud in pain and tears poured down her face. She was very still, swaying like a sapling in the morning breeze.

She cried out: "Mother, will I find him too?"

Trailing Sky gently held her beautiful daughter's tear-streaked face in her hands and said, "Yes my daughter – Eagle Speaker has traveled safely. We will find him."

Catriona was stunned, as she suddenly felt Trailing Sky's immense power as tangible, more than any words could convey. Rising Moon, however, was calmly composed. She had in that moment felt her father through Catriona's speaking. She silently thanked the Creator for bringing her father so close.

Then Rising Moon put her arms on Catriona's shoulders and looked directly into her deep blue eyes, "My gratitude to you Catriona, for your voice brought my father to me. I am so glad I did not send my arrow into your heart."

Catriona exclaimed, "Me too! You scared the living daylights out of me. You were so fierce and dangerous." Then she laughed, "I will keep my arms round your shoulders in case you change your mind."

They smiled together and felt a prolonged, profound moment. Rising Moon broke the silence by stepping back and drawing her long knife. Catriona was not afraid. For the first time a gentle smile appeared on Rising Moon's face. The smile lit up her high cheek bones and her dark eyes were now dancing with a strong inner delight.

"It was meant that I meet you in this future time and on this new planet. That much is clear to me. I must learn more about you and you about me. We are sisters through time and we now become blood sisters. This was told to me by my mother when my arrow was aimed at your heart. With my knife I will open a cut on my left hand, then on your hand. We will clasp hands for the remaining of time. Are you willing Catriona?"

Catriona without hesitation stepped forward and held out her left hand, hardly feeling the gentle small cut, then embracing her blood sister while they clasped hands, allowing their blood to mingle. She retrieved the first aid kit from the escape craft and placed gauze on the cuts they now shared with pride.

"I notice that you have a deep cut on your forehead. If you will permit me, I can stitch the skin together so it will heal better."

Catriona washed the wound with a disinfectant swab and carefully made four stitches to pull the wound together. She noticed the deft outline of Rising Moon's oval face. Long lashes concealed dark eyes set wide on high cheek bones. Her slender body belied her strength. At the same time Rising Moon perused Catriona, seeing how alike they were in body and power, only her blood sister had unbelievable red hair and the deepest blue eyes she had ever seen.

They sat by the fire next to one another and pragmatically planned what they must do to survive on this new planet. Catriona realized that Rising Moon had not eaten since her dramatic arrival at her fire by the lakeside beach. She gathered some basic rations, stating that while the taste was awful the benefits were valuable. Rising Moon wolfed them down. The fire was a great comfort, especially when Catriona dragged one of the parachutes out of its compartment and draped it round them. It was close to nightfall and neither one of them knew what to anticipate.

Rising Moon felt the texture of the fabric and remarked, "With this fabric I can build a tipi for us to live in. My people lived in such dwellings during the summer camps. We must find a good place for it – one that can be well defended and by a river. On my way to your fire I drank from a river that runs into the lake and it was good water. Do you know what a tipi is Catriona?"

31

"Yes I do – will you let me help you?"

"I will show you. I must make you a bow and set of arrows and teach you to hunt. There are fish in the lake and the river, birds and small animals in the forest. There is food for us here. I was taught by my mother about herbs and medicines. She would listen to the Sky People telling her what the plants were good for. I can do the same."

Catriona had a delightful habit of clapping her hands together when she was elated. She did so, "That is wonderful Rising Moon. I will show you what my escape craft has. Medicines, tools, basic rations that will last a long time, fabric from the parachutes and lots more. My father gave me something at the last moment and I have yet to investigate what it is. The escape craft converts to a boat once we remove the survival components. We can easily combine our different centuries – don't you think so?"

There was a long interval as she smiled to her blood sister. "It is also my intention to teach you to play the violin so you can make the songs the Creator speaks."

Rising Moon dropped all restraint and smiled with sheer joy. She said, "Do you see the two moons in the sky? That is so different from Earth. I wonder why my mother made sure I came here – was it to meet you? Are the two moons for us?" They smiled to one another somewhat shyly. They were in tune. Catriona sought more information about the Sky People.

"Can you tell me about the Sky People?"

"My mother became one of them when she passed from life," replied Rising Moon. "She was an extraordinary medicine woman and my teacher in communicating with the Sky People. They are the holy beings from different traditions all over Planet Earth. They are where my mother continued and from what she told me about the Sky People – they reach across the entire universe."

"Are they here on this planet then?" asked Catriona.

"Wherever there is life of any kind, there they are. They appear in different forms to different people. My mother actually saw them, whereas I only sensed them and saw them as a sparkling kind of energy but I could not communicate with them the way my mother did."

"So are they us?" enquired Catriona.

"Perhaps not you or me, but they are the all seeing people. They are a different kind of "us," not limited by time, space or by physical bodies. They do things with ease that we would consider supernatural and magical. That is the only way I can understand how I was plucked out of danger several centuries ago and transported to that high bluff above your fire."

Catriona smiled at this response, "So we were destined to meet one another."

"It would seem so. It was necessary to save my life and place me somewhere else. Here with your awful tasting rations." They laughed together.

Catriona became very serious and looked directly into Rising Moon's eyes. "Well my blood sister, I do not know how safe this new planet is, but I feel with every cell of my body that we were destined to be here together. Just how the Sky People knew to bring you to this new planet is a mystery to me, but I believe that will unravel." Rising Moon held the intense gaze, as her heart was moved deeply.

Catriona's curiosity continued, "Are the Sky People time travelers? That is what you seem to have done to meet me here."

Rising Moon paused for a while, "It is more than that. In our sacred tradition the medicine wheel is a ceremonial place yet also the gateway to transfer energy from one universe to another."

Catriona asked, "Can you explain that to me?"

Rising Moon collected her thoughts, remembering her mother's teachings, "The sacred Medicine Wheel is constructed with rocks placed in a circle around the four directions – East, North, South and West. From each cardinal point there is a line of rocks that connect to a smaller circle of grandfather rocks at the center. The central circle was a gateway for energy to pass through for those who were capable of doing so. Very few people could do this though my mother could. She would be in the medicine wheel physically while her energy traveled to other worlds. I have never done that or know of anyone else who could do it, so I do not completely understand. There would be shamans at different stations in the medicine wheel keeping my mother physically safe, while her energy went through the central circle of stones. She explained to me once that it was the Sky People who provided the pathways for her to travel to other worlds where she was needed."

Catriona was concentrating on what she heard: "I think I have a grasp on that. My father was an astrophysicist and a man of science about other worlds. He used to talk to me about "worm holes." This was the name given to passages between galaxies. But it was a mystery how they were formed or where they would appear. Perhaps the Sky People created them."

She paused for a while, "My father would have really liked to hear your explanation rooted in traditional ceremony."

Rising Moon said, "We must sleep now Catriona. Our first night on this new planet and we are both alive. I will build up the fire to keep us warm. We can fold the fabric on the sand and pull it over us. Do you agree my blood sister?" Catriona smiled shyly at her new sister. They were soon fast asleep next to a gentle bay where lake water softly rolled as music against the shore.

Catriona awoke and saw that morning had arrived. Rising Moon was sitting on a log across from her on the other side of the fire. Her dark braid was loosened and her lustrous dark hair hung down to her waist. Rising Moon's dark eyes bored into Catriona with intensity and then she smiled.

"You are awake my sister Catriona."

Catriona heard her and saw Rising Moon silhouetted against the morning sky. She had not been dreaming about meeting her the day before.

Rising Moon had risen early while Catriona slept. First of all she chanted her gratitude to meet the new day. She knew their present location was too exposed and explored their environment closely, finding the river she had crossed and how it meandered into a protected pool below a ridge that would be ideal to place their tipi. She slowly walked into the lake with a sharpened spear she had made, looking for fish. She cooked a large one on the embers of the fire and waited for Catriona to awake. Her simple greeting was welcomed by Catriona, as she took in this new gift of a blood sister.

35

"I am awake my sister Rising Moon." They both smiled at the gentle formality that naturally ensued between them. "I see that you have built up the fire," then Catriona clapped her hands in her delighted way, "Is that a fish roasting on the fire?"

Rising Moon nodded, "I was awake with the dawn of the morning and offered my daily chant of gratitude to the Creator for being alive and for finding you here. I chanted softly so I did not wake you."

"What a beautiful way to greet the day," Catriona exclaimed. "Is that your custom?"

Rising Moon nodded again. "I made myself a spear from a small sapling beyond the shore and walked into the lake. Small fish came to see me. They were very curious. I waited for a larger fish to come and feed on them and got this one. I also found herbs at the shoreline, similar to those in my homeland and crushed them over the fish. It will not taste as awful as your space rations."

They both grinned at the reminder. Catriona noticed a flat clean stone placed near her with a small bone handled knife in a beaded sheath.

"You may have my small knife to eat the fish when it is done. You are to keep the knife." Rising Moon continued, "I explored our surroundings. We must move from here as it is too exposed to wind and other beings. There is a river close by and I followed her and found the perfect place to build a tipi. The escape craft that brought you here must also be hidden. We can take it upriver to where we will build the tipi. Explain to me the materials in your space craft? I saw your violin case and looked in to see the beauty you shared with me. This slim case was there too. What is it?"

It was the case that Catriona's father had placed beside her before the escape craft ejected from the space craft. Rising Moon confessed that she was unable to open the box.

Catriona took the box and said, "That is understandable. My father would always build in puzzles for me to solve."

She inspected the latch of the slim metal case and fiddled with the code bar on the lock, finally putting in the name of her father, mother and herself. An omen of hope she thought. The lid opened and revealed two lasers that were obviously to be placed on her arms. There was a brief letter in Tom Hagen's bold script explaining how to use them. They were powerful, short-range laser tools that could split wood, sculpt stone and clear brush. In situations of danger they could be used as short-range weapons.

Catriona studied the instructions carefully before slipping one of the lasers over her right forearm. She walked over to a massive log with a six foot diameter. Standing ten feet away she squeezed the button in the palm of her hand. The laser beam spat out and in seconds the huge log was split into two parts. They both jumped back at the ferocity and power of the laser devise.

Rising Moon was the first to recover, "This will clear the trees from where we will place the tipi. I prefer that you operate it."

Then she mused, "This is also a weapon to be feared. I do not like the destructive weapon part of this devise. Let us use it to create and build. Not to destroy anyone."

Rising Moon reflected for a moment seeking the right words, then said, "Catriona, the way of my culture, passed on to me by my mother and father, was to respect all living things. Before I killed the big fish, I thanked it for its life so you and I may live. My father taught me how to survive and live well in deserts, mountains and forests. It was always vital to engage with creatures that support us. That includes plants, herbs, seeds, rocks, rivers, trees and all things. We see where they came from and treat them as part of the vast web that includes us."

"You know what Rising Moon, I have a similar attitude," Catriona said with understanding dawning in her mind. "When I was given my first violin, I saw and felt the tree it came from. I imagined it standing tall and noble in a forest. My feeling was that of gratitude. Often before playing I would think of the tree that gave itself to create my violin. That enables me to bring sounds of freedom into my music, which makes me different from other players."

"That's why you are a prodigy Catriona. See how I understand you. The Creator is happy."

Catriona clapped her hands in spontaneous joy. The both had huge smiles for one another.

Rising Moon said, "I will train you so that you come to know animals, the web of this new planet, to live simply without wasting lives. Now let us eat the fish before it burns black, then you can explain to me the treasures you have in your craft over there."

She carefully lifted the cooked fish, skewered by a sharp stick, and placed it on the clean flat rock and split it open so the aroma of herbs was released. They hungrily ate their first breakfast together. With her mouth full of delicious fish, Rising Moon shouted, "Better tasting than those rations!"

"I agree totally," said Catriona "Those rations taste awful."

After eating, they washed their faces in the lake and Rising Moon placed the remnants of the fish in the fire. Walking over to the escape vessel, Catriona noticed blood on Rising Moon's garment. She pointed it out and Rising Moon replied that it must be the blood of the soldier she killed. Her buckskin dress was also torn in several places.

Catriona stopped and spoke, "You are about the same size as me. I have two tunics in the escape craft. If you would like to wear one I can wash your garment and sew the rips."

"I can wash my own buckskin and do the sewing – my mother taught me well." Rising Moon replied sharply.

Catriona took her arm gently, "Please Rising Moon, allow me to do this. It would be my thanks for meeting you."

Then she giggled, "I also think you would look wonderful in a space tunic. You can choose a grey color or green." Rising Moon paused for a moment, then chose green and put it on, once Catriona explained how to.

"It feels like a second skin," Rising Moon observed "and very comfortable."

"That's the design," said Catriona. "When you get wet, it dries instantly. The fabric maintains a steady temperature for your body and protects you from most injuries. You are now a modern space woman, with your knife and beaded belt for additional elegance."

Rising Moon permitted a half smile to spread across her lovely face.

"Let's get right to work then. First of all I will need to find the tool box," Catriona said as she opened the escape craft. She pulled out a compartment that contained a variety of multi-purpose tools, selecting two solar powered screw drivers.

She explained to Rising Moon, "Each compartment is unique and comes out once the locks are released. The top part of the capsule comes off, leaving the lower part as a boat with a motor to drive it. Hold the lid while I unscrew the hinges."

The top layer was soon lying on the sand. The tool compartment was unlocked and lifted out, then the first aid compartment, rations, rope and twine, a complete sewing kit, lightweight strong nails in assorted sizes, clothing and basic cooking utensils.

Rising Moon was excited to see the twine. She felt it with her hands, pulled it taught to see how much stretch was in it, then looked at Catriona, "This is perfect for the bow I will make for you. Is there anything else here that we need?"

Catriona pointed to a computer console in the front of the new boat. "That is a communication devise powered by daylight. Something like the one I showed you yesterday. It is linked to the spaceship but there are no messages on it."

She bit her lip at this confirmation of the demise of PRIME 3 and the death of her parents. She was choking back her feelings of dread.

Rising Moon stepped closer to her. "I know the loss you are feeling right now Catriona. I feel it too as I lost both my parents while young. This machine stays with us to keep our horizons open. You must check what it has to say every day. Do you agree?"

Catriona reluctantly nodded through her tears.

Rising Moon, ever the pragmatist said, "We will also keep the cover of the craft. With a long pole it can be used as a raft for fishing. It is buoyant and strong, perfect for fishing and hunting close to the lake shore. The boat can take us further out with its motor, and you must show me how to use it. Is there anything else you have not shown me?" There was one compartment left.

Catriona unlocked the long box that she had been strapped to. The top cover of the box had the indented imprint of her body. She opened it and then started to laugh. Only her beloved father and mother could have done this. Densely packed were lightweight dishes and pots, cutlery, packets of East Indian curries she so loved, rice, maize and bean seeds, a flowered table cloth, a small Dutch oven for baking with packets of flour and yeast stuffed into it. Finally she discovered a powerful cross bow with instructions.

Catriona was now laughing and crying at the same time, as she explained to Rising Moon the love of her parents built into each item. Her father was a gourmet cook and her mother a national cross bow champion. She examined each item, explaining the meaning of her parents' love.

Rising Moon was very silent for a while before she spoke gently to Catriona, "Your parents are with you still and continue with you always. We will plant the maize, bean and rice seeds, and in seeing them grow you will feel your parents deeply. I admire your mother's cross bow and would like you to give it to me - a trade for my small knife. I can make better use of it than you and it enables me to carry your mother with me."

Catriona was growing to admire Rising Moon's forthright pragmatism. "The cross bow is given gladly from

41

my mother to you. We will find suitable ground for the maize and bean seeds, but will need irrigation for the rice. The river you located, do you think we could redirect water to grow rice? On my Earth History computer I can research irrigation methods."

Rising Moon smiled, "Your research is sitting right next to you. My main village had extensive irrigation channels. I would go with my father to inspect them and with my mother for the caring of seeds and plants."

Catriona was once again astonished, "For some reason that I cannot fathom, we have been placed together as a perfect fit."

Rising Moon's humor revealed itself, "Just wait until you try to teach me to play your violin. You may not find such a perfect fit as I may be terrible at it."

They both giggled like children at the thought. Leaving the precious compartments and their contents well above the shoreline, the two women walked along the shore for half a mile to the river that ran quietly into the lake. They noticed the variety of plants on the shoreline. Rising Moon dug up several wild tubers and placed them on the sand to dry. Then they followed the river for almost a mile. At a bend in the river Rising Moon pointed out how it embraced a broad expansive pool that was still, while the river ran lazily on the far side. They could see small fish swimming there and partridge like birds scurried away from them into the undergrowth adjacent to the river. Close to the pool was a long ridge with a wooded plateau.

Rising Moon pointed to the ridge, "That is where we can place the tipi. It will be easy to clear with your father's laser tool. There are enough tall, slim trees for the poles of the tipi, so our work is all here. We can bring the boat and the raft upriver to this pool. The stream does not run too strongly and there are no rocks to impede their passage."

They both felt entranced by the beauty of the place, noticing the flowers and the birds peeking curiously at them. The quiet pool with a river running on one side was a natural counterpoint to the wooded ridge, where Rising Moon intended to locate the tipi. They could see across to the other side of the river where a similar plateau lay ready for the future.

"Is this our first work together, building our new home?" Catriona asked.

Rising Moon smiled at her, "Yes Catriona, this is our new beginning."

As they traced their steps back to the lake shore, Rising Moon pointed out different herbs and plants she had already spoken to on her prior exploration. She knew their gifts. As they continued walking, Catriona stopped beneath a grapelike vine and reached up to pluck the fruit.

Rising Moon shouted out in alarm, "No Catriona that is poisonous. Please ask me before eating anything. The grey ones cannot be eaten, only the red ones which are further into the forest." The grapes were a hand's breadth from Catriona's mouth.

"How silly of me," Catriona muttered "that could have been disastrous for both of us."

Rising Moon quickly came to her side, "Forgive me for shouting at you my sister. Soon you will know all that I know. Just realize I have to keep you alive for now so that I get violin lessons out of you!"

They labored for the next two days, ferrying their resources by boat and raft from the sandy bay to the still pool at the bend of the river.

To Rising Moon's surprise the space tunic kept her temperature even, so that she hardly felt any fatigue.

They stored their precious cargo on the wooded plateau, making a fire pit close to the pool with the run of the river on the far side.

"Some rations and more fish to eat?" asked Rising Moon impishly on the first day. "The water is good, your rations are important, but let me show you how to fish."

She cut a small sapling into a six-foot spear with a sharpened point for Catriona and walked into the pool with her own spear. "Just watch for the small fish to come visit your feet and wait for a bigger fish to come after them. Then strike for the head of the fish. The water does not reflect accurately so your spear will get it in the middle of the back. Say prayers for the fish that comes to you."

Catriona did as instructed. She was intrigued by the small fish inspecting her toes and hardly saw the larger fish, some kind of bass, come close to her feet then quickly swim away.

"Never mind Catriona," Rising Moon called, "it will come back. Be ready. Did you say your prayer?"

Catriona nodded. She was too concentrated to speak but Rising Moon saw her intent. The large fish returned to seek out the small fish at Catriona's toes. With a swift strike her spear caught it in the middle of the back, right through. She lifted it out of the water screaming, "I've got one, I've got one. Look at how big it is."

Rising Moon laughed at her excitement, "That's a magnificent fish. We do not need any more. And Catriona do not clap your hands. You will lose the fish."

Catriona dared not to clap her hands at that moment, as her fish was flapping on the end of her spear. Rising Moon removed it and placed it on a rock and with a smaller rock killed it with a strike behind the head. She then showed Catriona how to gut the fish and allow the entrails into the water for other fish to eat.

Dry wood was plentiful, washed ashore by eddies from the river running past. Rising Moon built a fire and skewered the large bass like fish and rested it on a tripod of rocks on either side.

Catriona watched, then exclaimed, "Let me add something to the cooking." She raced up to the box of treasures from her parents and retrieved a packet of mild curry. "Let's smear this on the inside of the fish. It will take away the taste of our basic rations." And it did.

Rising Moon shouted across the fire, "I have never tasted fish like this – your rations even taste good."

They were full with fresh food and a sense of major accomplishment.

They looked over at their two sleek crafts, boat and raft, drawn up on the shore of the pool. They felt splendid to have so much for whatever was awaiting them.

As the day drew to darkness, they lay the parachute fabric on flat ground above the pool.

Pulling a top layer over themselves, the two young women slept deeply on their second night on the new planet.

2: The Tipi

By the end of their third day on the new planet they had transferred everything from the lakeside to their new haven. Rising Moon carefully removed all trace of their time at the lake. They awoke next morning to the wonder of what they were creating.

After a drink of water and basic rations Rising Moon announced, "We must start the work today on building our tipi, our home. I will need help from you, also tools from your space craft."

Catriona replied, "I am ready, just direct me."

Rising Moon needed twelve poles, three times her height. "They must be straight and smooth," she said. "Cut down the trees we need on the mound up there. Make sure the trees still standing will not shadow or fall onto our tipi. The poles we need should be the width of four fingers at the bottom and three fingers at the top. And we must peel the bark off so they can dry."

Catriona nodded her understanding." I can bring down the trees using the laser devise. What else do we need?"

Rising Moon replied, "We have my knife but will need a small axe and hammer. I have carved some wooden pegs to stich the cover together once I cut the big parachute to size. The circular bottom of it is perfect and the parachute strings will make good loops to fasten the bottom of the cover to the ground. There is plenty of fabric for an outside cover and an inside liner, you'll see all that soon."

47

She could see how excited Catriona was about building the tipi.

She thought for a moment, "I will need one of your strong coils of rope to grip the poles. It's in one of the compartments we carried from your space craft."

Rising Moon observed how quickly Catriona felled the trees on the extensive mound with the laser tool. She carefully selected twelve slim twenty foot saplings and they peeled off the bark.

She said to Catriona, "Use the small axe on any knots or bumps on the poles. The smoother it feels, the better it will be." They worked in silence. Soon there were over a dozen gleaming poles drying in the warm daylight. They stacked the rest of the timber by the fire.

"Perhaps we can place two of the bigger trees over the river as a bridge later on and use the laser to make it flat on the top," she said to Catriona as she was cutting a precise design from the larger parachute. Rising Moon was all business.

"We can get the cover ready while the poles dry. The door to our tipi will face to the East. We begin with three poles and I must mark exactly where they are to be placed. You can help me locate where the North, South and Door poles go in accordance with the movement of the sun and two moons."

Rising Moon carefully marked out where the first three poles would be placed in the central area of the cleared mound. She grinned to Catriona, "If we get the first three in the right place, the rest is easy."

Rising Moon continued with her instructions, "There is a special way to tie the poles, There is a shorter end of the rope, as long as I am tall, then a much longer end that we use to pull the first three poles up." She placed the North and South poles side by side on the ground with the Door pole across the top at an angle. She swiftly tied the three poles together at the top with a special binding.

She heard Catriona exclaim excitedly, "That's a clove hitch. My father taught me that when he took me fishing as a small child."

Rising Moon used the rest of the shorter length of rope to tightly wrap around the poles three times, sealing it with another clove hitch.

"This is where your strength comes in Catriona. Put one foot strongly against the bottom of the North and South poles and pull them up with the long rope. I will be at the other end of the poles pushing them up." Rising Moon used her strength to push the poles upright in co-ordination with Catriona's pulling on the rope. She shouted out, "That's it! Hold it steady now they are up. I will push the North pole away from you and the three poles will now stand on their own."

With that achieved, Rising Moon ensured that the base of each pole was exactly where she had marked. "It is steady. Now Catriona please swing on the rope. That pulls it tighter around the poles."

She carefully placed the remaining poles at precise locations, finally using the long rope to wrap around the top cluster of poles by walking around the tipi keeping the rope taut, finally bringing it over the North one to hang free. The beauty of the architecture was slowly revealing itself.

Rising Moon said, "The next bit is tricky. You see that sturdy pole I left out, that is the last one. It lifts the parachute cover over the tipi frame. I have to secure the cover strongly to the top of this pole, put it in place and then we spread the cover round the other poles. It all comes together at the Door pole and I will pin the two sides together with the wooden spikes I carved. We can then lace it together with your strong twine." This was meticulously completed and the majesty of the tipi emerged.

"If it looks good and stable, then we can stake the cover to the ground." Rising Moon went inside the tipi to check that all was in place. She had cut the tops from two of the poles to use as smoke flap poles for the fire pit inside. She was well satisfied with their work.

"We have almost finished the first part Catriona. Make sure you pull the bottom of the cover out at least a hand's width away from the poles. That lets fresh air circulate inside the tipi. Do you see the loop I made from the parachute strings?" Catriona nodded.

"Stretch it over a wooden spike, and hammer it into the ground. We have the inside liner to put on the other side of the poles, which will keep us cool when hot and warm when cold. That will only take a short time. Eventually we will sew the bottom of the inner liner to the outside cover. We can do that later."

Then she paused, thinking ahead, "I have yet to make a cover for the tipi entrance to complete our new home. All in good time my sister."

Catriona was elated when Rising Moon told her that once it all settles, they could paint the tipi from different colored juices from berries. When the last loop of the outside cover was pulled away from the poles and hammered into the ground, the two young women stood back and looked at their creation. They were awed by its beauty.

"It is so magnificent and feels totally sacred," whispered Catriona.

Rising Moon agreed, "When we step inside you will feel just how sacred this tipi is, though it is not yet finished. Before we do that I would like to give thanks in the way of my ancestors. That should be with burning sage and tobacco, but I do not have them as my medicine bag was ripped off me by the soldiers."

She thought for a while, "We can offer our gratitude to the Creator a different way. Do you have something precious that we could burn along with something from me?"

Catriona pondered for a while then picked up her violin.

"No, No, not that Catriona," yelled Rising Moon in alarm, much to Catriona's amusement.

"Of course not," Catriona laughed, "I have a piece of music written down. I know it by heart. It was composed by my mother for my sixteenth birthday four years ago. Here it is. She would be very happy that her music is used in such a sacred way. It also brings her and my father close to us."

There were tears in her eyes. She grieved deeply for her parents. She did not bother to wipe her tears as she knew Rising Moon was there for her. She said to her sister, "What do you have that you would like to offer?"

Rising Moon already knew, "I wear an amulet on my right forearm. It was carved by my father and strung together with leather and beads by my mother. It will bring both of them here to be with us. We must also find a hollowed stone to contain our offerings. We walk slowly

51

three times round the tipi while I chant our gratitude in my language. Is that fine with you?"

Catriona smiled confidently to her blood sister.

Rising Moon caught the smile, "I will hold the rock in my left hand, while I brush the smoke over the tipi with my right hand, then you hold it and do the same, then back to me. Just follow what I do. I will offer our burning treasures to the Four Directions, the Center and to the Creator. And I will chant for you."

They searched the river's edge for an appropriate hollowed stone. Rising Moon discovered the perfect one for their ceremony. It was lodged beneath a fallen tree trunk, just waiting to be discovered. She cleaned it in the river and dried it with grasses. Holding the greyish blue stone in her hand, she crumpled Catriona's sheet music into a tight ball and placed her amulet upon it with dried grasses and herbs to slow the burning.

A tangible silence settled upon them, enveloping the tipi, river and their lives with sharp anticipation. Catriona lit the tight ball of sheet music and it began to smolder, while Rising Moon chanted their gratitude.

Catriona carefully watched what her blood sister was doing and repeated it exactly when the grey-blue stone, now sacred, was passed to her, then finally back to Rising Moon to complete the three circles they traced with their feet and hearts. Rising Moon stopped chanting and placed the grey blue stone beside the tipi entrance and whispered to Catriona that the forest around the cleared mound received the blessing and the sky was listening intently. They stepped through into architecture of sublime beauty.

Catriona let out a cry of wonderment, "It feels like a cathedral, that's a sacred place in my culture. Look at how the light comes in from above and seeps up from the ground. I have never seen anything like this before."

Rising Moon smiled at her awe, feeling the same surge. "Let us sit over by the pool to take in this magnificent home the tipi provides. We also need to eat some of your awful rations."

Catriona laughed and brought out the nutriments they required. As she handed some rations to her blood sister, Rising Moon asked her, "How many summers have you passed?"

Catriona understood what she meant and replied, "I am now twenty years old. In the time calendar we use on Earth we are presently in the spring of 2085. It was five years ago, when I was fifteen, that I listened to my father give an important talk to the world. That was in 2080 and my father talked about the desperate and deadly conditions on Planet Earth endangering all life. He was asking the rich and powerful people to support a spaceship that would take pioneers to a new planet. That's how I got here."

Rising Moon did some calculations with a stick and several stones from the pond before speaking. "I have also passed twenty summers, so we are of the same age. My people did not have the time calendar of the white intruders, who were so careful to keep records of events, but we went along with that form. The year that I was hurled from Earth to here by the Sky People was 1781. My father died in 1771, when I was ten summers old."

She paused a moment in memory of her father and then began to laugh, "I am the older sister by some three hundred years and have full authority over my little sister. Did you know that younger sister?"

Catriona smiled back, "Do not push your luck in that direction, my blood sister. You might just get another kick on your head." They both laughed together.

Rising Moon's pragmatism asserted itself, "For the tipi we can make two wooden frames for sleeping, with some of your strong rope across to rest on. There is plenty of fabric left for cover and blankets. In our summer village we would put soft pine boughs on the ground to keep a good smell here and make it warm. When it wears out we just burn it and make another floor covering. There is much to do."

Catriona could hardly contain herself, "I am so happy with our home. Do you feel our parents smiling over what we have accomplished? I miss my mother and father terribly, but there is something inside me that insists that I will be reunited with them. Do you think that is crazy?"

Rising Moon gently embraced her without speaking.

Catriona said, "My father was an excellent craftsman with wood and showed me how to construct cabinets, chairs and tables – so tomorrow I will build our beds, while you find if there are trees that will offer us flooring. Does this sound like a plan my sister?"

Rising Moon's eyes sparkled at Catriona's sense of initiative. Next day they worked independently on their tasks. Catriona used the laser tool to shape the trunks of felled trees into robust planks, remembering the directions from her father to join pieces of wood with an interlocking bevel and groove construction. It needed only one slim nail at each interlock to make it solid. With the tools from her escape craft she carefully created two elegant and sturdy bed frames, drilling holes through the planks for the strong rope to weave a lattice to sleep upon. She applied the same care to cut fitted frame covers and blankets from the remnants of the parachutes. It took her most of the day, with all her concentration and memory of her father's patience.

Rising Moon was searching for trees with soft boughs but could not find suitable one's in the vicinity of their camp. Then she called to mind the trees where she had landed on the high bluff above Catriona's fire. There was a surprise waiting for her when she made her way back. Her medicine pouch was hanging from the branch of the perfect tree she was looking for. She thought she had lost it on the turbulent journey created by the Sky People and her mother.

She smiled, "If I was Catriona, I would now clap my hands," and she found herself doing exactly that. She laughed so hard she startled two partridge like birds, which were quickly dispatched with swift arrows.

She mused, "Food, tipi floor and medicine pouch. The Creator is truly pleased!"

She found some vines to tie the huge amount of soft boughs she had cut from the trees, akin to blue spruce. She returned to their new home tired from the weight of the boughs, yet very happy.

In the tipi she was amazed by Catriona's skill, astonished by the interlocking construction she carefully inspected. She began to weave the tree boughs into a soft floor around the two beds. When they stepped on the flooring there was a gentle bounce underneath their feet. She had sufficient to cover half of the tipi. When this was complete, she sat on one sturdy bed and told Catriona the story about clapping her hands when she saw her medicine pouch.

They laughed together until the tears rolled down their cheeks, rolling over and over on the new flooring with hoots of mirth until exhaustion took its toll. For the rest of that day they would return to laughter, while preparing the birds for roasting, moving their resources into the tipi, one would start laughing and soon the forest was filled with their exuberant joy.

To celebrate their first night in the tipi Catriona cooked a splendid meal of partridge, roots and special bread she baked in the Dutch oven. They thanked the Creator and their parents, eating together in respectful silence.

Catriona was sitting on her bed and asked, "Do you have fears and desires Rising Moon? Would you like to marry for instance and have children?"

Rising Moon snorted with mirth at the question, "Who is around here for me to marry? I do not see men seeking me out. I am just stuck with you!"

She laughed out loud then became more serious. "You ask good questions Catriona. Yes, I do have fears, mostly to do with my hate and anger for white people."

Catriona exclaimed, "I am white and you do not hate me do you?"

Rising Moon stared deeply at Catriona for a long moment, "You are the only white person who has ever honored me as a human being, even though you did kick me on the head while I was trying to kill you. Good job we are blood sisters."

That satisfied Catriona.

Rising Moon resumed speaking her thoughts, "My hatred and anger are for the white people who stole our lands centuries ago, who treated us as less than animals. My fear is that when I meet white people from your century, will I still carry the hatred and anger through to them?"

She was silent for a long time before she spoke less harshly. "I would like to marry, but someone of my own kind. Someone who had the qualities my father carried. Only I am not sure that is possible any more."

Catriona excitedly responded, "Rising Moon, there was a man from the Hopi people on the spaceship. His name was Manny Fredericks, a brilliant scientist who worked with my father to bring the space mission to fruition."

"The Hopi People you say?" Rising Moon asked incredulously.

Catriona nodded. "He would do fine as I speak Hopi. Do you think I should give him a chance my sister or do you want him for yourself?"

Catriona hooted with laughter at Rising Moon's earnestness. "I have no interest as I feel married to my music. Manny is a wonderful man, wise, kind and without a wife, so let us hope for your sake that he survived the explosion on the spaceship. He is all yours."

Rising Moon pondered in her practical way, "Maybe I will not like him, which means I have only you to put up with." They both laughed at their musings.

Rising Moon was direct, "You do not want a man?"

Catriona replied, "No, I do not perceive that in my life. My greatest desire is to teach a children's orchestra and see them grow with the music, just as you have grown with my violin."

Rising Moon understood and said, "And your fears, what are they?"

Catriona replied, "I think you know that. My greatest fear is that my parents are dead and I will never see them again. But there is something deep inside me that keeps a spark of hope alive."

"Keep that spark alive my dear sister," Rising Moon said solemnly. "It is time for our first sleep inside the tipi. Good night Catriona, my blood sister."

In the days and weeks that ensued, their camp on the bend of the lazy paced river blossomed into a safe haven. Catriona made a long table for the tipi, standing about two foot high. She showed Rising Moon how to use the carpentry tools to fashion it. Small stools were made, a tall rack for their bows, arrows and spears plus shelving for their containers. Catriona had learned how to hunt with the bow and arrows made for her by Rising Moon. She enjoyed the careful preparation of getting to know the animal or bird and blessing it before pulling the bow string back to her arm pit before releasing accurate arrows.

Rising Moon quickly became acquainted with the cross bow, having seen one before in a settlement close to a military fort during her life in the 18th century on Planet Earth. She studied it carefully, practicing with it by firing into strong trees. She knew this was ideal for larger game and went hunting further afield. She encountered a large male deer, half a day's walk from their camp. She was amazed that this new planet could be so like her own, similar animals, birds and plants but no evidence of people or tribes.

She and Catriona had long conversations about the similarities and the differences of the two planets they knew. Her thoughts were suspended as she stealthily stalked the buck, whispering her greetings to him, ensuring she was always downwind. He was aware of her, yet unafraid. She followed his trail carefully inspecting the dung left behind on the way. She found that it was healthy without any disease resting in the deer's waste. On hands and knees she crept within the range of the cross bow. The buck stood still, sensing her presence.

For her part she admired the deer standing tall between two trees. She released the bolt from the cross bow and the arrow struck the deer behind the upper right foreleg, penetrating the heart and killing him instantly. Rising Moon approached slowly, sad at the loss of his life, yet grateful that he would sustain her and her blood sister.

As was Rising Moon's custom, she cut out a piece of the heart and liver, placing it in the neck of a tree branch and chanted her gratitude. She gutted the animal, leaving the entrails for other animals to feed on. She skinned it and pinned the buckskin to several bushes to dry, knowing she would have to wash it later in the river. She sliced off the forelegs and put them over her shoulder. She would need Catriona's help to bring the rest. Catriona was shocked to see Rising Moon walk into their camp, alarmed by the blood on her tunic.

"It's not my blood," Rising Moon shouted, sensing the alarm in Catriona. "We can place the meat to roast slowly over the fire while we collect the rest of this noble animal."

On the journey to where the dead buck lay she spoke to Catriona about the hunt and her admiration of the creature that she first of all honored with a simple ceremony. They walked below a grey grape vine and exchanged a well understood grimace. The day's light was dancing through the forest and they listened to bird calls. Bold partridges ran across their path with impunity, perhaps realizing they had bigger things to cope with. It did not take long to walk directly there.

Rising Moon folded the buckskin into a large pouch where most of the meat was loaded. The rest was roped together with vines and Catriona carried it on her back. The return was slower as they stopped frequently to rest. Their conversation was lively as Rising Moon described how she would make a traditional dress from the buckskin for Catriona, remarking that she would look more like a woman than the boyish look of her space tunic. Catriona was quick to point out that her dear sister with long black hair hardly looked like a boy in the green space tunic she was wearing. They both laughed at that.

They stopped at the other side of the pool, next to the bridge they had built across the gentle river, and gazed with pleasure at their home. Their eyes and senses took in the fire pit on the bank of the pool roasting the meat from the deer, with a stack of firewood nearby. Then they glanced at their majestic tipi on the mound they had cleared, perfectly protected and solitary with a backdrop of rock and forest. Their two crafts, invaluable for fishing and hunting, were drawn up at the end of the shallow pool.

Catriona drew in a deep breath, "I can scarce believe that we created all of this. It is so welcoming and safe. Just look at our surroundings."

Rising Moon shared the deep feelings of her sister, yet her no nonsense attitude broke the spell, "We do not have all day for admiration, there's work to do. First of all, let us eat."

The meat was well roasted and they ravenously devoured it, forgoing the staple of space craft rations. Rising Moon was full and let out a burp that made Catriona laugh.

"I can do better than that, you know," said Catriona with a certain pride.

With no witnesses to the quality of their manners, a burping contest ensued while they cleaned the buckskin in the running water of the river. Catriona was declared the winner.

Rising Moon cut the rest of the meat into long strips and laid it out on a rock platform that she first of all covered with some of the tree boughs from the tipi.

"The meat strips will dry and be a ration that lasts a long time. We can easily replace the floor cover inside the tipi. Tomorrow let us go to where I found my medicine pouch and bring back enough tree branches to complete our floor."

Catriona happily agreed. She so enjoyed teaching the violin to Rising Moon, who preferred to have her lessons inside the tipi.

Meticulously, prior to every lesson, Rising Moon would clean and tidy up the inside of the tipi, explaining that if she was going to hear the voice of the Creator she wanted to be in a clean and sacred place.

Catriona had been patient with the beginning scrapes and agonizing sounds Rising Moon coaxed from the violin, but was surprised at how determined Rising Moon was when she started to catch the cadences. She decided not to teach her to read music first of all but simply instructed Rising Moon to follow her left fingers on the violin frets and right hand on the bow.

Rising Moon observed intently every finger placement, the angle and length of bow strokes. Although she struggled at first, she was soon playing simple pieces with adept fluency.

Catriona asked her once at the end of a lesson, "Is the Creator pleased?"

Rising Moon's eyes watered and one tear drop rolled down her beautiful cheek. "My tear of joy answers your question, my sister Catriona. Somehow this violin sound completes me. I am so grateful for that, and for your patience in the awful beginning."

Catriona was moved, "Thank you sister Rising Moon. Do you realize that you teaching me to talk to plants and the earth gave me something I never had? I know how to listen to the earth so only seeds that will be happy are placed where they can thrive. Our maize and bean plots are growing due to your knowledge. I deeply miss my parents, yet here with you I am strangely very happy."

With a gentle smile she added, "Let our journey to collect more cedar boughs tomorrow be a celebration of the gifts we have received from one another."

They went to sleep that night feeling happy, elated by where they were.

Rising Moon was always the first to awake, so used to the timing of morning dawn. She dressed and looked across at her beloved sister still sleeping, before slipping out of the tipi to greet the soft light of dawn that received her morning chant. There was a small ember in the fire. She placed small twigs around it and soon there were flames.

Rising Moon had fashioned a strong tripod over the fire, made from hard, fire resistant wood. One of the cooking utensils retrieved from the rescue craft was a pot they used to make a twig tea made from grasses, twigs and herbs. She thought it had a disgusting taste but Catriona liked it. Once the brew was ready, she poured it into one of the large cups from Catriona's box of treasures and took it up to the tipi.

"Here you are – the day is half gone already."

Catriona rubbed sleep from her eyes and sat up, gratefully holding her hand out for the cup.

"I don't know how you can drink that sludge, but it seems to wake you up." They sat in gentle, smiling silence. Rising Moon was on her bed across from Catriona on hers. She asked, "It looks like a wonderful day for our journey, but can we do the violin first of all before we go?"

Catriona looked into the intense face of her sister, "Of course we can. What a great way to start our day. I'll get up now and make breakfast."

"Already done," there was mischief in Rising Moon's eyes, "I have prepared something special for you. Come and see."

Over the fire she had skewered pieces of meat from the deer with herbs and tubers, sprinkled with Catriona's curry powder. She said, "This should fire us up for the day."

Rising Moon knew how Catriona liked her food in an orderly way with plates and utensils. She had laid them out on the colored table cloth placed over a plank of wood next to the fire.

Catriona saw the care and love from her sister and clapped her hands with that special delight. She did not have to say anything.

The skewer of meat, herbs and tuber was delicious. It melted into their mouths, as they ate in silence. Catriona had another cup of tea, at which Rising Moon grimaced with a deliberately anguished look on her face.

Then it was the joy of sharing music on the violin inside the tipi before they left to walk back along the trail taken by Rising Moon after her arrival on the high rock bluff. They were soon there. The view was breath taking. Catriona had not seen this expansiveness.

A string of lakes unfolded westwards as far as the eye could see. Catriona noted the directions on the compass embedded in her Earth History device.

They could see the bay where they first met, yet further upriver their tipi was partially concealed from sight.

They saw how the forest area on the other side of their river stretched to a mountain range set many miles back. Before them was the large lake where Catriona's escape craft had splashed down.

The two young women often wondered if they were the only people on this planet. They had not discovered any signs of habitation, just a landscape remarkably similar to sub-tropical regions of Planet Earth.

They did not feel lonely and easily adjusted to the two moons, twenty eight hour days and the largely unchanging weather patterns.

Rising Moon looked up into the sky, seeing something flying. It was not a bird or a cloud formation.

She touched Catriona on the arm and pointed it out to her, "What is that?" It came closer to them and Catriona could see it clearly, with excitement and relief mounting within her.

"It is a drone, a mechanical flying machine that is searching for me. There were drones like this on the spaceship. It has locked on to the signal from the console in our boat that you insisted we keep." Catriona took in a deep breath before speaking again.

"There are people from the spaceship who are alive and here on this planet. My mother and father may still be alive," she exclaimed and then shouted to Rising Moon. "We must stand apart and wave our arms like crazy, so it will come over and see us. It will make a recording of us standing here and take it back to wherever it was launched from."

They waved, shouted and cried out as loud as they could on that lonely promontory, jumping up and down like marionettes on strings.

The drone passed over them twice. First on its journey to pinpoint the location of the signal from Catriona's escape craft and then back over the two young women. Then it turned southwards to its point of departure.

3: Tom and Liz

Dr. Tom Hagen's blistering speech to an elite forum of political and corporate leaders at the United Nations in Geneva, Switzerland in 2080 changed the future of humanity.

Gathered before him were the power brokers from around the world. Tom was an astrophysicist, engineer and prolific author. He wrote searing plays about human fragility and books for children to inspire them to care for the Earth.

Tom's endeavours did not turn the tide of wilful ignorance about drastic climate change. This was despite his creation of detailed scenarios to adapt Climate Change and business ethics, both of which imperilled life on Earth.

He was also the chef-de-mission of the International Space Agency's PRIME 3 project to locate a suitable planet, as habitation on Earth was compromised. The entire project was outlined in Space Agency folders that each member of the audience had before them.

The International Space Agency had established research stations orbiting Mars and on Jupiter's smallest moon, Europa. It had an iron ore and rocky mantle, similar to Earth, yet the rocky interior was covered by a layer of ice 100-kilometers thick. An ocean was identified beneath Europa's frozen crust. Radical advances in space technology made this possible mid-century, through the invention of space elevator carbon nanotubes and revolutionary steps in nuclear fusion engines for spaceships. Station One at Jupiter was the key construction.

From there a probe, PRIME 1, was launched into the heliosphere through a wormhole into interstellar space. In a neighboring galaxy it had located a planet with two moons in an ecliptic plane with a dozen planets orbiting around a massive sequence star, the sun for this system. The planet had a liquid hydrosphere similar to Earth.

A more sophisticated probe, PRIME 2, sent back information identifying distinct zones from tropics to polar with evidence of oceans, forests and mountains. No sign of habitation was revealed. Both probes identified a dense particle field in the upper stratosphere of the planet, similar to a Van Allen belt. The long term plan was for Jupiter One to serve as a way station to ferry pioneers to the new planet. This project required massive financial support that Tom was trying to elicit.

Tom was standing quietly at the podium in Geneva, readying to speak. He had both good and bad news for his powerful and wealthy audience, deeply hoping that some of them would finance this late opportunity for survival of the human species. Tom looked at his carefully researched notes then put them to one side. This speech, the most significant of his life, had to come directly from his insight and heart.

He composed himself, standing still and silent at the podium, six foot three inches of intense focus, dignified and alert. He took his glasses off and placed them on top of his notes. Sian, his wife, sitting off to one side of the podium smiled in relief. Tom's fifteen-year-old daughter, Catriona, was sitting in the front row, dressed in a fashionable grey pant suit picked out for her by Sian to offset her lustrous red hair tied up in a bun. Her mother had fetched her from her boarding school in Switzerland. She knew Catriona would love to hear her father speak.

Tom looked around at his audience, one he did not particularly like, but one he had to convince. He saw Catriona in the front row beaming her smile to him and he relaxed a little. He breathed deeply and waited for that icy steel of reason and vision to ignite his insight.

Then he began to speak in a calm, clear baritone voice: "In this very moment what is left of the population in Australia is being evacuated. The sand storms and volcanic eruptions in the interior plus successive coastal tsunamis have brought an end to human occupation there. The inundation of Bangladesh, the Netherlands and coastal regions around the world are a direct consequence of the collapse of the Polar Ice Sheets, which increased sea levels by seven meters. Such cryogenic events have dislocated half the global population, ushering in plagues and pestilence that eliminated ninety per cent of other species and directly threaten human survival. These are facts that cannot be refuted. Furthermore we cannot turn away from the fact that our entire planet is suffused and overwhelmed with refugee camps and utter desolation."

Tom paused for several silent moments and made eye contact with the few individuals there who would support him. He glanced towards Catriona who adored him, and this helped him to gather his wits. The facts he had just delivered set the tone for what was to come. He knew many of his listeners would be offended. He slowly took a drink of water from the glass in front of him.

"In the early part of the Twenty-first Century it was possible to make the leap to a zero-net-carbon world. Yet the opposite trajectory was chosen with a rapid increase in greenhouse gases because wealthy nations and economic enterprises like yours doubled their production of fossil fuels."

He glared at his audience, "Did you not notice that degradation of the Earth's ecology was the catalyst for radical Climate Change? Did you not see that food crops were destroyed by horrendous heat waves? Did you not realize that food riots and world panic trace back to one cause, the economic agenda of your energy extraction? I know where your collective power was invested. It was in political, social and economic structures that centered on the carbon combustion complex. Did you not discern that this collective agenda was destabilizing world order?"

Several members of the industrial elite stood up and left. There was another pregnant pause, as Tom waited for them to walk out without comment.

"Your focus on economic wealth at all costs was stupid. With blindfolds towards the devastation caused, you directly went in the wrong direction. Your brand was, and is, a dysfunctional global financial system lurching from one disaster to another throughout the century, ignoring the welfare of populations and the ecological breakdowns caused by the consequences of your actions. May I remind you that the economy is a mere sub-set of the mother lode of ecology and you have successfully destroyed most ecosystems on Planet Earth. On your watch not only did financial collapses signal dangerous global watersheds, the world food system crashed along with the chaos brought in by climate change. Nobody moved to ask different questions and find different answers. The anger of the populace turned on their more powerful masters of capital and politics. At the extreme end of the spectrum of violence this anger has boiled over into lynching corporate and political leaders held responsible by eco-militias, the false defenders of the Earth who are basically anarchist criminals. The heinous actions of these black clad anarchists are certainly an extreme response to your control, lies and doublespeak. But none of you are safe from their reach."

That dangerous reality registered like a punch in the stomach with the rich and powerful still present.

Tom said, "Look back over this century and see why such violence has emerged. Millions of people have died from thirst, starvation and disease. Death arrived from every pestilence available, some of it created in your counter-intelligence labs. The countless millions who have died do not include the many wars waged over scarce resources, particularly water. The reason for such wars lies with your greed for money, control and power leading directly to the cascade of disintegrating eco-systems. Government, industry, banks and financiers grew wealthy while they permitted a systematic breakdown of failing ecosystems on Planet Earth. I have spoken before to gatherings of this nature and provided a reminder to us all about the course we are headed on. I will try one more time."

Tom felt exasperation arising within him but continued on the same track. "Your willful ignorance of warnings served to discredit climate change scientists and oceanographers screaming that eco-systems were disintegrating. You silenced and jailed citizens with the integrity to save the Earth. But it was never about the unanimity of science or free speech. It was about the brand of economics favored by your fossil fuel complex, a collective cabal of extraordinary power that extended its reach to encompass all-powerful corporate ventures. You know who you are."

Once again Tom paused to sternly stare at his audience. "You single-mindedly created a powerful culture of denial about climate change and how it has impacted the cryosphere to such deadly effect." There was an angry tone in Tom's voice as he stepped away from complicity with diplomacy.

"Social order broke down in mid-century ushering in the overthrow of governments, the establishment of martial law and Nazism. All of which increased the desperation of populations worldwide, who took to the streets in mass riots. In the vacuum of social order vicious warlords and militias took over many parts of the world. You have all suffered from the violence of so called eco-militias, which hunt down and string up in the streets those politicians and corporate leaders they hold responsible for the collapse of Earth's eco-systems. Let me be clear. These eco-militias do not serve the Earth. They are pathological criminals on the loose, yet in many parts of the world they constitute an ever present danger. You and I have lost many friends and colleagues to the murders they have carried out. They are extreme, but you are just as extreme. Somehow you inherited the Nero gene, fiddling with indifference while Rome burned. The entire planet has been allowed to burn on your watch. Perhaps at this late stage you can learn something from Rumi, the Sufi saint. He said, 'Sit down and be quiet. You are drunk and this is the edge of the roof.'

Tom allowed an entire minute for that to sink in before continuing.

"Your policies and brand of economics have forced humanity off the edge of the roof and you can now see the consequences worldwide. Big Oil and government create incredible propaganda campaigns to promote oil and gas extraction, irrespective of the damage caused to ecosystems and populations. They produced false images of reforestation, utmost safety, deep concern for wildlife, populations and clean water. This played to receptive audiences yet decades later we find rivers and lakes occupying a wasteland. Oil derivatives swiftly poured through interconnected waterways and aboriginal populations world-wide that once augmented their households with fish, game and forest products are no more. They either relocated or died. This effectively torpedoed any form of transition to a sustainable, renewable economy."

His explosive speech secured the exit of more power holders, though his next words caused a few of them to stop in their tracks.

"The billionaires amongst you have well equipped and tightly defended underground bunkers to escape to, but I have bad news for you. The deep core drilling for oil and gas all over the world, particularly in fragile ocean beds, has compromised the tectonic plates at the center of the Earth. The tectonic plates are now moving faster and rising closer to the outer crust of Earth. Wherever they collide precipitates world-wide volcanic eruptions and earthquakes that will first of all destroy your underground bunkers. It is estimated that billions will die from the volcanic explosions and many of those surviving will likely die from poisonous gases and the inevitable tsunamis in every ocean. Seventy years ago seismologists provided the critical evidence that deep core drilling and fracking were directly associated with the rapid increase in global earthquake and volcanic epicenters. Tectonic plates ride on a fluid like core, known as the asthenosphere, and the tectonic plates that are now colliding trigger massive earthquakes and volcanic eruptions. Repeated warnings from scientists to ban deep core drilling were ignored, bringing the unspeakable into reality."

Tom paused and took a deep breath before looking around at his depleted audience. "I ask you at this late stage to do one last noble thing. Take a good luck at the dossier provided by the International Space Agency. Support the PRIME 3 space project to the tune of fifteen billion dollars. That is what it will cost to build a new spaceship and create a viable outpost at Jupiter Station One. The very future of our species is at grave risk and presently lies in your hands. PRIME 3 is the last Hail Mary to begin anew without replicating the structures and policies that have led to the inevitable demise of Planet Earth."

Tom stopped talking. He was greeted by cold silence. There was no applause. No-one acknowledged him. He walked steadily to the side of the stage where Sian was standing. A look of sheer admiration lit up her face at his bravery. She embraced him lightly and sweetly. She held his hand as they left the podium.

Catriona stood up and took her father's arm and joined him and her mother as they walked up the center of the UN forum. She was so proud of her father but noticed that no-one would meet his eye. He strode purposefully as the rich, powerful and greedy studiously ignored him, or so he thought. Still, Sian sent a smile to everyone who appeared to be in some kind of shock, stasis or agreement. They passed through the security of the UN building and started to walk down the graceful stone steps.

Tom let out a long slow breath, as he glanced at Lac Geneva sparkling in the distance. "I sure blew that one Sian and Catriona. Hardly any one of those bastards allowed what I said to sink into their mind. I have no idea where I can turn to ensure the PRIME 3 project gets funded."

"Perhaps you may be wrong my dear Tom," Sian softly replied. "Look over there."

An armored limousine had drawn up in front of them. Heavily armed guards quickly fanned out in a defensive format. One guard opened the side door of the armored vehicle. Out stepped Seymour Hansen, the president of the biggest bank in America. He was a tall, commanding figure. His greying hair offset by deep flinty blue eyes that he now fixed upon Tom.

"Dr. Hagen, you do know who I am?"

Tom nodded.

"I just listened to your blistering rant. You may be surprised to learn that it impacted me deeply. I have sent a line of credit to the International Space Agency for the fifteen billion dollars required for your project. I am not buying a seat for myself on your space craft, as I doubt that I possess the necessary credentials. I have lined up a consortium of technologically sophisticated corporations. They will provide whatever technology and systems you need. They will deliver, as they are in my thrall."

Tom was stunned, yet asked, "Why are you doing this?"

Seymour Hansen replied, choosing his words carefully, "Your speech stung everyone, some more deeply than you realize. I admired your courage as well as your vision and precision. As far as I am concerned I would not trust anyone else with this space project. I may not be alive to see its fruition and neither will those who just listened to you. There are no strings to my offer. Just get it done."

Tom stood dumbfounded at hearing this from the most powerful oligarch in the world. He had no words or grace in that moment. Thankfully, Sian was endowed with both. She gracefully stepped forward to their benefactor and gently kissed him on the cheek, simply expressing their gratitude.

Hansen smiled, his flinty eyes softening, "It's good he has you Mrs. Hagen for the necessary graces." He held his hand out to Tom, who shook it firmly and gratefully, "Dr. Hagen, get it done."

Tom nodded, as his heart expanded with relief and determination.

Sian was delighted that Tom's vision had been supported. Catriona was jumping up and down with glee, laughing at the bewildered look in her father's face. Sian had to shake him by the shoulders to ensure it had sunk in.

"Tom," she spoke firmly, "this victory needs to be celebrated. Do you recall that astrophysicist turned artist you so wanted to meet?"

Tom said, "Do you mean Liz Abbot?"

"Yes, that is her name," exclaimed Sian, "There is a gallery in Geneva putting on a display of her paintings, and she will be there today to talk about them. Shall we make that our celebration? I feel it is important somehow."

Catriona clapped her hands and exclaimed, "Yes, yes we must celebrate this incredible breakthrough. I have heard of this artist at school and would love to see her work. Let's go."

Tom wholeheartedly agreed and summoned a driverless car from his watch. It arrived within minutes to take them to the gallery, tucked away in the charming center of Old Geneva. He had read reviews that extolled the artist's ability to think and express beyond the box and fascinate her audience with cosmic and mathematical perspectives.

Liz was standing at the entrance to the gallery and welcomed them in. Her deep dark eyes were a magnetic enhance to her beauty, with long dark, wild hair and a slim form encased in black leather with red Christian Louboutin's high-heeled boots. Catriona had never seen such an outfit and was astonished at their difference in fashion. Liz's outlandish outfit enhanced the graceful stone architecture of the gallery. Tom and Sian glanced in at the complex abstract detail of the huge canvases. Bold, near mathematical in nature, it felt as though they were observing different phases of cosmic design, explosion and fusion.

"Are you Liz Abbot, the artist?" Tom politely asked.

"Yes, I am indeed." Her grin embraced all three of them. She stopped smiling for a moment, pondering a further reply. "I would not really describe myself as an artist. I am a strategic thinker and roam outside the ordinary. Sometimes my focus is on cosmic art, at other times I design eco-communities and space craft, and also stand mathematics on its head."

The long pause between them brimmed with unspoken potential.

She said, "Do you recall that Alan Turing guy, who broke the Enigma code of the German Reich last century?"

Tom's attention was immediately engaged, as was Catriona's.

Liz elaborated, "Turing, along with a few other mathematicians in the 1930's showed that no system was closed. They took a big swipe at the Logical Positivists who felt they were in charge of science. Turing and his pals were thinking about mathematics only, but their views applied to everything, language, religion, music, art, space travel, astronomy, you name it. Systems are open and always were. That's why you cannot keep hackers out of computer systems. I was an ace at that, but it was way too easy for me."

Tom and Sian smiled at the addition of "hacker" to her extensive resume.

"My other passion right now is building a main frame for a computer so it can re-invent itself. It just needs an appropriate set of free floating algorithms to be built into its core structure. It was through art that I was able to crack this." She walked them over to another room in the gallery to look at her most recent work, which caused Tom's mouth to drop wide open as he could intuit where she was going.

"Look at this new piece in the puzzle. I have not talked about it to anyone. That is until you showed up." There was a long silence before Liz directed them to a mosaic of cryptic threads spread out next to one another in a tight circle. It had immediately mesmerized Tom, as he could see each unique strand and also see the strands disappear into a kind of vortex once he glanced at the whole.

Liz observed him intently and quietly remarked, "I think you have got it."

Tom chuckled, "I have stepped into something that I vaguely recognize, but do not know what it is. How did you come to create this masterpiece?"

Liz was forthright, "I was just waiting for my mind to switch into a different phase. It took dreamtime to bring it out. I dreamt over several weeks that I was in a monastery, most likely Old Tibet, as there were monks chanting and clashing cymbals. I was doing a formal martial arts dance in the dream, very slowly making a sequence of movements which never repeated. I always started from the center of the grand meditation hall extending to the periphery. I would dream several intricate sequences each night, picking up from where I left off the night before. On waking up I would write down in my own shorthand code precisely what I was tracing out with my movements in the dream."

She pointed to a thread of symbols on her painting as the first one, laid out in her own code of remembering. "Then I would dream other precise, unanticipated movements until I had a full circle of unique symbolic threads." Liz indicated the direction of the spectrum laid out with eerie precision on her canvas.

"It seemed to take on a life of its own, appearing as a kind of vortex driven by the sum of its parts. It looked like layers upon layers of Mayan Calendars and the experience was like the out of body experience you sometimes get in medicine wheel ceremonies or at drug induced raves." They all stared into the vortex created from Liz's dream dancing.

"What I think happened is that I dreamed the algorithms to expand the main frame of advanced computers beyond their built in limits. I have to take one more step, to turn each thread I painted into a mathematical form. Then I will have the algorithms needed."

Tom gasped at the erudite genius emanating from this young woman. Sian was smiling at Liz with the understanding of a Celtic Seer. Tom spoke first, "Liz, I am Dr. Tom Hagen, head of the International Space Agency project to find a new planet."

"Yeah, I know who you are, which is why I laid the Turing stuff and algorithms on you."

She then took Tom totally by surprise, "Now tell me, do you want me to work with you on settling this new planet you have already found with the PRIME 2 probe?" Tom and Sian looked at one another with amused amazement.

Liz continued, "Dr. Hagen I have read the books you wrote on establishing communities of different scales. I could design a better strategic plan for you. I also have a Ph. D. in astrophysics. I guess you know that or you would not be drawn here. My specialty was space craft design, most of which is baloney, but we can talk about that later." There was mischief dancing in Liz's dark eyes.

"Why did you need us to show up?" asked Catriona.

Liz looked at her somewhat waspishly, "It was your father who needed to see how my work coincides with the space mission. And what on earth are you wearing dear girl? With that red hair you should not be in a grey pant suit. This is the heart of European fashion, don't you know?"

Catriona was well able to stand up for herself and she shocked Sian with her reply, "I prefer to attend the UN not dressed like a prostitute." She eyed Liz up and down from top to toe much to Liz's enjoyment.

"Good one little girl. So, are you up for an adventure now that I have revealed my mind process for your father? How about you come on a shopping spree with me to get new clothes for you?"

Catriona carefully declined but Sian burst in, "I would certainly go with you."

Liz replied, "Naw, this would not be an adventure for old tarts, just for young ones."

Sian's mouth fell open. She felt offended by this suddenly strident, rude artist. But Tom winked broadly to her so she could catch on to Liz's ploy.

Liz looked at Catriona and said, "Look now, I can get real bitchy but just to find out who I am really talking to. Do you want to understand my paintings? Very few folk get to have the artist unfold the mystery. And hardly anyone gets an invite to go shopping with me"

While Sian and Catriona were startled, Tom was smiling as he had at last found the project assistant he was looking for.

Liz turned to Catriona with a different tone in her voice, "Now Catriona, how about that shopping spree? I heard you play solo violin with the Gothenburg Orchestra in Paris last year. I know you are a musical prodigy. You know I am the same in art and astrophysics. Do you really want to pass up a shopping spree with me? We will leave the old tart with the old fart and have some fun."

In spite of her elegant manners and sophistication, Sian burst out laughing and encouraged Catriona to take the outrageous offer. Catriona was smiling broadly, impressed by the exercise in adversity and nodded her assent.

Liz put her arms around Catriona, "OK, let's motor."

Tom with great equanimity announced, "This old fart is taking this old tart to the best winery in Geneva. And Liz, you are definitely hired for the PRIME 3 mission."

Tom had found the design scientist he had been searching for to get the PRIME 3 project moving. There was another strategic member to join his team that he had not yet become aware of.

4: The Transfer Particle

Manny Fredericks was of Hopi descent, a brilliant astrophysicist with a distinctive mystical flair. He published a provocative treatise on parallel universes and combined astrophysics with aboriginal ways of placing energy and intent from one universe to another. Manny alleged that the mystical native component mirrored the Transfer Molecule, a cross over particle that science had long sought for in its understanding of co-existing universes. The elusive particle was believed to have properties that enabled it to cross from one universe to another and alter energy patterns.

Tom had met Manny at a conference on Transfer Particles. Liz knew him well, and it was she who brought the published work to Tom's attention. He immediately tracked Manny through his advanced optic phone and explained the PRIME 3 space project. Their conversation focused on the mystical component alluded to in Manny's treatise. They were both excited at their blending of thoughts. The conversation ended with an invitation for Tom to travel to the Hopi Mesas in Northern Arizona to see and experience for himself. Tom jumped at the opportunity and days later he was at Phoenix International airport.

It was hot and dusty inside and outside the airport. The expansion of desert had penetrated from the Sonora right into the city. Such desertification was taking place all over the world as global temperatures rocketed ever higher with Climate Change. Manny was waiting for him. He was tall for a Hopi, over six feet tall. He wore a white T shirt with *'Don't Worry, Be Hopi'* emblazoned in black across the front. His long black hair was pulled into a pony tail and his chiselled face lit up with a smile when he saw Tom walking towards him, extending his hand in greeting. There was a helicopter from the Space Agency to fly them directly to the Hopi pueblos. On the flight Manny explained that his people had largely evacuated their villages with the encroachment of the desert.

They flew over a relentless scorched landscape that reached to the horizon until the six-hundred-foot Mesas loomed out of the dust and sand. One pueblo was still inhabited by elders who kept the ceremonial cycle alive and indeed evolved it further to anticipate Earth collapse. There was a cadre of supporters taking care of them. His grandmother had called in the elderly Keepers of the Energies. They were patiently waiting for Tom and Manny's arrival.

As Tom stared out the window observing the stark environs of the desert, Manny provided a brief overview of Hopi cosmology. Tom listened intently, fascinated by the year round ceremonial cycle that challenged humans to evolve through intricate and complex rituals. Generations of anthropologists who had researched the Hopi were baffled by the intricacy, not realizing that the obstacle to understanding was their lack of mystical grounding. Manny presented a rhythm of life through their chasm of disbelief, feeling certain that he and Tom would be instrumental in closing the lack of knowledge.

Times had changed radically since Hopi lore was first examined. There was openness about lack of understanding and a readiness from the Hopi Elders to fully share their mystical knowledge. In this particular moment the elders were prepared to assist the PRIME 3 space mission in a manner unexpected by either Tom or Manny. They had already been "seen" by the Hopi Elders, who were patiently waiting for the cosmic order to unfold.

Manny asked Tom, "Do you have the co-ordinates for the new planet's location? My grandmother will need to know that very precisely."

Tom did have the location specs, including the worm hole, but wondered why an elderly Hopi Elder would need them. He did not voice his query, but Manny picked up on the concern.

"Tom, do not be fooled by my grandmother when you meet her. She has a Master degree in quantum physics. She has made it clear what she needs from you. She may look like a traditional elder, but there is much more to her than that."

Tom smiled as Manny provided further information about this formidable woman.

"When she graduated from MIT her professors begged her to continue to a Ph.D., as they had rarely encountered a mind like hers. She declined, as her life trajectory was ceremonial and creating new vistas for harmony with what she knew from science and her Hopi tradition. Her entire thesis was grounded in ceremonial principles and built with impeccable logic to move the boundaries of understanding. She provided a new level of expression and intent and was the instigator for me to write the article that brought you here. You will find her an extraordinary woman."

Tom nodded and changed the focus by asking Manny whether he was choosing science over ceremonial.

Manny gave Tom a broad grin. "With a grandmother like mine, there was no choice to make. While I am devoted to science and love it, I do know where my starting point is. And if I ever forget, I have that steel trap mind of my grandmother to deal with." Manny dug into his pocket and pulled out an envelope addressed to Tom. "My grandmother has a message for you. Here it is."

Tom carefully opened the envelope and stared down at the neat handwriting.

"My grandson is integral to the ceremony we will create. It is necessary for him to accompany you on the journey to the new planet. He has the knowledge to provide a foundation for your enterprise. You will need him."

This note was not a request. Tom intuited that he was about to face the largest leap of faith of his entire life. He carefully tucked the note inside his jacket pocket and asked Manny to provide some details of the ceremony that was being prepared by the Hopi Elders. Manny composed himself and placed his mind in his grandmother's and began to speak the words she would use.

"My grandmother asked me to wait until you asked this question. She has four Sacred Keepers, including herself, and they have already prepared the kiva for a new departure in their ceremonial cycle. The kiva is a large underground ceremonial chamber. It is like a womb in the Earth body. It enables life and death to enfold in seamless continuity. It is built of stone and placed in the central plaza of the pueblo in accordance with the four directions: North, East, South and West. The ceremony takes place in the underground chamber. It has a sunken fire pit in the centre and this will be used as the central circle of a medicine wheel constructed in the kiva for the first time. My grandmother felt this was essential. Access to the kiva is by means of a ladder reaching into the upper chamber, which pokes up four to five feet above ground. This architecture is the heart of Hopi cosmology."

He placed his hand on the medicine pouch at his belt that he had received from his grandmother as a young initiate into the mysteries. Manny paused for several minutes, as though he was listening to his grandmother's voice before continuing the education of Tom.

"In the ceremonial chamber my grandmother has created a sand painting, using traditional symbols for animals, sea and lake creatures, corn seeds and plants, sky and earth. She has added new symbols for your spaceship and the new planet. You may understand now why she needs to know the precise location. You must inform her when you meet."

Tom leaned in closer to Manny so he did not miss a moment of the archetypal knowledge that was being shared.

Manny explained that the four Sacred Keepers were unanimous in their enthusiasm for the interstellar venture. Manny's grandmother was the Keeper of the Sky People and would be sitting at the North stone of the medicine wheel. She would track and find the energy passage to the new planet once she was provided with location specs. The Keeper of the animals was already gathering their essential energy to transport it through time and space. He would be at the East stone. The Keeper of corn, plants and trees had spoken with these families and requested their co-operation, which was granted. That Sacred Keeper, an elderly woman elder, would sit at the South stone. The Keeper of the Earth would be located at the West stone for her to usher in the energy of new beginnings.

Tears suddenly began to run down Manny's cheeks as he realized the immensity of what the Hopi Elders were offering.

"I will be at the fire pit right in the center of the chamber. My task is to keep the inside circle of the medicine wheel open so there is a portal for the energies to pour through to their destination on the new planet. The Sacred Keeper at the East stone will also concentrate on the spirit world energies to assist me. My grandmother called me in to do this, as I have been trained by her and have the spiritual strength to hold the portal open. The four Sacred Keepers have specific energies to concentrate upon and send through the portal."

The tears had not stopped as Manny said, "The Keepers are elderly, all in their 80's, and I now realize that this ceremony is their last before departing this life."

They were both acutely silent, struck by this blow of terrifying dedication, taken aback that the Four Sacred Keepers were offering their lives to enable a renewal on a distant planet that none of them would experience.

Tom asked: "Manny, will you survive the ceremony?"

It was Manny's turn for silence. Eventually he answered slowly, "No, I will not die in the sacred kiva, because I am coming with you to the new planet. You did get the instruction from my grandmother did you not?"

They both permitted a grim smile, but were overwhelmed by the intentions of the four elderly Sacred Keepers of the Hopi.

The helicopter hovered over the dusty main plaza in Orobai – the only inhabited pueblo. The Hopi villages clung precariously to six hundred foot high escarpments looming out of the desert terrain, distributed on three rocky mesas. The buildings in Orobai pueblo seemed almost surreal as they poked out of the desert overwhelming the escarpment. Sunlight glinted on old vehicles and modern trucks, barely reaching inside the remaining dwellings which were shuttered against the desert.

Orobai pueblo was the center of the annual cycle of ceremonies and this was where the remaining elders and their supporters now lived. They could see a gathering of people off to one side of the plaza when the helicopter was put down to the north of the kiva. The four Sacred Keepers were standing there wearing traditional garments, white tunics with dazzling Hopi woven blankets thrown over one shoulder. Their demeanor, calm and unworldly steadiness struck Tom forcibly as he looked over at the four incredible people who had offered to help his mission.

He was introduced to Manny's grandmother and the three other Sacred Keepers. They had dark wrinkled faces and they spoke to Manny in a deep guttural manner that felt as if it emanated from an ancient time, which it did. Tom sensed their all-seeing wisdom and deep stillness. They had something outside of time and space about them and cast an eerie presence that made Tom shiver in the heat of the desert. When he looked into the eyes of Manny's grandmother, Tom sank down to his knees before her and wept, just as Manny had wept on the journey there. She calmly held out her hands to him and stood before him. He looked up into the eyes of wisdom, beauty and power.

She spoke to him in perfect English. "Manny has instructed you well." She chuckled with that deep guttural sound he had heard before. "You have the new planet's location for me."

Tom nodded. There was nothing he could say as he passed the co-ordinates of the new planet to her.

She understood and said, "We know what is to be

created here and treat it as an honor to be part of it. It will be your task to place it in order on the new planet."

Tom was included in a circle of the most magnificent people he had ever met. The tears continued to flow down his face.

"This is good," remarked the Keeper of the East.

"Dr. Hagen, do not lament that we will not return from the kiva," Manny's grandmother said. "I reassure you that this is what we want. We are ready to move on and become part of the Sky People. That is something all four of us have yearned for. We gladly reach for that transformation. We cannot invite you into the kiva. You must stay outside, next to where the North stone is placed. I will show you."

She took Tom by the hand and pointed out the chair placed right above the North stone in the subterranean chamber. Her smile was all embracing. "We will be inside with the ceremony for the rest of the day. It will be completed by morning. You are to stay at this location throughout. Our people will bring you water and sustenance. At daybreak Manny will come out by the ladder. There is a flat stone that fits the top of the kiva perfectly. You and Manny will place that over the entrance, as this kiva becomes our tomb, though it is only for our dead bodies. We will have gone elsewhere by dawn."

She looked deeply into Tom's eyes and he felt he was gazing into universe after universe. "I have one request. Do not ask Manny what took place in the ceremonial chamber of the kiva. When the time is right he will inform you. Until that time, please resist all curiosity about the Transfer Particle. The fact that you land safely on the new planet in the next galaxy is proof enough."

90

Tom relaxed for the first time, "I now understand Manny's reference to your steel trap logic!"

She smiled again and he felt the deep love she extended to him and to all beings. She summoned her three companions and they nimbly climbed down the ladder into the womb of the Earth. Manny was the last to enter the kiva, pulling a wood and vine cover over the top opening.

Tom took up his station at the North apex. For the first time in a long time he began to pray. He was not particularly spiritual but at that moment he was. He remembered the chants and sutras from his flirtation with Buddhism much earlier in life and reflected on the teachings of impermanence and emptiness. In that long night under the desert stars he internalized all that he had ignored for so long. He knew his contribution to the Four Sacred Keepers was stillness and the absence of thought. He allowed his scientific mind to recede and felt deeply in his body the unification of universes. Tom opened up to a reality of something he had no prior knowledge of.

The taste of the burning fire pit at the center of the medicine wheel was pungent in his mouth. Although the night was cold, beads of sweat broke out on his forehead and ran down his cheeks, splashing onto his buttoned shirt. He was starkly aware that the Sacred Keeper of the Sky People was directly below him. Manny's grandmother had given him specific instructions and he kept to them as though they were sacred vows. He was in unfamiliar territory, which became more and more unusual as the night proceeded. Yet he was prepared to make that leap of faith to completely trust the elderly Hopi Elders who were offering their lives.

Deep sobs arose in his chest and he cried uncontrollably several times during that long dark night.

The first light of dawn on the desert horizon was not a relief, just a marker of the most significant act of his life. The morning breeze raised a brief sand storm. He gripped the wood of the sturdy chair upon which he sat. He felt the knots of the hard wood with his two hands. This grounded him deeply to the experience of the four Sacred Keepers who he knew were now dead. Humbled by their nobility he waited patiently. He made it so through the night until he heard Manny's steps on the ladder and was there to embrace him as he climbed out of the sacred kiva.

His new friend looked gaunt and bereft, yet had a steely determination in his eyes. Between them they lifted the stone slab and placed it on the top opening of the kiva. They sat at the North apex where Tom had been stationed, very quiet, full of wonder and not a little grief. Breakfast was brought over to them by the other elders remaining in the pueblo, who knew what had taken place. The coffee was good, as were the corn tortillas. There was no need for any conversation or analysis. Tom and Manny entered the helicopter and were quickly ferried to Phoenix International airport. It was a silent journey. Both men knew they had been radically changed. They looked down on Planet Earth in all its devastation and glaring beauty, knowing that soon they would leave it behind and there was no coming back.

Progress on the PRIME 3 space project had quickly accelerated after Tom's 2080 speech. The project was surrounded by the devastation of Climate Change and a world of refugees on the move or in camps. The rapid decline of safety on Planet Earth added a sense of urgency. Liz and Manny provided precise protocols to carefully scrutinize the many pioneer applicants for this new venture for humanity. They checked background and career, eventually choosing one hundred individuals with a similar desire to begin anew with principles rooted in ecology, caring and sharing.

The engineering team enlisted Liz's expertise and created a sleek craft, much smaller than intended with reinforced tungsten plates on the hull and nose. This was to more easily penetrate the dense particle field identified in the upper stratosphere of the new planet. Tom also designed a self-contained laboratory that could be jettisoned from PRIME 3 in an emergency. The lab had space for fifty persons in addition to seeds, plants, fertilized embryos in deep freeze, sophisticated communication consoles and small fruit bearing saplings amidst other essential requirements for a new settlement.

The launch of PRIME 3 from the International Space Agency HQ in 2085 took place on the Colorado plateau. It was surrounded by a USAF base and was not publicly announced. This denied the opportunity for militias to interfere with their progress. The travel sequence involved a series of steps. The first stage took approximately one month to the Mars station with technicians on board in addition to pioneers. All systems were double checked for the more severe strains anticipated for the longer space flight to Jupiter One. The journey to Mars Station went very smoothly, just as planned.

During the long two month flight to Jupiter One there was training for everyone: escape crafts, martial arts, emergency procedures and daily seminars of expertise from the carefully put together contingent of pioneers. Those not in training were entranced by seminars on the use of drones, the skill of councilors, eco farmers, irrigation experts, yet by far the most popular were the talks by Manny on his Hopi heritage and how it was based on respecting the Earth Mother and bringing forth the best in people. Liz and Tom discussed the type of community they could establish. Liz spoke eloquently about the pros and cons of a communal structure as opposed to an eco-town structure. There was much discussion as preferences coalesced on trying out the communal structure first of all.

At Jupiter One Station there was a change in flight deck personnel. The Russian pilot and all American flight crew that had brought them from Earth were replaced by Captain Thomas Murphy and four astronauts, two couples from the Russian and Chinese Space Agencies. They met and mingled with the pioneers who enjoyed this respite from space travel before PRIME 3 continued its journey through interstellar space.

The technical team that completed all the checks was replaced with another readied technical team at Jupiter Station One. Both teams, flight deck and technical, spent almost a week together to ensure everyone was on the same wavelength.

There was also a sad farewell, a mourning of Planet Earth and the way of living that was no longer viable.

Tom and Sian spoke at length to the pioneers of the immensity of not going back to what they had left behind.

In their different ways they emphasized that the ties that drew them to this human experiment were a mix of ethics, respect for ecology and for communal integration. This was a time to reflect on their bold adventure to begin anew for humanity.

The discussion was quiet, respectful and determined. They all realized that things would get difficult, stressed and likely break down at times. Yet their resilience was the glue to re-integrate and persevere. The staff and personnel at Jupiter One Station participated fully in this discussion, as they saw themselves as an extension of the pioneer community.

This essential time phase also enabled the pioneers to be conducted around the vast complex built at Jupiter's Station One. Captain Murphy and Tom were close friends and overjoyed to be on the same mission. They co-designed the protocols for pioneer behavior on board the space ship, making life safe and enjoyable.

Captain Murphy acquired the nickname of Cappie from Sian and could never shake it off, much to everyone's amusement. As a pilot, he was in a class of his own in the International Space Agency, meticulous and adventurous.

The careful specs identified for the wormhole preoccupied Captain Murphy's attention. He was shown the location on a space chart where it was most likely to appear. On sighting it, he would have to execute a specific split-second sling shot manoeuver to pilot PRIME 3 through this conduit into the next galaxy.

Captain Murphy pored over charts with his crew and the scientists at Jupiter Station One to ensure he had the exact location of the vicinity of the worm hole in interstellar space. The worm hole had received prior PRIME 1 and PRIME 2 probes. The question was whether it would receive a vessel much larger than a probe. This worried him and he knew he had to find the exact route in the center of the worm hole to get through in one piece.

His meticulous preparations paid off. After spending a relaxed time on Jupiter One, it was time to get the pioneers on board and ready for the next stage. PRIME 3 blasted off from Jupiter One and Nikolai, the navigator from Russia, called out the prior space markers that preceded the entry to the worm hole. It was right where the scientists at Jupiter One had mapped it.

Captain Murphy very carefully allowed the spaceship to overshoot by a slight margin before he banked PRIME 3 into the slingshot manoeuver he had practiced diligently on the simulator prepared for him on Jupiter One.

His flight deck crew from Russia and China held their breath and then cheered wildly as the spaceship banked off the rim of the wormhole right into the center. They were elated and relieved, as this was their first encounter with such a space phenomenon. The pioneers were not privy to the drama on the flight deck. They were firmly strapped in safe harnesses, as they had anticipated a bumpy ride through the wormhole. Yet the journey into the next galaxy was surprisingly smooth, almost as if the new planet was welcoming them into its orbit. Once through the worm hole, Captain Murphy asked his Russian navigator to lay in the course for the new planet.

The young people were excited to be on the last leg to the new planet. They eagerly participated in the many training exercises, yet had occasion to bring their gifts to the other pioneers. Catriona gave a violin concert, Nikolai's son Igor organized a chess competition, Sian talked about meditation and therapy, and Captain Murphy started sing-a-longs, which were a hit with everyone. There were daily chores, which emphasized the ethics of caring and sharing.

They were two weeks away from the new planet when Manny brought Tom's attention to four young men, rugged, extremely fit and in a state of constant readiness. They were kindred to his experience as a Navy Seal in the US military, a prior life to his university studies. Manny noticed that they did not draw attention to themselves and merged quietly with the crowded throng of pioneers. They were super-alert, did not engage too much, but would meet for a meal every few days. Manny recognized the mannerisms that reminded him of his own military training.

Tom surveyed them and approached them in the dining area. "Gentlemen, may I join you?" said Tom as he placed his tray on their table.

The tallest one made room for him and replied, "Of course Commander Hagen."

Tom replied, "I will come straight to the point. The four of you are obviously a Special Forces unit. I need to know who you are reporting back to. Are you a Black Op that the Pentagon and CIA know nothing about?"

He glanced at each one of them before stating that the spaceship communications operator had detected encrypted messages coming to and from a console not on the flight deck, but traced to their quarters.

Tom said, "Given the deteriorating situation on Planet Earth and the difficulties we may face on the new planet I need to count on your skills and not anticipate a separate agenda. I know the credentials you embarked with are certainly accurate, but you bring much more with you to this mission."

The tall, fair haired man looked up, "Commander Hagen, with all due respect we must discuss this and report back to you." There was no denial, just plans for a rendezvous the next evening. Manny was at a nearby table and had monitored the brief exchange. His intuition was confirmed.

The flight deck communications operator alerted Tom and Manny that encrypted messages were exchanged shortly after this conversation.

The next day, at the same time and place, Master Sergeant Marshall Edwards introduced himself. "I am in command of this unit. To my left are Martinez and Chung. On my right is Johnstone. You were correct."

He smiled and looked over at Manny. "You can bring Manny over from the next table. Just as he recognized us, we saw clearly that he was of a similar training."

Manny grinned and came over to sit with them.

Marshall paused and glanced at his three men. "Last evening and this morning we communicated with our handler. Our orders are simple, to support and protect the PRIME 3 mission. We are instructed to work closely with you sir, in whatever way you wish. I am authorized to reveal who we report to and that is Seymour Hansen."

Tom looked at Marshall with surprise at hearing Seymour Hansen's name.

Marshall said, "We have special skills quite apart from what is on our resumes, which are totally legitimate. In addition to my expertise on eco-communities, I am a specialist in drone usage and have two of them distributed in parts amongst the four of us. They are much more sophisticated than the four Space Agency drones you have on board. I am also an expert in advanced communications. Martinez is an agronomist and an ace tracker. Chung does have legitimate credentials in Chinese Medicine and acupuncture yet his capability in weaponless combat is unsurpassed. Johnstone has credentials in irrigation systems but his military skill is that of an ultimate survivalist."

Manny was carefully studying Johnstone, noticing how this soldier's face held sharp angles with no warmth in his eyes. Manny, with his mystical indigenous background, felt he was looking at a dark skull, a dangerous quality in his culture.

98

Manny addressed the Master Sergeant directly, "Is it necessary for your ultimate survivalist to be carrying three knives under his shirt and one larger knife attached to his right thigh?"

Johnstone stood up angrily, "Mind your own fucking business! I carry what I need!"

Tom interrupted, "Johnstone, I am the commander here and there is a rigid protocol that weapons are not be carried by any pioneer on board."

Johnstone sneered, "I ain't a pioneer – I'm part of this unit that has a job to do. So call off your hound dog." He glared at Manny.

Marshall Edwards intervened quickly, "Johnstone, hand your knives over to me immediately, then return to your quarters where I will speak with you personally."

Johnstone angrily divested himself of his weapons and requested to be dismissed. This was granted by his commanding officer.

Then, Johnstone stood up and intentionally stepped in the direction of Manny as he turned. Manny was carefully watching for this and easily sidestepped him.

Johnstone's fists came up but Chung and Martinez swiftly restrained him. Johnstone glared hatred at Manny and the sinews in his arms almost popped before he walked off in the opposite direction.

Marshall apologized and noted it's his responsibility to restrain Johnstone.

Tom said, "Marshall, keep an eye on that man. He seems to be like an explosion waiting to happen."

The tension round the table receded, though Manny had heeded Johnstone's warning signal. "Mr. Hansen asked me to pass on a communication to you sir. I think this will provide a different view of him and perhaps of us." Marshall pulled out his console and placed it before Tom.

Dear Tom,
The four man unit on board is reporting to me. They are there to support and secure your mission on PRIME 3. Personal tragedy now places me in a similar position. My wife, children and grandchildren were all massacred by an eco-militia at our family compound in Maine. This was well defended with state of the art surveillance and commandos chosen from Special Forces. The eco-militia had, over a period of time, tunneled underneath the guarded perimeter and came out at a small copse of trees by the kitchen. They were well armed and ruthlessly killed every member of my family. I had been called away the previous evening for a meeting with the President, so their main target was not available. On hearing multiple gunshots from the house the commandos went on the offensive, too late to save my family, but they killed all the militia and blew up the tunnel.

With great internal turmoil and grief, I decided not to pursue hate and revenge. Instead I liquidated my assets on Earth and placed that fortune to service the Jupiter One Station and your mission. This is what my wife and children would have wanted me to do. I arrived on Jupiter One several weeks ago after your departure in PRIME 3. I am communicating with you from there. My organizational and financial skills now serve the new beginnings you have eloquently spoken and written about. I am also doing my fair share of cooking and cleaning on Jupiter One as prescribed in Jupiter One's charter – I thought such intel may lighten your day!
Sincerely,
Seymour Hansen

Tom passed the console over to Manny so he could read the communication. Tom felt the grief and turmoil described by Seymour Hansen and quietly marveled at his choice of transformation. After their initial meeting in Geneva, he and Sian had spent several holidays at Seymour's compound in Maine. A deep friendship had developed, as they found themselves on the same page on many issues. Tom looked over to Marshall and asked quietly if he could reply to Seymour Hansen. Marshall passed over a keyboard and connection. "Commander Hagen, we will leave you for a while and return later." His unit and Manny walked away to provide privacy.

Tom stared at the keyboard. He was completely distraught by the massacre of his benefactor's family, so took time to settle into steadiness and compassion.

Dear Seymour,

My heart is very heavy right now, learning of the tragic loss of your family. I am humbled by your resolution to support the new beginning we hope to establish on the new planet. You in fact are the person who made it possible. The Jupiter One Station can only be enhanced by your presence and acumen. I wish there were more people like you. I will talk to the pioneers on board PRIME 3 about the example and support you have provided this mission. You chose not to hate and pursue revenge. You placed everything you have into the rebuilding of human society with caring and sharing. Your wife and family will be so proud of you at this moment and all of us here are deeply grateful. We offer our love and sincere condolences for your grievous loss.

My wife Sian and I are so much richer from the knowing of you, and indeed look forward to your cooking! We remember the salmon dish you cooked for us when we last visited your home and family several years ago.

Your friend,
Tom Hagen

Tom sat very quietly with the communication from Seymour Hansen and certainly did not anticipate the desperate turn of events awaiting them.

He was suddenly roused by an alarm from Captain Murphy. PRIME 3 had run into major damage as it entered the dense particle layer in the high stratosphere of the new planet. It had lost the thrust of one of the nuclear engines. There was a hull breach next to the damaged engine, which killed thirty pioneers.

Tom's engineering skills along with Liz's design faculties had adapted PRIME 3 to be compartmentalized into unique units that could be isolated when necessary.

The rear of the spaceship was locked down.

Sian grabbed his arm to help their daughter Catriona into an escape craft. There were ten still functioning and all ten were quickly occupied by the youngest members onboard and ejected into space. This was completed like clockwork as the children and their parents had been trained meticulously for such an outcome.

Tom and Sian then raced to the laboratory, ushering in the remaining pioneers who knew what to do. They had run repeated drills of where to strap themselves to the lab wall. This unit was placed close to the hull.

Cappie – Captain Murphy – was in constant and precise co-ordination with his Commander. He waited for the last frantic seconds of getting the lab door closed and spoke to Tom through his earpiece:

"Commander Hagen, on my count I will open the hull hatch right next to the lab container and you can fire the explosive ejection charges. My flight crew has already ejected in the escape crafts on the flight deck. I have one next to me. Once you are clear and I can see you, I will use it to exit the spaceship and hopefully find you in a day or two. I have set PRIME 3 on destruction mode two minutes after that. Precisely in one minute I will have a position over the sea adjacent to a sub-tropical zone. You will hear my countdown and then wait ten seconds before the lab container is ejected."

The calm, steady voice of Captain Murphy was the salve required by Tom in that instant. Marshall's unit on Tom's instruction had brought in the two remaining escape crafts to assist navigation of the clumsy container now crammed with people and specimens.

Tom and Manny waited for the Captain's countdown, plus ten seconds, then simultaneously fired the ejection charges that threw the titanium water-tight laboratory beyond the trajectory of the failing spaceship.

Through the small windows Tom could see, several minutes later, the destruction of the spaceship. Tom whispered a prayer that Captain Murphy got away in time.

He felt a heavy burden of responsibility at losing thirty pioneers. Doubts and regrets filled his mind as to whether sufficient thought had gone into the space ship design.

He struggled with his sorrow and felt alone, so alone. Would he ever see his daughter again?

There was a sickening dread in his stomach that they had come so far but was the price in human lives worth it?

He bowed his head and then felt Sian's hand on his chest. He held her hand tightly and wept in her arms.

5: Marguerite Bay

The lab was equipped with four massive parachutes which opened once it was clear of PRIME 3. The splash down was almost an anti-climax. So gentle, as the buoyant lab submerged under the sea and then surfaced. Hatches at the top of the laboratory were opened by Marshall and Manny. They pulled in the huge parachutes to eliminate drag and placed the two escape vessels in the water facing towards a shoreline some miles away. Chung and Martinez from Marshall's Special Forces unit quickly entered the escape crafts, activating the motor drives and towed the clumsy lab unit towards the nearest land mass. Marshall was watching their progress from the front hatch at the top of the lab's roof. Manny was lookout on the other side.

A tree fringed bay stretched before them for approximately five miles. With binoculars Manny could make out slightly elevated ground beyond the white beige sand, sheltered by a limestone cliff formation to the south. The water was a calm turquoise with a gentle rhythm rocking the structure of the lab. The elevated ground onshore gave way to alluvial slopes that merged with a valley beyond. He was looking at a lush sub-tropical paradise.

Manny called across to Marshall, "The sand is flatter on your side. The sea is at high tide and receding. If we empty the container of people's weight, the lab would be more buoyant and we could move it to the south end near the limestone cliffs. We are in shallow water. I see that

105

Chung and Martinez have beached the escape crafts and are bringing ropes to fasten to the lab."

Marshall shouted down to the remaining pioneers to climb out through the top hatches and down the ladders on the outside. Manny mused to himself that this exit was very similar to his leaving the kiva in Orobai.

Chung and Martinez fastened their ropes to the bottom of the outside ladders. Only Tom remained inside to open the main door once the lab was beached. Soon there was human muscle power round the perimeter of the lab. Following Manny's directions they pushed and pulled the now buoyant lab through the water to the south end of the pristine bay. Once beached, the sea water receded leaving the lab close to the high tide line. It was safety roped to large trees on the shoreline. At Manny's call, Tom opened the front sliding door of the lab and stepped out.

Tom knelt and picked up a handful of wet sand and smiled wearily to his friends and looked around at the unbelievable beauty they had been delivered to. "Thank you my friends for preserving this laboratory intact. We have emergency rations for everyone. Sian and Manny will bring them to you. I know the taste is not great, but the proteins, liquid and sedative will settle you, as we take a moment to gather ourselves."

They rested on the warm sand, gratefully receiving basic rations. Then they listened to Tom's calm voice saying. "We are here at last, safe on this new planet. But we have lost special friends. Ten of our younger people, including my daughter Catriona, left PRIME 3 by escape crafts. Sian and I are praying for them all to survive. I know there are parents who are feeling just as distraught as we are, but please know we are determined to find these young people."

Tom paused as he and Sian embraced all the parents. They hugged and shed tears, sharing the same ordeal.

Tom continued, "Captain Murphy and his crew make five more in escape crafts. Each one has a tracking device that connects to the console in the lab. My fervent hope is that they will find us."

He paused for a moment, thinking of his daughter clasping her violin case, as Sian placed the oxygen mask on her face. He stifled the gasp of fear and grief of losing her. He continued to speak in a steady tone. Only Sian knew of his inner turmoil.

"The hull breach and engine explosion in the rear of PRIME 3 took the lives of thirty friends. We are now seventy in number," he said grimly. "Yes, I have done the math and it deeply disturbs me. Our first priority is to create shelter and support for everyone. We must take time to remember and honor our lost companions. I suggest we each pick up a stone for everyone we were close to and together make a small pyramid. I see lots of dry driftwood above the shoreline. Let's make a large bonfire over the stones. This evening we can say or sing whatever is in our hearts as we comfort one another. It is also essential for everyone, and that includes me, to receive support from our wise councilors. Sian will now talk to you about that."

Sian gently looked around her friends, sitting and lying on the white beige sand.

"Dear ones, we have come through a severe ordeal and will be feeling shaken and disheartened by our losses and the worries about our children's safety. Fortunately we have skilled people who can help in this situation. You know that I am a music teacher, but more significant is that I have practiced as a therapist for many years. I encourage you to come and talk to me about how you are feeling right now. Rather than bear the pain alone, it is so much better to share it with skillful therapists. There are several amongst us who can do this. Do take a moment to enjoy this glorious setting, but I encourage you not to neglect deep feelings at this time."

She gestured to two women standing next to her. "You know that my two friends, Maggie and Mary are skilled therapists. They provided counsel on our long space journey. We lost many good people in the explosion on PRIME 3, and deep down that has shaken all of us. I will be speaking to Maggie as I am deeply worried about my daughter Catriona. They both will be consulting with me. None of us are exempt from the grief and loss. Maggie, in addition to her therapeutic skills is a wonderful gardener and naturopath. Mary has created abundant permaculture domains in all kinds of climate zones. I have worked professionally with them both and it was always a treat to discover their other gifts. You can consult with any one of us, individually or in small groups, whatever you are most comfortable with. Confidentiality is assured."

Sian smiled to everyone and presented her fellow councilors as M and M, much to everyone's amusement.

Maggie was a tall woman with vibrant blonde hair. She introduced herself as M1 and Mary as M2 because she was so much shorter. She explained their particular skills in neuro feedback procedures. It used mind feedback systems to deal with emotional grief, trauma and anxiety. She talked about how the therapy encouraged the brain to adapt from distress and reorganize itself in an organic manner. She and Mary had worked to good effect in post tsunami situations as well as war zones. Their main focus was to release the places where one had got stuck, by improving neural plasticity.

The audience knew about this therapy as M and M had offered a number of intriguing seminars during the months of space travel. Mary emphasized the bounce back feature and the use of software that created gentle music patterns to bring the brain to a "reset" mode. They worked from a base line established by tiny sensors placed on the client's skull and ears that picked up the electrical activity of the brain. Mary quietly looked around her many friends and said. "We are here for all of you and I entreat you not to shove your grief and feelings down. Please allow us to provide some assistance."

Once Mary stopped talking, Tom thanked the three councilors and asked Mary to keep a space open for him. He encouraged everyone to swim, relax, or walk along the beach and to ensure that they talk to one of the councilors. He postponed assembling their well-practiced and prepared teams until later and walked over to Mary to start the process of releasing personal and collective suffering.

He said very quietly, "Mary, I am trying to keep up a good front for the pioneers that are left, but my guts are churning with fear, guilt and suffering. I keep asking myself if the design team of PRIME 3 missed some strategic safety measures. What more could I have done to protect those killed by the hull breach. Help me Mary, please."

Mary gestured to Tom to walk with her to a quiet spot away from the beach then gently spoke to her good friend. "Tom, you do not have to put up a brave front. These people know your character and bless your leadership. That leadership can come out strongly this evening when we honor our dead companions and you must let it out how viscerally you are grieving. They can all identify with that and are waiting for something authentic to emulate."

Tom nodded and sat still while Mary retrieved her small case that held the sensors she placed on different parts of Tom's skull. Mary asked him what hurt him the most. Tom took a deep breath and his eyes watered.

"It is the fear of never seeing my daughter again. I know she is resolute, smart and brave but I do not know where she landed and what is around her. There is no way I can protect her."

Mary took note of the sensor receptors, played several chants on the feedback monitor to calm Tom and said. "Tom, trust in the training you and others provided for Catriona and all the other children. They know how to survive. They are resilient and far stronger than you give them credit for. You passed on to Catriona all your expertise and do you not think that is enough? The other children are capable and smart. They may well surprise you, though perhaps not their parents who know how skillful their kids are. "

Tom replied slowly, "That much is true Mary, but I feel I do not have it all together to lead this community at the present time. Thirty pioneers are dead and that is on my conscience. It is my fault they are not with us." He put his head down and gripped his knees to regain his composure. Mary waited patiently until his breathing evened.

"Tom, do you think you are the only one in charge? The only one who is responsible? That is not so. We are all in charge and we are all responsible, not just for the grief but for creating a renewal in this magnificent environment. Sian, Maggie and I are working hard to keep this community afloat and integrated. Why don't you delegate the immediate task of shelter to Marshall's unit? They are soldiers and better placed than you to restore order. Lean on all the leaders that are around you and stop thinking that you are the only one in charge. Chef-de-Missions have to step down now and then and this is the time for you to take that step down. Now close your eyes while I play some gentle rhythms to calm your worried mind."

Mary continued, "This is hardly the arrival you anticipated, Tom. But look around you. Could you possibly be in a more beautiful environment? After a long space flight you have arrived at a holiday camp of extraordinary beauty. The natural surroundings provide a glorious opportunity to bounce back. Think of how lucky you are. Walk around and experience where you have arrived. Consider offering blessings for all of that rather than dwelling totally on the grief and loss."

Mary smiled, "You are much calmer Tom. Put into practice the guidance I have provided and come back and see me on a regular basis."

Tom thanked her and received a gentle hug from his good friend. He walked over to Marshall and passed over a flat metal box, the same as he had given to Catriona. He said, "This has two prototype lasers that can clear brush and trees. They can split wood into planks and simple beds can eventually be made. For now, we need temporary shelter until we get a better sense of what is around us. What do you think?"

Marshall nodded and added, "The parachutes can provide fabric for tent and ground cover. We know what to do."

Tom reminded him to read the instructions carefully for the laser tools. Marshall examined the lasers before replying, "We will need to cut down some of the trees so we can make rollers to put underneath the lab and move it onto land, and we can make use of the rollers afterwards as benches and tables. I think we must be scrupulous about cutting down trees. Remember the Easter Island folly where the Polynesian population cut down the trees and could no longer build canoes for deep sea fishing"

Tom smiled in agreement, "Yes, let us start right at the beginning with an environmental ethic."

Marshall said, "We are on the same page Commander. Thankfully the lab is placed at the top of the shoreline, which makes it easier. We will need no more than ten rollers to move it."

He and his Special Forces unit took off to the tree line, while other members of the mission relaxed in the warm sea water. Then without any directions from Tom, small teams of gardeners and eco-farmers began to explore the surrounding area looking for suitable planting areas and fresh water. The cooking team started to gather rocks to make a large fire pit. Manny made a number of spears from nearby saplings and taught his foraging team how to harvest the curious fish exploring their unexpected presence. There was a lot of joking about the huge fish that got away. They presented twenty large gutted fish to the cooking team, who were excited at the feast they would prepare. The cooks opened a container in the lab delivered to them by Liz. It revealed eating utensils and a stack of aluminum trays that would serve as plates.

Marshall and his unit found a mixed composition of trees and brush on the elevation beyond the tree fringe facing the bay. Johnstone pointed out certain trees that should not be touched, as there were bananas and coconuts to be harvested. That was their first discovery. Johnstone and Chung took this unexpected bounty to their fellow pioneers. Marshall and Martinez carefully cleared the brush with the laser tools, taking down selective trees to make rollers. Their initial clearing created space for a camp to emerge. They dug latrines at either end of the elevated mound with palm branches woven over a wooden frame as a screen for privacy. With great care they created a design of tents in a semi-circle facing the beach from the slight elevation of several feet. Using the laser tools they made rough-hewn tables and benches and placed them in the middle of the semi-circle of tents.

Several small tents for couples and four large dormitory tents for men and women were quickly built. They worked through the afternoon making their makeshift camp simple yet spectacular. One large parachute was cut into tent size portions for smaller units, while the dormitories were open at the front with fabric stretched over wooden frames. There was sufficient fabric for ground cover to sleep upon. The climate was warm and little else would be required at this time. Marshall looked around for Johnstone, but he was nowhere to be seen. Johnstone had his knives returned to him, but burned with resentment that he had been publicly humiliated.

Marshall walked back to the shore and informed Tom that the camp was almost ready, though Johnstone had disappeared. Tom said, "He will return once he gets hungry. He is a different kind of person. A loner, he has to investigate his surroundings for himself. We must keep a sharp eye on him and not put too much of a restraining leash on him. What do you think?"

Marshall replied, "I have been on many military missions with Johnstone and he is the ultimate professional soldier. I did not notice this side of him before. If I had I would have advised that he not be on this mission. But that is too late now. Here he is."

Johnstone walked towards them carrying several dead animals he had hunted.

He said, "Sir, here is some protein for the community. I had a hunch there was game beyond the ridge."

Marshall took the kills from him and said calmly, "Thank you Johnstone, this will go over well at this evening's meal. Please ensure you let me or other members of the unit know when you are hunting."

Johnstone took this direction as a rebuke and abruptly walked back to the camp to assist Martinez with the final tasks there. Tom and Marshall exchanged knowing looks, but remained silent.

Manny and Liz were establishing the lab as a HQ for medical care, research and communications. They walked back one hundred yards with everyone else and there on the elevation above the shoreline was their camp. They exulted in the beautiful quarters established for them so quickly.

Marshall and his company were somewhat embarrassed at all the praise and thanks.

Sian was delighted with the tent for Tom and her. Everyone found a resting place that pleased them.

Marshall pointed out where a fire pit could be placed adjacent to the tables and benches. The cooking team got to work, built the fire pit and prepared a great feast with fish, meat, bananas, coconut and just a few rations for their first meal together. It was soon served.

Tom asked Manny to say a Hopi Blessing before they ate together in silence, in gratitude, before talking.

Manny stood up and said, "This blessing is the Hopi Prophecy from the beginning of this century. That would be June 8 in the year 2000. I feel it is appropriate for our first taking of food on this new planet." Then he began to speak with great reverence the words of a Hopi Elder.

"You have been telling people that this is the Eleventh Hour, now you must go back and tell the people that this is the Hour. And there are things to be considered.

Where are you living?

What are you doing?

What are your relationships?

Are you in the right relationship?

Where is your water?

Know your garden.

It is time to speak your truth.

Create your community.

Be good to one another.

And do not look outside yourself for your leader.

Then the Elder clasped his hands together, smiled and said, "This could be a good time! There is a river flowing now very fast. It is so great and swift that there are those who will be afraid. They will try to hold on to the shore. They will feel they are being torn apart and will suffer greatly. Know the river has its destination. The elders say we must let go of the shore, push off into the middle of the river, keeping our eyes open and our heads above water.

And I say, see who is there with you and celebrate. At this time in history, we are to take nothing personally, least of all ourselves. For the moment that we do, our spiritual growth and journey come to a halt.

The time of the lone wolf is over. Gather yourselves! Banish the word "struggle" from your attitude and your vocabulary. All that we do now must be done in a sacred manner and in celebration.

We are the ones we've been waiting for."

This and other blessings became the regular feature prior to meals with different friends who presented a grace, song, poem or reading. The silence too was preserved, so discussion afterwards came from a deep, quiet place.

Manny sought out Tom after dinner and sat beside him. He had carefully observed Tom addressing pioneer gatherings on the long journey aboard PRIME 3, and saw how he had continued on the new planet under such great pressure and sadness.

He marveled at the manner in which Tom led from the center, to establish a course while not insisting on a particular agenda, his presence, attentiveness and humility allowed inspiration to seep through from all quarters. He noticed that Tom did not criticize opposing voices, that he was patient and solid with generous smiles, as he encouraged ways to arrive at consensus.

Manny said, "Tom, the Hopi Blessing that I recited before eating talks about leadership. Would you tell me more about your leadership?"

Tom looked at him steadily for a while. "Manny you must find your own balance, so that you are authentic. With "authentic" you will find humility and steadiness alongside.

116

It took me a while to find that stance for myself. I studied several role models: Gandhi, Nelson Mandela and Martin Luther King Jr. You can find their life stories and speeches on your Earth History console. Just take what appeals to your heart and mind. Do not posture or engage in political theatre. Never, ever do that."

He smiled to his young friend, "We can talk more about this, as I think it coheres with your traditional Wisdom of the Elders." Manny carefully took this in.

Tom said, "We have much to do to settle our community on this new planet, but very soon we can talk more about this. Perhaps we can make it an issue for discussion amongst the community. What do you think?"

Manny replied, "I think that would set a good precedent Tom."

Before people left the dining area Sian asked aloud to everyone, "Can we build our pyramid of stones and firewood here, in the center? It just needs the tables and benches to be moved back a bit. I feel it would be appropriate to keep our memorial alive in the middle of our first camp."

Everyone agreed and moved the new tables and benches, while the cleaning up team cleared the trays. The pyramid of stones and rocks appeared at the center from people's hands. It had grown and was covered by dry driftwood to make a pyre of remembrance.

Mary exclaimed, "Tomorrow morning when the stones are cooled, let us take the stones back into the ocean where we arrived. Their memory will be intact."

"Bravo Mary," called Manny.

The pioneers assembled around the pyre, which had been lit by Marshall. Sian read out in a quavering voice the names of the friends who had perished. She had to stop herself several times as the tears rolled down her cheeks. When she got to the end of the tragic list she asked if anyone wished to speak. Johanna, a botanist, with a shy smile spoke about her friend and fellow scientist Marguerite.

"My dear friend Marguerite enhanced whoever she was with. I would like to name where we came to shore as 'Marguerite Bay.' It is beautiful as she was. It is welcoming as she was. I propose that we keep our friends alive in our minds by naming different parts of our new home after them."

Johanna broke down and cried, quickly surrounded by her friends who held the same grief. They unanimously agreed with her suggestion.

Names gently followed and were bestowed on their surroundings.

John Tinsley, an astrophysicist named the limestone cliffs after two of his colleagues who had perished. They became known as the McIntyre and Gallagher cliffs.

Joyce Melville had great fears for her four children and prayed for the safe landing of their escape crafts. With her husband Robert holding her, she named the pasture newly found inland as Children's Paradise, not in their memory but for their coming home.

Robert said, "Our greatest desire is to show our children the pasture now named for them."

The other parents gathered around them, all deeply fearing the worst and longing for their brave children to be safe.

Robert also dropped two stones in the fire for the Patterson couple who had died in the explosion. Their two sons had been safely placed by Manny in the escape crafts and then ejected into space.

Speeches, songs and anecdotes were in flow for several hours until a natural silence crept over everyone. Everyone fell silent as Tom walked slowly to the bonfire.

He took a few minutes to compose himself. He held open a bag with thirty stones that he emptied into the bonfire.

Tom then spoke to his community, "Dear friends, I remember and honor the thirty friends who perished aboard PRIME 3. I feel gut wrenching responsibility for their death and question in my mind if there was anything I could have done better. After talking to Mary this afternoon, I found something beyond the grief and I have now grasped on to. It is to keep alive the names of our children who bravely went into space on their own in escape crafts. I certainly fear for my daughter Catriona, but know that she is smart, resilient and strong like all the children. They are well trained and will see their landing on this planet as a great adventure. I pledge to all of you that I will never stop looking for them. I will be tireless on your behalf to track their crafts with communication devices and by drones. I will never cease this search as the children are vital for our future. We must support one another in our grief and loss. But not lose sight of our mission to build a home on this new planet. I do not have stones for the children as I intend to bring them home. That is my promise to all of you."

The bonfire burned down to embers over the commemorative stones, as people went to their tents to sleep. The deep gravitas of grieving lifted a little after Tom had spoken, but it needed something more. It was Liz who provided this from the women's dorm.

She shouted into the night, "This is Liz saying good night to Sian."

Sian sang back, "This is Sian sending sweet dreams to Liz as she sleeps." It caught on with gusto and some laughter.

Marshall and his soldiers entered the novel game, "This is Marshall saying good night to Commander Hagen."

Tom bellowed back, "This is Tom, do not use the Commander moniker, good night Marshall."

Marshall shouted back, "Aye, aye sir, good night Tom."

Maggie got into the mood, "This is M1 saying good night to M2." It continued until everyone had been named and called out their greeting. The only person who did not engage was Johnstone. This was carefully noted by Marshall, Manny and by Tom.

Sian whispered softly to Tom, as they lay side by side in their tent, "Now, can you believe this is the new beginning? Catriona will come home to us. I know and feel it, so let the sadness, guilt and uncertainty go. She is alive and her return will be so wonderful for all of us."

6: Liz and Marshall

The early morning breakfast next day was a somber and quiet occasion. The stones were picked out of the bonfire's embers and reverently cast into the ocean. There was heaviness in the hearts of the grief-riven pioneers. They talked quietly to one another about how they were feeling while the cooking team did their best to provide a joyful start to the day with pineapple, coconut and tropical fruits mixed in with basic rations.

It was a beautiful morning at Marguerite Bay after the early mist had lifted. As the community was finishing breakfast they suddenly all froze into silence. They could hear, and then see, one of the escape crafts from PRIME 3 approaching from the north end of the bay.

It was Captain Thomas Murphy bellowing as loud as his voice allowed. As he approached ever closer to the shore, several men plunged into the gentle surf, plucked the Captain from his small vessel and carried him on their shoulders to the beach. The sheer delight of everyone was delirious, tangible proof that indeed they were renewing. Mary brought him some fresh water in a coconut shell and all gathered round the benches to listen to his news.

He told them he had found his flight deck crew. Co-pilot Subing Chen, her husband, communications officer LongFu, and the Russian co-pilot and navigator couple Elena and Nikolai Chutskov were all safe. They had landed in the ocean within communication range. The escape crafts tracking devices enabled Captain Murphy to retrace the last stages of navigation on PRIME 3 and find them North West of where his escape craft landed in the ocean.

He related their story of swift rescue. Subing and LongFu had splashed down next to one another in the sea. They saw another escape craft hit the ocean close by, Nikolai's, but no sign of the last one. They quickly motored over to Nikolai and fanned out to find Elena. LongFu saw where her craft had crashed and lodged into trees, neighboring a sheer rock face. She had been pitched face down into the ocean.

LongFu had quickly pulled her in to his craft and started CPR on her chest. Minutes later Nikolai was alongside, lashing his craft to LongFu's before starting mouth to mouth resuscitation. Subing strung a rope to the two small crafts and kept them from crashing into the rock face on the island. After five minutes Elena took a deep breath and vomited over her saviors. After regaining her breath, she was able to put their minds to rest by saying she had not been in the water too long. She was just stunned when she went head first into the ocean after stepping out of her space craft.

The Captain said, "Elena soon recovered and they will be here soon, maybe tomorrow. I thought it necessary to get to your co-ordinates as soon as I could." Then he chuckled, "But I tell you something, I have never in my entire career seen such Russian–Chinese accord." They all laughed at Cappie, as he came to be known by the name bestowed upon him by Sian at Jupiter One Station.

He looked around with admiration at their camp and then asked, "Is there news of their children, Igor and the twins Lan Lan and Bao and the other children?"

It was Sian who replied, "Not yet Cappie, we need your navigation knowledge to pin-point direction. I feel confident that we will find them all, my daughter Catriona too."

Cappie said, "I have the sequence and navigation for each escape craft in my memory." Then he smiled to Sian, "I see you have christened me as Cappie, so no-one will ever refer to me as Thomas. So be it. You can put me to work but I have one request. If I was not a pilot I would have been a chef, so is there room for me on the cooking team?"

Not only did the cooking team embrace Cappie, they congregated around his skill and acumen. In the days following, Cappie had the eco-farming team create two compost bins for cooking waste. Marshall's unit built raised kitchen beds that were filled with fertile soil and the first plants, herbs and seeds from the lab began their life. The cooking team became the natural hub for the entire community. Cappie had a motto – If your belly is satisfied then we can create wonders!

Cappie's team cooked nutritious food from their rations and what could be harvested from the sea and the land. He established a rhythm of entertainment: story-telling, dancing lessons on the beach, mealtime protocols, a forum for discussions and frequent music evenings. Community solidarity was all beginning to happen with the cooking team at the center. Cappie was in his true element. He was a large, burly man of Irish descent and had the humor and grace to set everyone at their ease.

The laboratory was moved on tree rollers off the sandy beach onto a flat rock promontory after the joyous welcome for Cappie. The entire community used their skill and muscles to achieve this. They felt so galvanized by the arrival of their spaceship Captain. The rollers were then fashioned into benches and tables placed above the five-mile beach and ocean. Heavy rocks were piled around the lab's perimeter to provide a firm foundation. It was constructed as a giant solar panel providing energy for the stockpile of plants, saplings, seeds and fertilized embryos of chickens, sheep, goats and even two dog species. A border collie for work and standard poodle for hunting, though Sian was sure that family pets would perhaps be the main priority.

Tom was deeply encouraged by the visible co-operation of the community. He met with Liz and Marshall to set up the lab as an operations center. Cappie joined them as his expertise was required. Tom held up a wooden plank that he rested on their main console. "The names on this plank are our first priority."

He had inked in the name of each one of the children and spoke their names, "Catriona Hagen, twenty years old; Igor Chutskov, nineteen years old, the twin seventeen year olds Lan Lan and Bao Chen; the Robertson boys – Andrew is seventeen and George is fifteen."

Tom paused for a moment and then spoke again: "May I remind you that the parents of the Robertson boys perished in the hull breach, so we will have to take special care of them once we bring them to this new home." They all took that to heart.

Tom finished the list, "Finally we have the four Melville children, James seventeen, John fifteen, Joan is thirteen and the youngest pioneer Ruthie is ten years old." Tom looked around at his friends. "We have to secure our camp on Marguerite Bay, explore our surroundings and establish a community rhythm, but finding the missing children is the top priority." Everyone nodded in assent.

"Let us talk about our communication systems. Can we reach their escape craft modules? I know they have limited features but can we somehow upgrade them through the systems we have in the laboratory? The same applies for the drones."

Marshall had retrieved the drone components from his small company of commandos, and said, "These drones can fly over areas within a fixed range. They send back live stream and photo data images. I can interpret the data on the communication console I have with me. It was built by a genius so it can upgrade itself through complex algorithms programmed into it."

Liz's eyes sparkled before she entered the conversation, "I can help you with that, as the genius you are referring to is right here." She was smiling broadly. The early light caught her wild hair pulled back into a pony-tail. "How come you have this devise in your possession, Marshall?"

He hesitated for a moment, "My team was brought together by a wealthy financier who supported the PRIME 3 project. He wanted us to have the ability to communicate in a manner never thought possible."

Liz mused for a moment, "Hmmm ...that would be Seymour Hansen would it not? That was the guy who asked me to create it. I thought the devise was intended for your hands Tom, or on the flight deck of PRIME 3, not in the hands of this cowboy."

Marshall looked up, smiling at his new status.

Tom added, "For Liz's computer skills Seymour Hansen agreed to provide food, shelter, medicines and education for immigrant camps in two war zones. I encouraged her not to compromise that leverage. For now, we have an extraordinary control device. Liz, can you tell us more about the system you built?"

With an impish grin she explained what she had created. She reminded Tom of the Art Gallery conversation in Geneva. "Remember my ideas about communication systems being open?"

Tom nodded and waited for Liz to continue. She said, "I built into the main frame of this devise a matrix of three hundred floating algorithms that would coalesce and create something different when it encountered new phenomena." She explained how she mapped her dream patterns first into a piece of art and then into algorithms. "Tom, you saw some of them in my painting. Do you remember?"

Tom smiled to his outrageous assistant. He could never forget her moment of sheer genius. "I do indeed remember and am still amazed at the outcome of your dream dancing."

The first drone was quickly assembled by Marshall and Liz in a matter of hours. It was launched on a trajectory over the valley inland. Marshall was impressed by Liz's adept assembly of the drone and complimented her on her engineering skills.

She brushed it off brusquely, "I know lots of stuff." After a moment she relented and smiled to him, "You know what Marshall, we make a good team. I actually like cowboys."

There was something about this tall, handsome soldier that resonated deep within her, only she did not know how to get close to him. She helped Marshall interpret the live feed and data sent back by the drone. It revealed a glorious vista of lakes, rivers and plateaus. Robert and Joyce Melville had joined them as they wished to explore inland from the five-mile beach. They were elated at the potential paradise unfolding before their eyes on Marshall's monitor.

Tom remarked, "There is more potential here than I ever anticipated." He turned to Cappie and grinned, "You sure knew what you were doing by dropping us at this location."

Cappie chuckled, "There is no substitute for preparation. The scientists on Jupiter One picked out this region from data provided by the PRIME 1 and 2 probes as possibly the most supportive ecosystem on this planet to establish our pioneer community."

Tom hesitated as another thought crossed his mind. "Could the drones connect to the consoles in the ten escape crafts the children were in? I am thinking of my daughter Catriona, as well as everyone else."

Liz placed her hand affectionately on Tom's shoulder. She knew how much he missed his daughter and worried about her safety, as did she. After the Geneva shopping spree in 2080 she had become a role model for Catriona. She was happy to bring comfort to Tom in this moment.

Marshall answered the question, "Tom, it is a matter of range, as we need to bring the drone back each time. Also the communication capacity in the escape consoles is fairly small. Liz and I could build a composite drone to increase range. Perhaps she can open up another means of communication by using her magic algorithms to transfer larger capacity to the small consoles in each escape craft."

Liz was nodding, "Sure can try, cowboy."

She was thinking along a different tangent. "We need your navigation skills Captain Murphy. You very carefully landed us right here, so we should have a precise navigation route. We can work out a timeline and trajectory back to the first ejection of the escape crafts before PRIME 3 self-destructed. Do you have those specs handy Cappie?"

Cappie confirmed that he did. Liz continued her thoughts, "If we can put time and navigation together we would have co-ordinates of where the escape crafts came down and know where to send the composite drone we have yet to build."

Tom clapped his hands and said, "Go to my friends. There's much work for wicked dancers and cowboys." They laughed at his pointed humor. Then the screen went blank on Marshall's console.

"It has gone done some five miles north of here. The last image provides the location. So I will go and retrieve it." Marshall readied to leave.

Liz piped up, "You are not thinking of leaving me behind are you?"

Marshall smiled, "Good footwear, body length tunic and water is all you need."

Robert asked if he and Joyce could join them as he had been examining the hinterland through binoculars and had spotted a range of plateaus that the drone had just confirmed before it crashed. He said, "I would like to take some soil samples and bring them back to the laboratory for testing."

Marshall smiled, "Please join us. I do not think it will take us too long to hike inland for five miles. You can educate me about the eco-village you established in Scotland. I remember your fascinating talk about that on the spaceship."

The small party of four quickly gathered what they needed and set off inland. Marshall had pored over the drone data to find the best way in and saw that the river meandering into the north end of the five mile beach would take them close to the drone. Marshall checked Liz to ensure she had sturdy walking shoes, space tunic and water. She looked dazzling in the mid-day sun with her wild hair caught back in a bun.

"Well," said Liz "Do I pass muster for this journey?"

Marshall smiled and tried not to show Liz the impact her presence made upon him.

He set off to the river and they followed him. Robert and Joyce were overjoyed to see the lush landscape beyond the camp. From the vegetation they could deduce that the soil was highly fertile. They took soil samples as they walked inland close to the river and surprised Marshall and Liz with their constant recognition of plants and possibilities.

Robert said, "This land between the two rivers – see the other river to the south of us - it is bound to be highly fertile and we can grow practically anything with good horticulture."

As they climbed higher they could see a series of linked plateaus. Joyce could hardly contain herself, "That is where we can establish permaculture and orchards, a sort of wild cultivation of the land harvest. This could not be better."

Liz and Marshall listened intently to the education they were receiving from Robert and Joyce. Marshall saw that the river was running through a deep ravine, so they had to climb up the surrounding cliffs protecting the run of water. He warned everyone to be careful where they placed their feet. Liz was walking behind him and bent over to inspect a purple orchid. The surrounding rock gave way and she plunged head first down the cliff. She landed with a thump on a grassy ledge jutting out from the cliff on the other side of the river.

Marshall called to her inert body splayed face down on the small ledge. "Liz, speak to me. Check for injuries so I know what we are dealing with."

Liz responded with a tremulous voice, "Nothing broken. Just bruised with a few cuts. This ledge is not very sturdy and it feels as though it cannot support my weight."

Marshall shouted instructions for Liz to slowly stand up and flatten herself as close to the cliff wall as she could. He bellowed that he was going to abseil down the other side of the ravine and then swing across to get her. While he was shouting instructions to Liz he had pulled the coils of rope from his and Robert's packs.

"Robert there is a large tree behind us. I will use that as the belay post for the rope. You and Joyce will let the rope out on my call as I abseil down. Once I am opposite Liz, I will push off from the cliff face on this side of the ravine and swing across to get her."

Robert nodded, "Understood. We will have to pull you up, is that correct?"

"Yes" answered Marshall, "I can use my legs to walk up the side of the cliff but you must keep the tension taut in the rope."

"I have done this with sheep in the Scottish Highlands many times, so I have some basic training." Robert said.

Marshall was soon abseiling down the side of the ravine cliff. He heard Liz's frightened voice yelling out that the ledge was crumbling. As soon as he was opposite, he pushed off strongly against the cliff face and swung across. He was almost too late as the ledge supporting Liz started to crumble. With a scream Liz felt herself falling as the ledge disintegrated underneath her feet. Just as she started to plunge downwards, Marshall reached the end of his swing across the ravine and caught her as she was falling. Liz clung to him tightly as he roped her in to his body.

The pendulum of the rope swinging across the ravine came to a stop. Marshall shouted to Robert and Joyce to haul them up. He could use his hands and feet on the cliff face, as Liz was lashed in to his body. The climb up was slow and meticulous as Robert and Joyce carefully pulled the two of them to the top. Once on firm ground next to Robert and Joyce, Marshall said, "That was close, Liz."

Her faint voice replied, "It was very close Marshall." She felt that they were talking about different experiences. Liz was grateful to be alive and uninjured. Beyond her fear the closeness to Marshall was soaring right through every fiber of her being. She had felt his heart and bravery as well as his strength. She did not realize that the closeness had also rattled Marshall, who had experienced exactly the same as she. She drank some water and allowed Joyce to examine her for injury. Joyce was a doctor and a vet. She had medical supplies in her pack. She pronounced Liz as sound apart from a few cuts and bruises that she tended to.

Joyce's authority extended to Marshall, "Your turn Marshall. I saw how you slammed into the rock face when you caught Liz. Turning at the last moment so that Liz did not receive any harm. So I need to inspect your ribs for injury."

She carefully examined Marshall's upper body, noticing his winces as she examined his chest. "Hmmm, it does not look like you have broken anything, but you may have cracked two ribs on the left side. You are very lucky. I will put a temporary plaster on the two damaged ribs to hold them in place."

Liz was almost speechless. She said in a quiet voice, "You did this for me Marshall?"

He simply smiled, "Yes." His eyes and hers fused together and drew a knowing smile from Robert.

Robert whispered to Joyce, "I think we are witnessing the beginning of an overdue love story."

Marshall thanked the two of them and was immediately all business. He said. "The drone is not too far away from here so let us move on, so we can be back by evening to Marguerite Bay." They proceeded to the drone under Joyce's protective eyes. It was soon found. Liz and Marshall examined it carefully. Liz observed that the small solar power unit had disconnected from the "eye" of the drone.

She said, "That is easily fixed Marshall. That scare in the ravine has got my brain cells humming and I just thought of something."

She mused for a while as she caught Marshall's attention. "We have four short range drones and your two military drones. We can make a composite drone out of two of them. I can boost the solar unit and reduce the weight. I think the drone was not designed for this kind of climate. Here it is denser with rainfall and humidity, not a feature found in desert terrain. What do you think?"

Marshall pondered about her suggestions. "I wonder why we did not do that in the first place. That is wonderful technical logic."

Liz replied, "Had we already done that, you would not have had the opportunity to save my life."

Although she said this in a flippant tone, she knew that she loved him. Marshall did not know what to say, so he simply smiled at the woman who totally dazzled him. They were silent on the hike back to Marguerite Bay. Joyce and Robert intuited that something very deep was moving in these two young people, so they wisely took up the conversation. They talked about what types of crops and orchard could grow in the open pasture between two rivers. Joyce had a beautiful contralto voice and she sang some walking songs, much to the pleasure of Liz and Marshall.

Marshall and Liz continued their work together and while Marshall learned a great deal about Liz, he was very reserved about himself. He was courteous and soft spoken, yet quietly admired Liz and not only for her extraordinary mind. She sensed something about his demeanor that was not in sync with a Special Forces operative. Liz approached Sian one evening while she was walking along the beach and requested her to shine some light on the turbulence she was feeling.

"Sian, I am falling for that tall soldier, but somehow cannot click on a level I feel we can. I feel that we both fell in love at the ravine incident." She stopped speaking for a moment collecting her thoughts and emotions, then said, "When Marshall saved my life at the ravine, his body and mine made a contact that only lovers can recognize. I know he felt just what I felt. It was something mutually transcendent, outside of ordinary experience. It filled my whole being, all my senses with such tenderness. And here we are working in the lab, day to day, just as though we are colleagues working on a project."

Sian asked Liz to sit with her on the beach and listen to the evening sound of birds calling to the waves gently reaching their feet. She took Liz's hand and looked deeply into her young friend's eyes and heart. "Marshall is a very fine man Liz. You already know that. But there is something in his past you must know in order to understand him."

She was silent for a while. "I did the final debriefing of Marshall before he joined this space mission. His credentials were impeccable but Tom felt there was something deeply hidden and requested me to find it. And I did?" There was a long silence between the two women. Only the sound of the waves could be heard.

"Marshall was happily married to his high school sweetheart and they had a glorious life together. She too was as brilliant as you, but in a different direction. They had a cabin in the Santa Fe Mountains and it was destroyed by a volcanic eruption five years ago. She was there and fled for safety. Marshall was on his way to meet her but was delayed. He drove like a mad man through the blockades, ran in and found her on a Forestry Services road, scarcely alive. He carried her out for five miles before the paramedics met him and relieved him of the dead body he was carrying. He was crazed with grief and guilt. The military saw to it that he got the best therapy available to recover, but I do not know how much lingers in his mind."

Liz chewed on her lip then asked Sian very intensely, "Is he still carrying the dead body of his wife?"

Sian answered, "Only he can tell you that Liz. I will relate to Marshall that we had this conversation." She put her arms around Liz, as she saw the depth of her unhappiness.

In the following days, Marshall did not intimate to Liz that Sian had spoken with him. He continued with his courteous and respectful manner, enjoying their walks along the beach, at times joining in with Manny's boisterous foraging team where they learned to fish with spears and baited lines. They were becoming good friends. He was fascinated by her ability to derive algorithms from her dream dances, intuiting that her self-created shorthand was the key to her art and science. He mentioned this insight to Liz and she was startled by what it awakened in her. She realized that Marshall was not just seeing into her scientific skills. He was seeing into her.

Liz brushed her feelings to one side and said, "The shorthand system I created must have begun way back when I was in art school yearning to be an astrophysicist. It was an intuitive means of mapping form, movement and numbers that I made up for myself. It just evolved while I was doing my art work, meditation and dancing. And it was just for me to know what it meant."

Then with a spark of insight she turned to him, "Why don't you create a shorthand system that is unique to your thoughts and imagination Marshall, and see for yourself what happens?" She did not realize that the consequences of her challenge would encounter all of Marshall's carefully built walls and ultimately change both of them. She was prompting him to trust his heart again.

Marshall struggled with portraying form, movement and numbers in a shorthand mode and only progressed when he stopped wrestling with it. He sat over the table inside the laboratory with specimens, computers and soil samples scattered all over the table surface. He tried to configure his military training and the impact of Liz upon his heart into a condensed form of shorthand unique to him.

Liz had shaken him deeply. He had never forgotten the blaze of energy that surged through him, when he caught Liz's body falling into the ravine, but did not want that to come to the surface. And so he kept his feelings under wraps.

He was getting nowhere with the challenge from Liz. Remembering the breathing exercises of his early military training as a sniper, he placed himself in calm states and the symbolic representations slowly began to form in his mind, like a subtle Koan. Rather than stifle them he allowed the symbols to emerge. That allowance enabled his deep feelings for Liz to come to the surface He left a file for Liz with a cryptic note in his newly shaped shorthand writing.

"I do not dream dance, but can wait for inner symbols to express in my own shorthand."

She studied his newly created short hand and was astonished by its elegant depths. She scribbled a reply in cursive English,

"My eyes see this."

Writing backwards and forwards at this moment was better for Liz than speaking. Her deep feelings for Marshall were not reciprocated, or so she thought. Next time she saw him, she simply smiled not knowing that the symbolic shorthand had shaken his restraint. Next day he gave a note to her, written in a beautiful calligraphy,

"I thank you for your eyes."

Liz stared at the beauty, seeing beyond the depth of his calligraphy into the intimation of something profound and life changing between them. She took in a deep breath, steadied herself, and stared right into him with her dark hazel eyes. "Marshall," she asked sharply, "Are you still carrying your dead wife in your arms?"

He stared in surprise at her for a long time. His green eyes opened wide, taking in everything about her. She knew he would not walk out and be lost to her, as she trusted the deep feelings within herself and within Marshall. It felt like an eternity before Marshall spoke quietly.

"No Liz, I am not carrying the dead body of Amber, my wife. I was overwhelmed by grief and guilt at that time. I carry her love within me and thought that would sustain me for the rest of my life. But I was very wrong, for I have met you. I came on this mission to be of service and to find a way of moving beyond the sorrow. I thought I was done with love without any desire. Yet my fears, sense of loss and inner pain did not go away. That is until I met you, Liz Abbot. I lost one woman I loved deeply. I was not going to lose you at the ravine"

Liz was speechless with astonishment and gratitude.

Marshall took a deep breath, never taking his eyes from the luminous dark eyes of Liz. "The calligraphy is incomplete. I left something out that will express what I feel for you." He spoke it from memory:

"I thank you for your beautiful eyes

I thank you for your lips that I long to kiss

I thank you for completing me."

She gasped at his spoken words and could not say a word. Tears welled in her eyes as her heart burst wide open.

Marshall said, "Dear Liz, I have a thousand and one things to say to you..." His voice petered out as Liz flung herself into his arms. They collided like wind and fire, immediately transported to another realm.

Liz whispered, "I have the rest of my life to hear your words. Just kiss me." He did, gently and deeply. So tenderly did he kiss Liz that neither of them heard Tom enter the lab. He smiled at their beautiful embrace and quietly left, walking back to Sian at their tent. He carried good news.

Marshall and Liz left the lab and sat side by side on one of the benches overlooking the five mile beach. They listened to the magnificence of the ocean rolling onto the beige colored sand. "I honestly thought you would never wake up to love," Liz confessed, leaning her head comfortably on his shoulder.

"What would you have done if I did not wake up?" enquired Marshall playfully.

"I would have chased you down and knocked you into the surf dammit!" With that Liz pushed him off the bench and Marshall convulsed with laughter. This was how Sian found them and she embraced them one by one.

She declared, "This is a time when only good things can happen." Her words were strangely prophetic.

The various work teams at Marguerite Bay continued with their tasks. Robert spoke to them at an evening discussion about the potential further inland for a new settlement. There was consensus that they would eventually build a more substantial community on the inland plateau that overlooked the two small rivers with extensive pasture for planting and irrigation.

Joyce pointed out that on a higher plateau there was the opportunity for permaculture and orchards to be planted. The elevation made it quite a bit cooler.

The excitement was palpable and the planning began.

There were a surprising number of pioneers who were excellent carpenters and builders. With Liz's design help they mapped out a central gathering place for meals and gatherings in the new settlement with plans for simple, elegant cabins, strategically placed around that hub.

It would be impossible to move the lab there, but Marshall and Chung suggested that it should stay where it was and the scientists could be caretakers of an ideal vacation camp. That received a unanimous seal of approval.

Liz joined Marshall early the next morning in the lab to interpret the latest drone data, which showed more details of the planned new settlement. Liz looked up from the console and waited for Marshall's full attention.

"Can you tell me just one of the thousand and one things you have to say to me?"

Marshall turned the console off, looked down at his feet and smiled to himself, wondering how much he should reveal. He received his prompt from Liz when she called out, "I want to hear the biggest thing."

Marshall felt her penetrating eyes upon him and he slowly exhaled. "I trust I do not cause any shock but you did ask for the biggest." There was only a brief silence as he collected his thoughts. "Liz, shortly after I first met you I had a dream about the two of us being married in a ceremony conducted by Sian. It was in a field bordered by a river that tumbled down a waterfall and made a small lake on the bend of the river."

He stopped speaking for a moment, not daring to look at her. "When we started to interpret the drone data recently, I saw exactly what I had dreamed, the waterfall, river, lake and pasture very close to the new planned settlement."

Liz wondered for a moment if Marshall was teasing her. "And what was I wearing?" she boldly asked.

He turned his gentle green eyes to her and replied gravely, "You were wearing a golden silk dress and you were barefoot." From his expression and quietness Liz realized this was no tease.

She whispered, "You really want to marry me?"

His eyes sparkled and his face lit up. "Yes I want that more than anything else in this universe. You already know that answer Liz, but there is something I must ask of you. I still have the wedding rings from my marriage, also the engagement ring. I know Amber would be overjoyed that my life continues with yours. She would offer the rings to you if she could, but this is not something I am insisting on, just asking you."

Liz put her face in her hands and rocked back and forth before speaking, "My dearest Marshall please forgive me for being flippant a moment ago, but you must know that I cannot replace Amber."

Marshall quickly interrupted her, "There is no replacement Liz, you complete me in your own right. I refer to Amber only to relate how happy she would be that I blend my life with yours. Forgive me for my clumsy expression. You must feel in your bones how much I love you."

She slowly nodded her head as Marshall said, "First thing in the morning when I wake up I greet you with "Good morning beauty" and at night I whisper for you to sleep well. You are there with every breath I take. Manny and my team, who are sharing a tent with me, sometimes hear my words. They must wonder what is going on, but I do not feel foolish at all."

He finished lamely, "I also do not see any place around here to get a ring for you."

Liz was moved to giggle at his earnestness, realizing he was desperately floundering with his proposal to her. She looked up at his lovely face and green eyes. "Hey cowboy, let me show you the way." She went down on one knee and held him tight with both her arms wrapped round his legs.

She looked up at him, "Marshall, your words are sheer music to my ears. I could be with none other. As for the ring, I have no logical objections. It just feels strange to me. But here we are on a new planet with different boundaries, so I will allow it."

Marshall picked her up and she lovingly put her arms round his neck. He carried her to the ocean where they had come ashore. He strode into the surf still carrying her. "The ocean blesses us," was all he said. He stopped and felt the engagement ring in his chest pocket. He could not remember placing it there but solemnly asked if he may place it on her finger. Liz was beyond words, smiling consent to her tall, loving soldier.

When she looked closely at the ring, she exclaimed, "Marshall that is exactly what I would have chosen." They returned to shore to find Sian waiting for them. Liz held out her hand to show the beautiful ring, three emeralds embedded in gold.

Sian held her hand in both of hers and winked to Marshall, "You two bring so much happiness to all of us. We see your unity. The ocean does indeed bless you. Hmmm... look at this, three emeralds no less. For you, that means three babies." They all laughed, but Sian knew what she had seen.

"I suppose you will be thinking of a wedding ceremony, but can that wait until we finish the new settlement on the plateau?"

Knowing their consent, Sian linked arms with her two young friends and insisted on a walk along the beach. Drone data could wait for a while. On the way back Liz asked Marshall to show her the location where they would marry, so they returned to the lab.

He switched on the console and immediately looked over to Sian with suppressed excitement. "Sian, please come over here and see this latest drone data." It was from the composite drone that he and Liz had programmed to extend its range to locate Catriona's escape craft. There was a photograph. Sian looked at it and put her hand over her mouth in shock. It was Catriona with another woman, waving and jumping in the series of images recorded by the drone.

Manny and Tom were drawn to the lab at that moment and shared in the sheer joy and relief. Manny held Tom and Sian in a warm embrace, as they wept with joy at their daughter's image.

Tom's eyes shone and the severity he carried on his face melted. His beloved daughter was safe.

142

Sian slumped against his side with relief and said, "At last my fears can be let go. I have been trying to keep up a good front about Catriona and the other children, but my guts have been in knots with anxiety, always fearing for the worst, though saying the best."

Tom started to hum the tune of their favorite waltz and slowly danced Sian around the lab, taking care not to knock over any specimens.

They came to a stop at Manny's voice. He was focused on the other woman in the photograph. "She was not on PRIME 3 and looks aboriginal, like someone from my region a few centuries back. We know where they are. Is there a way to communicate?"

Liz spoke rapidly, "The console in Catriona's escape craft is not designed to receive communication over this range, but maybe I can change that. Marshall my love, can you bring me the console from Cappie's craft? I can experiment on that to see if I can transfer algorithms from this master computer. This might upgrade the capacity of the modules in each escape craft."

Marshall did as requested. He and Liz worked tirelessly through that day and night, succeeding the next dawn. Liz found a way to place several key algorithms into Catriona's console and sent her a brief report that her mother and father were alive.

There was no response, though they sent messages every day for a week. Tom felt sure that Catriona would diligently check in once she had seen the drone overhead.

The messages had indeed gone through, but Catriona and Rising Moon were elsewhere.

7: The Children

After yelling and screaming like mad banshees at the drone, Catriona and Rising Moon rushed back to their camp to monitor the console to see if any messages had been sent to the escape craft. There was not a flicker.

Catriona immediately began to monitor the console on a regular basis. She removed it from her escape craft and placed it in the tipi, ensuring sufficient sunlight reached its powering facility. Rising Moon was intrigued by the Metal Bird, as she referred to the drone. She already knew from Catriona that there were other young people who had left the spaceship along with her, as Catriona had told her of the many training drills for this emergency on board the spaceship. Her sharp instinct led her to ask Catriona what direction was the spaceship tracing in the sky and was there an ejection sequence for the escape crafts.

Catriona carefully pieced it together. "There were ten escape crafts for the young people on board. Mine was fired first of all, then the others at thirty second intervals. The spaceship was on a North West to South East trajectory as the pilot was taking the space ship to the best location for the laboratory to be ejected."

She explained what the laboratory was. Rising Moon took a stick and drew her understanding in the soil. She traced an arc to show that if Catriona had splashed down at the top of the arc, then the other escape crafts must have landed to the South East from where they were standing.

Rising Moon said, "I have dreamed about people from your spaceship to the South East of our tipi. I saw five young people on a large island in my dreams. My mother taught me to pay attention to these kinds of dreams. And I have dreamed this dream two times in the last week, but did not think to mention it to you until now."

In a determined voice, Catriona picked up on Rising Moon's sense of urgency, "We must find them Rising Moon and bring them here. My hand device is good for navigation so we will not need the weight of the console in our boat. It is getting dark now, so let us prepare to leave tomorrow. We need to organize rations and water and make a start in the morning."

On the next day they quickly closed their tipi, walked their boat full of supplies down river to the lake and climbed in. Rising Moon was fully equipped with her weapons and two spears. At Catriona's surprised look, she answered, "It is best to be prepared."

They motored past the high cliff where Rising Moon had landed, after being hurled there from the eighteenth century. On a clear sparkling day they traveled parallel to the shore, noticing animals and trees not present in their vicinity. Rising Moon pointed out mountain sheep on the rocky cliffs and many different species of birds. She stored them in her mind for future hunting. With most of the day gone they had spotted no trace. Then in the distance a large island loomed out of the early evening light and there was a large parachute displayed prominently on the side of a cliff.

"Your dreams were right on Rising Moon," exclaimed Catriona with admiration at her blood sister's capacities to "see."

With great excitement they steered towards this display to find escape crafts tethered to a pontoon floating off a beach of mixed sand and rocks. There were four people waving to them. As they got closer they could see the twin girls, Bao and Lan Lan, daughters of Subing and LongFu. Next to them were the two brothers, Andrew and George Patterson. They were all astonished to be reunited and warmly embraced one another.

Rising Moon then asked, "Where is the fifth one?"

Andrew pointed to a forlorn figure sitting on a rock fifty yards away. "That is Igor. He is grieving the loss of his parents, Nikolai and Elena Chutskov. Igor saw PRIME 3 explode and seems to have slipped into a depression he cannot get out of. We take care of him as best we can, but we do not have the skills to help him."

Catriona walked slowly towards Igor and sat down on a rock facing him. "Igor, it is Catriona here and I have good news for you. People from PRIME 3 made it to the planet after we escaped. Just a few days ago a probe flew over our camp. Perhaps your parents and my parents are alive and trying to find us."

Nothing seemed to register with Igor. Catriona knew she had to desperately draw on her mother's skills.

She said, "I remember playing chess with you on the space journey. You were always so kind, allowing me to take a few pieces before wiping me off the board. You even let me win once or twice, but we know who the ace was." Igor nodded, recalling that memory.

Catriona spoke further to her troubled friend. "I also cried and grieved for my mother and father. It was my friend Rising Moon who pulled me together. Here she is." Rising Moon had quietly come over and sat silently on the other side of Igor. She listened intently to Catriona speaking.

147

"Igor, we think it is a state of mind called depression that has got hold of you. It can be brought about through trauma and grief. Without Rising Moon I could have so easily slipped into the same state. My mother is a skilled therapist and I used to listen to her talking to her patients. She always encouraged them to concentrate on other things in addition to what they were suffering from. So let's try that shall we? Concentrate on how your breath comes in and then concentrate on how your breath goes out. Will you just do that with me for a few minutes?"

Igor said nothing yet responded by following her example. Catriona then encouraged him to concentrate on his left leg with the in-breath and then his right leg on the out-breath, as all three of them walked along the rocky beach. "That's wonderful Igor. I will do that with you several times each day." This did not register with Igor who sat down on his rock and slumped again into depression.

Rising Moon, with understanding, spoke to Igor and struck a spark within him. "My new friend, would you like to learn how to hunt with me? You will have to concentrate on your every movement, then on the creature that is hunted, getting to know it. To pull the bow you need to concentrate so the arrow flies true and the animal does not suffer."

Catriona clapped her hands in awe at her sister's swift intuition. "That would be wonderful Rising Moon. Igor, the more you get your mind to concentrate on other things, the less you allow your grief and trauma to overwhelm you. And just think about it, you do not know for sure what has happened to your parents. They could still be alive. So place that doubt in front of your grief. We will stay here with you to move things in your mind. We have built a beautiful camp not far from this island and you can join us if you wish. Shall we try the concentrations again?"

Lan Lan, Bao, Andrew and George listened attentively and committed to help him. Igor did not speak and sat vacant on his rock but stood up when Rising Moon gestured to him to follow her. She said quietly to Catriona, "I will pull him forward when we hunt."

Rising Moon took Igor on his first hunting training on the nearby hill, returning with a partridge and two rabbit like creatures. She had Igor concentrating on keeping his breath steady, telling him to breathe with her as she pulled the bow string back. She also explained the honoring of each animal that gave its life so they may live. Igor carried their dinner with pride and helped Rising Moon to skewer the meat on sharp sticks that were placed across the fire. Their camp was in a cave above the beach and they had survived on fish and crabs along with their rations.

They talked about their experiences on the new planet while they ate and joked about advertising it as a resort for astronauts. Andrew and George had made hand lines and spears to harvest the lake and their cave was well protected from rain. Lan Lan and Bao had harvested the land when they recognized herbs their mother had taught them to use. That evening Igor seemed to be a little more settled. Andrew made a small bonfire and they sang songs from their different countries, which Igor ignored. Before sleeping, Catriona proposed that they stay on the island for a few more days to help bring Igor back to himself.

In their cave, the morning unfolded with tea, rations and crab meat. A sudden flash of intuition seared through Catriona's mind and she spoke to her friends, "What is the one thing that Igor loves the most?"

Lan Lan replied, "Chess of course. He used to beat all of us at once on the spaceship."

"That is what I remember," said Catriona. "I have a laser tool that can carve out a wooden chess board. We can make the chess pieces and that will surely give him a boost in the right direction to move out of his depression. What do you think?"

"That's brilliant," exclaimed Andrew.

Catriona brought out one of the laser tools from her satchel and went to find a suitable piece of wood. She found the right sized log on the stony beach and made a wooden board that she presented to Igor. She said, "Here is another concentration Igor. This is your new chess board and you can divide it up into the necessary squares. We will all help make the pieces, pawns, kings, queens, knights, bishops and castles. One set dark, the other light. You have to promise that you take it easy on us when we play chess with you."

Igor smiled for the first time in a long time. Bao and Lan Lan had fun searching for small white pebbles, then darker ones for the pawns. Rising Moon was not sure what this was all about. Andrew and George whittled different colors of wood into chess pieces with their knives and soon it was complete. On receiving the chess set assembled by his friends, Igor slowly became diligent with his concentration exercises with Catriona and with Rising Moon, who had taught him how to use her bow and arrows in hunting. He sparkled at the chess games with each one of them, though Rising Moon did not participate as she did not know the rules.

They knew he was ready to leave when he remarked to Rising Moon one morning, "I would like to teach you how to play chess, but you will need to concentrate." He started to laugh and it was contagious. All of them roared with gusto at Igor's steps on the road to recovery. They left early next day. Rising Moon very carefully cut the parachute down from the cliff, knowing it would be needed for the tipi to be built.

Their flotilla of escape crafts reached Catriona and Rising Moon's camp by afternoon. Their friends were in awe of the beauty of the tipi and layout of their safe haven. Rising Moon told the boys about the new tipi she would build for them. The three young men were shown where it would be, across the bridge on a facing plateau.

Rather than intrude on the young women, the boys decided to sleep under the parachute fabric right where their tipi would be placed next day. Lan Lan and Bao prepared the fire and started to make dinner from Catriona's supplies. Catriona walked straight away to her console and was stunned to see daily messages from Liz.

She shouted excitedly across the bridge, "Come Igor, Andrew and George, I have news that my parents are alive and I bet yours are too." She was beside herself with utter joy and could scarcely calm down as everyone packed into the tipi she now shared with Lan Lan, Bao and Rising Moon. She screamed her delight to the universe, to the trees, her friends.

It was Rising Moon who brought her feet to the ground. "Send a message about who is here with us and find their parents."

Catriona was flustered: "OK, OK, what shall I say?"

Andrew, the steadiest person at that moment showed his maturity as he spoke to Catriona, "Use the keyboard on your personal device and lock it into the console. Keep your message simple." He dictated to her, "Catriona and Rising Moon here with Lan Lan, Bao, Andrew, George and Igor. Confirm presence of their parents. Igor is beating us all at chess. Now click on the Send button at the bottom of your hand held device." Andrew spoke calmly, "There may not be a reply until morning, so let us rejoice with Catriona tonight and may she rejoice with us tomorrow."

Liz was in the lab when Catriona's response arrived. She was elated, as a special bond had been struck with Catriona in Geneva during their shopping spree. Liz immediately called for Tom, Sian and Manny to come and bring the parents of Igor and the twins with them. She knew that Andrew and George's mother and father had perished on board PRIME 3. Before they arrived there was further communication from Catriona explaining the state of Igor. Liz carefully presented all the information. The parents were overcome with relief and could at last relax their worst fears.

It was Nikolai who spoke after tears receded. He conversed in Russian with his wife Elena before speaking in English. "Sian, your daughter has learned well from you. My son Igor is a kind, sensitive boy and we both feared for his despair at losing us. The Patterson boys and he are good friends. But we cannot bring joy to the two girls and Igor with devastation to Andrew and George at the same time."

He paused and cleared his throat, "Elena and I wanted many more children but Igor was the only one to come. We would like to adopt the Patterson boys, Andrew and George, so they can be part of our family. I love them both already." Nikolai requested to join the expedition so he could personally welcome Andrew and George into their family. Subing added her presence to the rescue party.

Liz was moved, "I will communicate your precise words Nikolai." She looked to Tom and Manny. "Shall I tell them that we will send someone to bring them here?" Tom nodded.

Manny interjected that he would like to do this as he wanted to know more about Rising Moon. "OK then," Liz replied, "The message will affirm the parents here, Nikolai's proposal and Manny's question about Rising Moon – is that correct?"

Subing the co-pilot of PRIME 3 insisted gently, "Liz, the message must contain our love and joy, also our sorrow for the Patterson boys, as they will need our compassion and attention." Nikolai and Elena agreed.

Liz smiled to them and said, "What about this? Liz calling, Igor's parents are here with Catriona's parents and the twins' mother and father. It grieves us deeply that the parents of Andrew and George did not survive the explosion on Prime 3. Our sadness and sorrow are for Andrew and George. Igor's parents would like to adopt both boys and include them with Igor in their family. We are sending a rescue party that will include Manny, Subing and Nikolai, the prospective father to Andrew and George. Manny requests information about Rising Moon's history. The journey to your location will take about two weeks. The entire love of the community is with you."

Liz mused "I think that covers everything for now. Yes, it is much better. I will send it now and report back to you when I get an answer."

***

Catriona received Liz's communique next morning and paused before relating it to anyone. She decided to speak to Igor who was immediately buoyed up by the news that his parents were alive and well. The stress and fear he carried just dropped away. When Catriona asked him if he would communicate his father's request to Andrew and George, he rose beautifully to the occasion. He knew Andrew and George well and presented the news of their parents' passing very gently, as he knew they would be totally upset. He told them he would love it if they would join his family. Andrew, the older brother comforted George while Igor embraced both of them. The beginning of a new family was sealed amidst the grief.

Lan Lan and Bao were delighted to learn from Catriona that their parents were alive and brought their gentle energy to the three boys they cared for. Bao invited them to join their ceremony for the ancestors. She looked at the Patterson boys with great compassion in her eyes. "This is for all our ancestors, yours too Andrew and George. Catriona and Rising Moon are doing this with us." The simple heartfelt ceremony to honor all ancestors from their Chinese tradition touched everyone. Andrew and George were closely held and comforted by the others, as they cried at the grievous loss of their parents.

Catriona briefly described it in her cryptic message to Liz, "Ancestors honored, Andrew and George supported. Come and get us. Manny, read Trailing Sky Six Feathers and "see" Rising Moon. Our love is booming for all of you."

At Marguerite Bay Marshall mapped a route for Manny, who now included Chung in the party. From drone footage a chart was pieced together that would take them due north along the coast until they came to a slow moving river coming in from the west to empty into the ocean. Further inland there was a tributary that would take them to an east-west chain of interconnected lakes. Catriona's location was four lakes to the west and was the biggest one in the chain. The enhanced console that Liz had experimented on was placed back in Cappie's craft for communication. Subing was pilot and navigator for this craft along with Manny. Nikolai and Chung followed in another vessel. They left at dawn next day, knowing it would take approximately one month for the journey there and back.

They were entranced by the terrain on the northwards stretch, noticing the abundance of fruit trees and other potential settlement areas. It felt as though they could inhale and touch the dense sub-tropical forest lining the banks of the slow, lazy river once they found it. They could see mountain ranges in the far distance shrouded in clouds and recorded the dazzling flora and fauna they passed by. To hasten their journey they motored through the night when the light of the planet's two moons permitted. The dark around them was penetrated by the moonbeams casting light on the canopy of trees bordering the river. The majestic buttes inland and limestone cliffs were etched beautifully by the moonlight, a contrast to the darker recesses across the river hiding their secrets. The landscape they travelled through had a rare beauty with much noise from animals and birds objecting to their passage.

They were surprised by the abundance of flora and fauna and it registered that without human interference a different ecological face would present itself. There were varieties of monkeys no-one had ever seen. The glorious riot of tropical flowers made Subing gasp at their beauty, especially the giant orchids growing by the river bank. They had been warned by Marshall to stay clear of whirl pools in mid-stream and to keep close to the river banks to avoid being sucked in.

On finding the westwards tributary, Manny noticed a plume of smoke that could only come from a camp fire. Subing set a course in that direction. This was much too soon for Catriona's location, but they had to investigate.

155

They were being carefully watched from the river bank, then an explosion of yelling and waving came from four young people. Manny recognized them immediately and waved back. He was soon embracing the four children of Robert and Joyce Melville. This was such a welcome surprise, as the communications team at the lab had been unable to connect to the escape craft consoles of the Melville children. James was the oldest brother at seventeen years of age, followed by John fifteen, and their two sisters Joan and Ruthie, thirteen and ten respectively.

Manny came straight to the point, "Your mother and father are alive at the settlement of Marguerite Bay far to the south of here." The news was like the slow spreading light of dawn, as it sunk into the minds of suddenly happy children. The younger girls burst into shrieks of excitement and tears and were comforted by their brothers. Nikolai and Chung arrived at the river bank and embraced the now radiant children.

Manny briefly explained the purpose of their expedition and was impressed by the camp this young family had created for themselves.

James saw the inspection and offered an explanation, "Fifteen years ago my parents established an eco-village in the Scottish Highlands and we were brought up to be resourceful and resilient. That's why our camp looks so cool." He grinned to his four visitors and directed them to look around and see how they had harvested the land and river.

Manny was aware that the consoles in the children's escape crafts had all malfunctioned so he told them he could communicate to their parents with the console they had borrowed from Cappie's craft. He asked, "What would you like me to say?"

The youngest, Ruthie, piped up, "Tell them we're coming home and we have managed fine with all they taught us. Oh yes, we love you to bits."

James smiled at her outburst, "That's a perfect message Ruthie."

Subing quietly spoke to the four children, "We have to push on, but one of us will take you back. Are your escape crafts in good order and could you be ready to leave soon?"

James spoke for his siblings, "Before you move on, please take tea and food with us. That's what our mum and dad taught us. Our vessels are in good order, although the consoles did not operate well. We kept the parachutes. We can leave camp quickly, but first of all permit us to break bread for this awesome occasion. Who will take us back?"

"That would be me," spoke Chung. "You can call me Chung. I am from Korea originally but served as a Special Forces soldier in the US Army, so you will be in safe hands. We will get to know one another on the way to Marguerite Bay. It is about a four-day journey from here. Did you say you had bread?"

Joan broke into the conversation, "My mum and dad put packets of baking flour in our escape crafts. We are down to the last packet and this is definitely the best occasion to bake bread."

Her younger sister Ruthie had the final word, "It will not take long, so please sit round the fire and my brothers will serve you tea and fruit. We made a fish stew today and the bread will be yummy." She giggled and then got busy.

Their visitors felt as though they were being treated as royalty. With exquisite politeness the four children served a splendid meal, engaged in conversation about the new planet and warmed the hearts of their rescuers. On their journey south with Chung, they indeed got to know one another. They came to address him as "Uncle Chung." He had never encountered such smart and resilient children.

***

Two weeks later Manny, Nikolai and Subing arrived from the east at the bay where Catriona had landed and met with Rising Moon.

The anticipation by both parties was palpable, until their two crafts were spotted from the promontory at the east end of the bay.

Catriona and Rising Moon waved excitedly and Manny raised both arms as a salute to them. The two young women ran from the high bluff and were standing at the shore where Subing, Manny and Nikolai beached right in front of them. There was such delight in their meeting.

Manny gave a letter to Catriona, "This greeting is from your mother and father, from all of us." He smiled respectfully to the Native American woman standing next to her. He spoke to her in Hopi, which she understood well.

Rising Moon replied politely in the same language, "My father was a friend of the Hopi, and the elders there respected the medicine power of my mother."

There had been an instant spark of mystic knowing and recognition between Rising Moon and Manny, who had read about her mother Trailing Sky Six Feathers. They remained silent, staring at one another from across time and space. Catriona broke the strange silence that had settled around them, repeating what she had learned about Rising

158

Moon: this young woman had come to the new planet from the Eighteenth Century.

Manny could scarce contain himself. He spoke directly to Rising Moon in English so everyone could understand the significance of what he had to say. "My grandmother's great-grandmother was trained by your mother in medicine power. The Hopi Elders sent her to learn from Trailing Sky Six Feathers. Your mother's wisdom and medicine were delivered to future generations of Hopi medicine people right down to my grandmother and then to me."

Rising Moon's mouth dropped open at the unexpected recognition of her lineage. She could not speak. Her eyes were riveted on Manny. She felt his words coming directly from his grandmother's mind.

"I know that the spirit of your mother traveled to the twenty first century to find the reincarnation of Eagle Speaker - your father. She became two distinct entities as her gifts were also incorporated into the Sky People. That is where my grandmother and three Sacred Keepers chose to go after a ceremony that seeded this new planet with abundance. My grandmother knew the location of this planet. Time, Space and Form do not restrict the Sky People so her knowledge would immediately be part of their entire spectrum. That is how the Sky People knew where to hurl you, Rising Moon, when your life was endangered. My grandmother knew you had to come to this new planet."

At last Catriona had an answer to why Rising Moon was transported by a hurricane of energy to this planet. The silence between Manny and Rising Moon was a shock wave of mutual and stark understanding. It felt as though the lake stood still in the shimmer of sunlight. The birds and wind were silenced until nature conveyed the significance of what Manny had just said to Rising Moon.

After these startling revelations, Nikolai and Subing were led to the camp from the shore to meet their children, and they were exhilarated by the two towering tipis and careful construction of this concealed haven.

Subing met her daughters Lan Lan and Bao. They prostrated to one another with delicate intent before embracing in a hug of tears and laughter.

Nikolai was very moved to witness it. He was directed over the bridge and found the three boys in the other tipi playing an intense game of chess.

Igor jumped to his feet yelling "Father," and was swept around in a huge bear hug from Nikolai. He put his son down and looked over to Andrew and George.

"Dear Andrew and George, let me greet you as Subing just greeted her daughters Lan Lan and Bao." He went down on his hands and knees and placed his fingers on the feet of Andrew, then of George. Nikolai stood up and spoke simply to the two boys, "My whole family is here for you and will support you in every way through the loss of your mother and father. I knew them and lost many a chess game to your mother. We love you both already and I want more than anything else in the world to bring you into my family. My wife Elena feels the same way." The brothers were deeply impacted by this giant of a man.

George answered with tears in his eyes, "We feel sad and lost that our parents died on board PRIME 3. Your warmth is helping us to cope. Igor has told us so many stories about you and Elena. We feel that we know you very well and are happy to be included in your family."

Nikolai picked them both up in his strong arms with a yell to the evening sky, while Igor beamed his gratitude for such a father.

Catriona called everyone for supper. "Lan Lan, me and Bao have prepared a special meal, so let us eat while we talk."

They were treated to a feast of wild roots, curried fish and baked flatbread from Catriona's well used Dutch oven.

The conversation was lively and their stories unfolded with lots of laughter and happiness.

Subing with her soft, intense voice asked if they wanted to move from their magnificent location to the Marguerite Bay settlement, two weeks to the south.

"We love this place," responded Catriona "but we wish to be with everyone. Rising Moon and I have talked about it at length ever since we exchanged information with Liz." With her usual excitement she reported, "I have just learned that the four Melville children are reunited with their mother and father at Marguerite Bay. The children refer to Chung as "Uncle Chung."

Catriona had to clap her hands at that. "I have sent a message that Manny, Subing and Nikolai have arrived here, that Nikolai and Elena have two wonderful new sons and Igor is looking for a chess rival."

Nikolai let out a roar of delight and applauded the young people.

"We have our children back. I feel totally drunk. Our children are safe."

8: Sian and Rising Moon

Sian, now in her middle years, carried her Celtic heritage gently and obviously. The traits of mysticism were very strong in her. She was tall and slender with auburn hair streaked with grey. Her hazel eyes could be soft and gentle, then hawk-like in an instant.

Her diplomacy and grace were features shared with Tom, though it was Sian who convened the community council gatherings where everyone had a voice. This body framed intentions, priorities and policies that the Care Taking Council implemented. By consensus Tom, Liz, Cappie, Robert and Marshall shone, as they organized resources and personnel to establish a balanced community.

Every morning on rising from the tent she shared with Tom, Sian would give thanks to the land, ocean and other elements that so kindly received their presence.

Marguerite Bay, on the five-mile beach, sparkled with the same gleam of joy in her eyes. She would close her eyes in silent prayer before the ocean and then open them wide as she turned around to take in the valley stretching inland to where the new settlement was being built. She often recited out loud a passage from her favorite systems ecologist; Howard Odum's masterpiece on *Environment, Power and Society*. She would chant softly to herself while she breathed the morning in and out:

"In-Breath: With the turning of the earth, the sun comes up on fields, forests and fjords of the biosphere. And everywhere within the light there is a great In-Breath as tons upon tons of oxygen are released from the living photochemical surfaces of green plants that are becoming charged with food storage by the onrush of solar photons.

Out-Breath: Then when the sun passes in shadows before the night, there is a great exhalation as the oxygen is burned and carbon dioxide pours out, the net result of the maintenance activity of the Living Machinery."

Tom once asked her why she did this. Sian thought for just a moment, then replied that such attention kept her humble and grateful for every moment of the day, so that epiphany became the mark of her life work. Her daily recognition of the Living Machinery included all that she loved in an earth-based spirituality. Tom had smiled gently, listening to her and asked her to chant for him also.

Far in the distance Sian could see the outline of plateaus set at different altitudes stretching inland for thirty miles to a ten thousand foot mountain range. The vista thrilled her to the core, as stretching before her every morning was a cascade of climate zones permitting untold possibilities. Her eyesight was deteriorating ever since the landing, but she could discern enough to feel the gratitude swell in her heart. Their new settlement was almost complete on the nearest plateau flanked by two rivers that emptied into the five-mile beach. Liz designed the simple elegant structures that were built there.

The settlement received its name from two of the Melville children, James and Ruthie. They had hiked in with their parents to inspect their new home. The children both called out in unison, "What an Oasis" on seeing the new settlement and the expansive home provided for them. They stayed several days and helped their parents set up their new home. On returning to Marguerite Bay, Oasis became the name for the new settlement, which delighted everyone. The exodus of families and other personnel had yet to take place, as the community preferred to wait for the return of their friends and children. Sian was ready for the joy of seeing her daughter Catriona and pondered on her new daughter Rising Moon. The anticipation was palpable, sparking a deep chord in everyone, especially after the celebration of greeting the four Melville children with Uncle Chung.

Fourteen days northwest at the haven created by Catriona and Rising Moon, no-one was in a hurry to leave. Rising Moon continued Igor's education in hunting, extending his appreciation of being close to earth and animal rhythms. Manny felt his ancient culture resonating within himself as he observed Rising Moon. He paid careful attention to this startling young woman. He also noticed Catriona taking the young people to learn the lessons of the land taught to her by Rising Moon. Nikolai and Subing were happily tending to the cooking and preparation for departure. They were so relieved to find their children in such balance and maturity.

One morning Rising Moon called out, "Manny, will you come with me to collect healing plants for the journey to Marguerite Bay, you ready Manny?" He smiled at her assurance and brought his knowledge to hers as they found specimens of healing plants, all the while talking about medicines for the body and mind.

"Fish would be good for us right now," Rising Moon commented.

Manny disappeared silently and then found her, still gathering medicine plants and herbs. He had two splendid fish on his makeshift spear.

Rising Moon flashed her grin to him, "That is perfect for the body medicine I will make for us. Did you know that Catriona, my blood sister, knows almost as much as me about medicine plants?"

Manny knew how the two young women had first met, but did not know the extent of Catriona's medicine lore. He was impressed by Rising Moon's skills and felt drawn into her orbit. His attention was noticed by Rising Moon. She allowed it to resonate around and within her, then surprised him.

"Manny, you are older than me, twice my age. Why have you not married?"

He was taken aback and spluttered a reply, "I never found anyone who would put up with me. I was completely immersed in science and Hopi ceremony. I was happy with that, though it did consume most of my time and energy. The years just rolled on and I never found a chance to be with anyone."

Rising Moon looked at him shrewdly, "Is it the same for you here, on this new planet?" "I am not sure about that," he said, "There is a lot of work to do to establish healthy communities." He realized that his words sounded very lame.

Rising Moon tapped her fingers on her bowstring, before she turned round and her beautiful dark eyes bored right into him. "OK then, you might have a chance with me. But that will take some time."

No woman had ever spoken to him in such a forthright manner. He found it exhilarating, overwhelming. He had no words and just stared at this regal, composed young woman standing before him. After gazing at her beauty he quietly said, "I appreciate the chance you offer and will do all I can to not disappoint you."

Rising Moon was not finished, "Yes, I already know that, but there is a test you must pass."

Manny rolled his eyes, "And what would that be Rising Moon?"

She answered, "My blood sister Catriona has to approve of you being with me, also my Mother Sian and Father Tom." Manny was convulsed with joy and laughter at where this was going.

Rising Moon realized she had placed him on a rack and looked into his handsome face with much gentleness. "I am sure they will let you through. Our first child will be a girl, she is to be named Catriona, then a boy to be called Tom, the next girl is to be named Sian. There will be one more girl that you can name after your grandmother."

Manny recognized prophecy when he heard it coming straight from Rising Moon's heart. In that instant his entire life changed. He took her hands in his with great respect, love and reverence. "I will be there with you and with each child. You have totally changed my life." He was completely smitten, happily realizing that he had been waiting his whole life for her. And he told her so. He also said a silent prayer thanking his grandmother for her connection with the Sky People who brought Rising Moon to this new planet. He shared that with Rising Moon, as she knew that her mother and his grandmother were both with the Sky People.

Rising Moon read his mind and started to laugh, "You know what Manny the Sky People are dancing for us right now."

Soon they were ready to leave. Rising Moon and Manny said prayers of gratitude for the place that had so nourished them. They both knew, without speaking, that one day they would return to establish a community in this haven with their indigenous roots. On Igor's prompt his father Nikolai took young George on his vessel, as Igor wisely pointed out that the youngest brother needed parental presence the most. Lan Lan and Bao shared a boat and followed their mother Subing who had the lead boat for navigation. Manny and Rising Moon were at the tail end of the flotilla with Catriona. The boys had their personal escape crafts and were in the middle, under instructions not to stray from that position.

They passed without incident through the lake system to the tributary that led to the camp secured by the Melville children. It took them fourteen days to approach Marguerite Bay and they fished and hunted between camps. Manny sent daily communications to the lab describing their progress. The entire community was waiting for them on the five-mile beach. Tears of joy, shouts and yells greeted them, as friends and parents swam out to guide their vessels to the beach.

Catriona broke down in her parents arms, so relieved to find them alive. Sian saw Rising Moon standing apart, tentatively waiting. Catriona gestured, "This is my blood sister Rising Moon, your daughter."

Sian opened her arms and murmured, "Welcome my daughter." Rising Moon discarded all restraint and fierceness. She clutched Sian tightly. This tall, elegant woman reminded her so much of her own mother. Her head on Sian's breast, she allowed her tears to flow like a river.

Manny took all this in, marveling at the depth of the young woman he loved. Her sobbing ceased and Sian sang a soft Gaelic lullaby to her. She kept her arms around her new daughter until the tempest receded.

"Mother Sian, I'm here now," Rising Moon said.

Sian smiled and placed her hands on Rising Moon's tear-streaked face. "I see you my child and my heart is full." Catriona noticed the instant depth of feelings between Rising Moon and her mother. She tugged her blood sister by the arm to present her father.

Rising Moon collected herself and said, "You must be Father Tom, I am here now."

Tom held out his hands and took hers in a respectful embrace that said everything. "I have made a tent dwelling for you and Catriona, next to ours. It is not as grand as your tipi, but I hope you will like it."

"Father Tom, I have waited for this moment for a long time and I thank you." Rising Moon always addressed them formally as Mother Sian and Father Tom.

Cappie and his cooking team created a dinner that never seemed to stop, as the community listened to stories, song and music, while families blended and no-one chose to sleep until long into the night. As the two moons cast their light over the gentle bay, Catriona pulled out her violin and played her Mendelssohn favorite. It stunned everyone. She passed the instrument to Rising Moon who played the final movement, not with the same skill but enough to marvel the audience. They were home.

The arrival of the young people revitalized the community and the steady exodus to Oasis began. Although there were a dozen children who had made it to the new planet in the lab, the potential loss of ten young people had sucked the energy right out of the community. Their energy was diminished because the young ones ejected into space were considered as the next generation of leaders. To lose them would be a disastrous blow to community dynamics.

The feeling of loss undermined even the leaders. Maggie and Mary were lesbian partners, yet were sleeping in the women's dorm. They asked Sian what was the best thing they could do with the community pulse being at such low ebb. This was before the young people were found.

Sian provided gentle advice, "I do know what you are talking about. In the move to Oasis I will make sure that a cabin is made for the two of you. Whenever you feel the energy of the community changing for the better then make a statement of your true relationship. Or you can do this at the orientations that will take place on a regular basis for pioneers coming in from the Mars and Jupiter One stations. I can guarantee you will receive a warm reception. It is just for you to decide the timing."

The community felt and expressed the joy of the young people returning to them. The presence of the ten young ones galvanized the community as a whole. It made the transition to the new settlement of Oasis a joy to look forward to. The trail between Marguerite Bay and the new settlement stretched along a ridge overlooking the ocean on one side with the excitement of the valley before them and distant plateaus on the horizon.

The walk never seemed long, as flowers, birds and animals entranced the pioneers. The view of the ocean and inland mountains was breathtaking and there were many stops to take in the extraordinary beauty of their new home. They were met by the building team.

Two members of Marshall's unit, Martinez and Chung, and scientists John Tinsley and John Barclay were in charge. All were skilled carpenters and builders, happy to make adjustments and extensions where needed. Oasis began to buzz with this new life injection at the return of the young people.

Tom had made a humble request to the building team to build him a wood working shop close to the dwelling that would house Sian, himself and their two daughters. He was a master carpenter and working with wood was his way to simply be. One compartment in the lab was a tightly packed set of fine wood working tools that were his first load to carry to Oasis. Little did he know that "Tom's Shop" would become the hub for the community to gather, talk and sometimes learn the finer aspects of carpentry. A great variety of tables, stools and shelves made their way into different dwellings, but it was much more than that. Tom's Shop became the venue for plans and visions to emerge and take root.

Robert Melville and his family gathered there one evening after dinner. Robert was a dynamo of energy in establishing their two locations, but he was thinking beyond that. He and Joyce talked to Tom and Sian about the eco-village they had established in the Scottish Highlands and that was what they were really good at. It was a different structure to the communal organization of Oasis, with small holdings for each family to grow crops, raise animals and establish artisan enterprises. Each holding would be owned by a distinct family and they relied on an ethic of inter-dependence. Robert and his friends had explored beyond this plateau with the help of drone footage and found an ideal region for an eco-village to be established.

Tom and Sian listened carefully as they stained some wood destined to be a cabinet.

Tom said, "That is wonderful Robert. You know the lab has a store of seeds and fertilized embryos of farm animals in deep freeze that would support your venture. We will help in whatever way we can."

Sian added thoughtfully, "I think this provides an opportunity to express to the community what our vision is on this new planet. It is not to have only one form. It is to establish different kinds of communities that are balanced, healthy and respectful of the environment and others. It needs to be addressed to everyone."

"I agree with that Sian," Tom said, "And I think that you are the one to do this once we have settled into this new place."

Robert then chuckled mischievously, "Do you know what we found on a plateau near where we would like to locate the eco village?" In the pregnant pause it was Joyce who revealed that one of their botanists had discovered a small copse of coffee bean bushes.

Tom let out a long slow breath, "That is reason enough for you to do this. I would love to taste coffee once more." They laughed at his whimsy, as he paused from his task of staining wood with dark berry juice, dreaming of a steaming hot mug of coffee.

"There is one other thing that the children would like to ask you, if you do not mind," said Robert. Tom and Sian gave their full attention to the four children. Ruthie had been chosen to speak. She gathered herself and on prompting from her older brother James she began her rehearsed request.

"Mr. Tom and Mrs. Sian thank you for listening to my mum and dad. There is something we would like to request. Uncle Chung has become part of our family. We want him to come with us when the time comes for us to move to an eco-village. Is that OK with you?" Her bright blue eyes sparkled above her freckles and no person in the world could refuse her.

172

Sian kneeled down to Ruthie and put her arm around her, "Ruthie, your Uncle Chung is a wonderful gentleman but it is not up to us to decide where he goes. You must ask him yourself and we are fine with whatever he decides. Look he is over there at the dining area helping with the washing up team. Will you run over and bring him back with you?" Ruthie and Joan raced over to where Chung was working and brought him to Tom's shop. The girls had grasped each one of his hands, so he knew this was important.

Sian smiled to him, "Uncle Chung, the children have a question for you." This time it was James who spoke on behalf of his siblings and he outlined their long term plans and how the entire family would like him to come with them when the eco-village became a reality. The children adored him and waited expectantly for his reply.

Chung smiled at the gathering that had grown as the discussion deepened. He thanked James for the invitation and spoke quietly to the family, "I am honored that you wish me to come with you. I feel part of your family and you have enhanced my life so much."

He beamed to the children, "Let me tell you something you do not know. Before I became a soldier I was a Buddhist monk in Korea since fourteen years old. My marital arts training was part of it and that led me to enlist in the US Army Special Forces. The time for me to return to being a monk is close and I have not spoken about it to anyone. You are the first ones to know. I have thought a lot about this and intend to request the community if I could build a hut for myself close to Oasis. From there I would give training in Buddhism and martial arts to anyone who is interested. So long term I see that Oasis will be my home."

173

He saw the disappointment in the children and the tears at the corner of Ruthie's eyes.

He knelt down in front of Ruthie, "With your permission Ruthie I will come with your family when it is time to establish your eco-village and help with building it. I will stay for quite a while but will return to my hut at Oasis. But here is the thing that may make you happy. I would ask your parents to build a hut for me at your new place so I can spend three months there every year."

Ruthie and Joan rushed into his arms and knocked him over as they screamed with delight. They had not lost their Uncle Chung. Once their excitement had calmed Robert and Joyce gave their blessing to Chung and assured him that once they were ready to make such a move they would build him the best hut ever.

The bond between Rising Moon and Sian deepened, much to Catriona's delight. They shared their different knowledge and Sian intimated how much she admired Trailing Sky Six Feathers.

Rising Moon's matter of fact reply was, "Mother Sian, you can meet Trailing Sky though me. You are very much like her, which is why I am so at home. And Father Tom is a source of amazement. He knows so much about the stars and is best friends with Manny."

Sian glanced at her and asked about Manny. She had noticed the deep love between them and mentioned that Marshall and Liz would have a wedding ceremony soon and left it at that.

Rising Moon was thoughtful and remained still before replying, "Manny and I know one another from across time and space. There is no impediment to our union, but we are not in any hurry. Sooner or later we will return to the tipi settlement fourteen days from here and it is there that we will have our marriage ceremony. So there is plenty of time to understand each other. But Manny must ask permission to marry me from Catriona, you and Father Tom."

Her sense of mischief then revealed itself, "Can we make him sweat a little bit before you give consent, just so he does not take anything for granted?"

Sian laughed out loud and readily agreed to bring the co-conspirators together before Manny approached them. That did not take long. Manny visited their new home and formally asked Tom, Sian and Catriona if they would bless his future union with Rising Moon.

They put him through a steely inquisition that surprised and shocked him. Just as he wondered if they would deny him, he heard the muffled laughter from Rising Moon coming from the adjacent room she shared with Catriona. He then relaxed and joined in the laughter. Sian, Catriona and Tom took him off the hook.

As Rising Moon came into their large living space and into his arms, he said, "You arranged this torture for me?" She nodded and he lifted her up in his strong arms. At last his soon-to-be extended family was free to express their love and happiness.

At the first community gathering Sian offered her deepest gratitude to Liz and Marshall. Their wish to marry as soon as Oasis was settled had taken place several days ago. The pasture by the lake in the bend of the river provided the perfect place. Subing had a roll of silk fabric in her sparse belongings and sewed the golden wedding dress Marshall had seen in his vision. Their vows of devotion to one another and to the community were deeply moving. They declined to spend their honeymoon at Marguerite Bay when they saw their simple dwelling in Oasis adorned with tropical flowers placed there by their friends. The music from Catriona and opera arias from Elena and Joyce created a palpable ambience of love.

Sian said during the ceremony that she could reach out her hand and touch their deep love, as could everyone there. She reminded the gathering of this, "For Liz and Marshall to bestow their union on the beginning of Oasis is a taste of beauty I will never forget. We have a foundation speaking to us very clearly. Oasis is a new beginning and I wish to talk to you about the Vision we hold dearly. The return of our children and flight deck crew together with the beautiful marriage of Liz and Marshall enable us to recover a bit from the severe losses and crises we have endured. We know the conditions on Planet Earth that made the PRIME 3 mission essential."

She waited a moment for that to sink in, "On this new planet we wish to establish community here that takes care of the environment, bound by caring and sharing for one another. The ecology of this new planet is a vital relationship for all of us."

She stopped and concentrated on the threads of vision that had brought them together. "Our first communities are of a communal nature. We discussed this in detail on the long space flight from Earth and there was consensus about the principles to live by. The communal structure is only a beginning, though I consider it to be very important. It may not appeal to everyone's preference. Offshoots to establish eco-villages, small towns and ultimately eco-cities are eventualities I anticipate and fully support. They will each take on a different form and structure to the one we have at Oasis, but I hope that a strong code of ethics can flourish in each settlement we create."

"I also expect that businesses, currency and financial institutions will be necessary and have learned from our friend Seymour Hansen that there are ways to strictly regulate capital so that it does not become an overwhelming paradigm of greed. He has drawn up a schedule of restrictions on the use of capital and he should know better than most as his financial empire was the largest in the history of the Earth. Seymour is now based on Jupiter Station One and we can consult with him, even better bring him to our new planet." That news was warmly received.

"Here at Marguerite Bay and Oasis we are training ourselves to move away from the mental attitudes that destroyed much of Planet Earth. That will not be an easy step for some, so we have to struggle with our previous mental attitudes." She paused for a moment and saw that everyone's attention was fixed on her, "I would like to mention a scientist whose words still ring in my ears. Francisco Varela was a biologist and visionary. One hundred years ago he made a statement about humanity and Planet Earth that has echoed through the collaborative science of brain and consciousness:

'The chance of surviving with dignity on this planet hinges on the acquisition of a new mind. This new mind must be wrought among other things, from a radically different epistemology, which will inform relevant actions.'
Sian allowed her words to resonate with her listeners then said, "You know full well that his words were ignored, as survival with dignity was not an option on the planet we all came from. We now have the chance to put his views into action. It is not so difficult, as we are self-selected by wanting to be pioneers aboard PRIME 3. Oasis provides a taste of what the new mind feels like. There are rules and regulations for our daily conduct. They are laid out clearly in the Earth History modules you all have. Policies and

preferences are discussed in this general council where everyone has a say. The Care Taking Council, which we elect, is a smaller body that carries out the tasks recommended by the community. It also arbitrates disagreements, conflicts and serves to provide security and safety. One of our scientists, John Barclay over there, is our official historian and has registered the land from Marguerite Bay to Oasis, between the two rivers as being owned by the Township of Oasis. The area has been identified from drone data."

She stopped for a moment and looked over to the newly-weds standing by Tom.
She said, "Tom, Marshall and Liz have created different plans with appropriate regulations for many kinds of community structures from communal all the way up to city and state. But Oasis is where the rubber meets the initial road, as they used to say in times gone before."
This brought a chuckle from older members of the audience.

"There are pioneers on Mars Station and Jupiter One waiting to join us. Their first destination will be Oasis so that the basic foundations we are agreed upon are learned and appreciated. We cannot control what may evolve in generations to come, but we can be clear about the principles and foundations that brought us here in the first place. There is, however, one structure that we did not anticipate. That is the Wisdom of the Elders from the Native American realm. I have learned much about this from Rising Moon and Manny and request that they talk to the community in the near future." The community applauded and approved such an event.

Sian continued, "I have outlined and emphasized what you already know, but I feel it necessary to discuss it openly at the beginning of the Oasis settlement. I know Cappie has a few suggestions he wishes to bring forward."

Cappie stood up, first congratulating Liz and Marshall on offering their marriage to the new community before bringing up an issue that was new. "We have brilliant scientists and physicians here and there are many of us, including myself, who would like to learn from them. This could be through apprenticeships and mentoring relationships. Is this possible?"

Sian asked the scientists present to respond and they were more than happy to establish training for anyone who aspired to it. The discussion then became one of ways and means. There was no issue with the Vision presented by Sian, as this was deeply held and fully endorsed by all present. There was a humorous suggestion that Tom's Shop be expanded, as not everyone could squeeze in at the same time. Tom laughed and promised that he would train would-be master carpenters so they could build their own shops. The meeting ended with many promises and commitments to create mentoring opportunities, a young scientist's group and all agreed on a delivery by Rising Moon and Manny about their Native American village structure.

Tom and Sian's new home was on the inland edge of Oasis, set back close to the forest and adjacent to one of the two rivers. A small waterfall sang them awake each morning and Sian would often sit there to meditate and be clear. Their cabin had a large open space for chairs and table with a simple kitchen area. Spacious rooms led off to one side, one for Sian and Tom, the other for Catriona and Rising Moon, which became a music room for the young women. The wooden cabin was topped with a thatched roof of interwoven palm branches with an open structure for air to circulate. Tom's carpentry skills enhanced this environment with grace and elegance. His "Shop" was an open structure set twenty feet away that allowed the evening crowd of eager friends to learn wood-craft. On the morning chosen for the address by Manny and Rising Moon, Sian felt a strange premonition arise to her attention. Tom noticed her concentration and stern focus.

"Dear Tom," Sian said, "could you introduce the talk by Manny and Rising Moon this morning? Something dark is arising that needs my attention."

Tom knew her well and glanced at her, "You need solitude to dig this out. I am happy to take your place this morning."

Rising Moon stepped up to Sian, "Mother Sian, we can postpone what Manny and I have prepared."

Sian was quiet and intense, "No my daughter, I need to focus on seeing into what is arising. It is something that I cannot evade, as it will drive me into seeing further. This does not interfere with the opportunity you and Manny will offer. I just need to see clearly. You understand don't you?" Rising Moon knew better than most when shamanic voices called for attention, though they all underestimated the danger that Sian would soon face.

Rising Moon and Manny had discussed their proposal with Tom and Sian, who knew that sacred earth traditions were always conveyed by creation stories in tribal communities. Manny felt that Rising Moon was the one to speak. "You are closer to this than I, Rising Moon. I would prefer to be there to support while you tell the story. Is this agreeable to you?"

Rising Moon's dazzling smile was the affirmation everyone sought. Manny's talks about his Hopi culture on the space journey had intrigued the community and now they had Rising Moon's more immediate experience. The pioneers gathered in the open dining space to listen to her. All the children were there as they had been taught several traditional dances by Rising Moon and were eager to hear more about her culture.

Tom opened the presentation by observing that the community presently had the opportunity of space technology, sophisticated communications and simple living with the land to place into balance.

He said by way of introduction, "To reinforce the relationship with the land I have asked Rising Moon to talk about the Creation Story of her people."

Rising Moon was greeted with instant respect. She burned some of her sage and offered it to the Creator with a simple chant. She said, "This is how my people honor and welcome every aspect of life. In tribal cultures like my own and Manny's there are Creation Stories, which are road maps for how to be. The purpose of a Creation Story is to establish a way of living with the land and with one another. I think you would call that earth ethics. Am I correct?"

There was a resounding "Yes" from the children, while everyone else smiled.

Rising Moon resumed her address to the community, "The Creation Story lays out clear guidelines for organization, work, ceremony for people to mature, protocols for justice and relations with other people, all creatures and the land. Most Creation Stories are ancient, based on myth and the past, yet the Creation Story for my people is different. It was a new creation by my mother Trailing Sky, my father Eagle Speaker and their friend Long Willow. After a brutal attack on our summer camp by

Apache raiders, which killed many people, they escaped to a cave in the Sacred Canyon. There they planned a renewal resting on the equality of women and building a strong community based on new visions of well-being."

She looked over to Manny and saw the confident smile on his face and then continued. "Manny and I have talked at length about establishing such a community at the safe haven Catriona and I created fourteen days north of here. That is the reason I talk to you about this Creation Story as some of you may wish to participate in such a venture."

Rising Moon saw that she had the community's rapt attention. "Here is the story of how my parents escaped from the massacre at their summer village. They retreated to a cave in the Sacred Canyon and from there they created a new design for living with the Earth Mother that called on the ways of the Creator."

She then related the story that had been told to her many times. "During the massacre my mother, Trailing Sky, said to my father, Eagle Speaker, "Put your weapons down, my husband." Rising Moon indicated to the rapt audience that she was switching into her parents' words, allowing them to speak for themselves.

Trailing Sky said, "The Sky People taught me how to make myself invisible. Concentrate and look only into my eyes so you may not be seen. Otherwise we will both die. There are too many of them. Look into my eyes and no place else."

Alert and watchful they waded into the river that sheltered their summer settlement. All they heard was the murmur of the river flowing over rills of rock and the pounding of their hearts. The canopy provided by the large oaks and maples kept them from view once the river turned sharply upstream, narrowing through red buttes that soared on either side. Pinon pines dotted the unique rock formations as Trailing Sky looked for the cut through the rock wall.

After several hours they found it, left the river and headed to the sacred canyons to the west, climbing to the ponderosa pines close to the canyon rim.

As night fell they settled under a large rocky outcrop sheltered from view by a clump of juniper trees. A curious desert badger came close and inspected them, grunting and growling. They saw the outlines of mule deer in the valley below, as they listened to the evening chorus of insects, cougars and birds. In soft voices they at last spoke to one another."

Rising Moon related their words. "You knew this was to happen?" Eagle Speaker asked.

"No," Trailing Sky replied. "Not even I could see this. I knew there would be an end to how we lived. My spirit guides warned me, instructing me to prepare. I found a cave, high in the sacred canyon, very close to where we are sitting. During my last six moon times I did not join the other women. Instead I carried seeds, plants, tools and blankets to the cave to ready our new home."

He remembered how tired she was, returning from the seclusion of her moon times. He had not asked, as this was women's concern. He simply made her comfortable with extraordinary tenderness. Trailing Sky treasured that care, as she could not say what she was seeing, hearing and sensing. She journeyed six times to the sacred canyon, ensuring that when the inevitable catastrophe befell, they would be able to flee lightly.

During that long night Eagle Speaker's thoughts turned from revenge and rage to quietness vaguely remembered. He recalled how he felt when learning the old ways from his grandfather. His anger, fear and shame fell away.

When Trailing Sky woke in his arms next morning and looked into his eyes she asked, "You traveled through the darkness while I slept?"

"I did," was his reply.

They left their rocky outcrop and walked stealthily as the sun climbed high above them. From his grandfather he knew how to extract water from the nearest saguaro. She thanked the giant cactus for the refreshing taste of water.

They continued to climb higher up the canyon until they were there, suddenly at the cave. The entrance was small, yet opened up into a wide expansive cavern. The recess of the cave had air outlets to the other side of the canyon. Water that filtered through from rain and morning dew collected in a rock pool below these openings, the overflow carefully draining into the pots she had placed next to it. The daylight coming through the air vents and entrance enabled him to see the wonder created by her.

Dry wood lay next to a small fireplace at the rear. Baskets of seeds and plants surrounded the rock pool. A blanket was thrown over bundles of reeds for their bed. His bows, arrows, spear and long gun were on a rock ledge next to sharpened staffs, some with cloth dipped in fish oil to provide light when needed.

Beneath a rock cache dried meat and fish had been stored, with maize, beans and roots to sustain them. He paused, looked around him and silently gave thanks to her.

She said, "When I first found this place there were many creatures here. It was their home. I prayed to the Creator and placed sweet-grass for all of them by the entrance to the cave. I then sang a request that they permit us to share their home. By the time of my third journey here, most of them had vacated it for us, even the scorpions," Trailing Sky smiled.

Soon after they had settled in the cave Trailing Sky was collecting herbs and berries before dawn when she noticed a woman last seen at the summer settlement doing the same. She cried the small grouse call, a woman's call.

The answer came quickly and she swiftly reunited with Long Willow, a tall angular woman known for her sharp tongue. There was nothing sharp left as she wept in Trailing Sky's arms.

On the first day that all three were together, Trailing Sky said, "The knowledge of the elders, shamans and medicine people is in me. I know the annual ceremonies and ritual passages that will provide stepping-stones for boys and girls to mature into adult men and women."

She collected her thoughts into the right vessels for speech. "We must establish a new village based on the fact that the Great Spirit is in the wind, the sky, in everything around us. The plants and animals, the materials for our winter and summer homes are all sacred. This is our guidance for how to live. I feel strongly that women must have a decisive role in planting and harvesting cycles because they know the behaviour of plants. We must educate our people about the sacred inter-connection of all of nature. They easily neglect this, walking through the connections as innocently as children running through a spider's cobweb. I see the year round cycle of ceremony creating daily life from a deep spiritual link with all that the Earth Mother provides for us. These are my thoughts."

Eagle Speaker glanced to the horizon and the length of the sacred canyon before speaking, "What you have said to me will come about. I agree, there will be a woman's council and no decision can be enacted until the men's council and women's are in accord." He traced a map of the future village with a burnt stick on the lip of the stone cave.

He proposed a village of four clans as their tradition was based on the four main directions: North, East, South and West. There would be a central location for the home of The People's chief.

Long Willow added, "An elder and chief holds wisdom from the Great Spirit and knows the spiritual link between the cosmos, people and the earth. It cannot be any other way without disaster happening to the land. The elders and medicine women have investigated the threads of natural order and know they are woven into one single garment. This can only be understood through the eyes of humility and reverence for all of life. We must ensure that the People are in gratitude for the garden bequeathed to them; to care for the earth and gather seeds for the next season's planting. Slain animals are to be respected through rituals that keep the creature and the human as one linked being. The earth nurtures us. There is enough as long as we share with respect and always circle back to the Wisdom of the Elders."

Long Willow was encouraged to continue. "As a community we must learn to defend ourselves better against attack. At present we rely upon our men to do this, neglecting that women and girls should be trained in combat. This must change from the old way of leaving it to

186

the men as we can double the number of warriors by including women."

Eagle Speaker replied, "There will be training for both men and women. The clan chief will be responsible for teaching close combat to both men and women. This will be a regular preparation. In the second phase of every moon cycle, I propose that every day one of the clans will be in training, while the other three clans complete their work. At the end of four days the next two days will co-ordinate all warriors, men and women. We will need to train scouts and sentinels to be alert to any hostile intrusion into our territory and village."

He explained the foundation from the elders and the clan structure, right down to the details of continuing it in a way to resolve conflict.

From the four Clan Chiefs, the wisest and most able would be selected by the men's and women's councils to be the central chief. The clan that offered their leader after such deliberations would then select a new clan chief. This allowed all clan voices to be heard. He described his plans for managing the irrigation of their crops and the creation of a women's council that would regulate the cycle of planting and harvesting. The medicine people would be authorized to oversee and regulate the establishment of a rich ceremonial cycle to celebrate each season of nature and each phase of life from birth to death.

He said, "Each clan has much autonomy, yet it is only one strand in the web of our village. The center is balanced through the men's lodge and the women's lodge. All clans participate in these two councils for shared ceremonies and for making decisions."

Rising Moon stopped talking and looked at her entranced audience and allowed the comfortable silence to extend before continuing. "The ceremonial cycle was the jewel from the many plans laid down in the sacred canyon by my mother, father and Long Willow. The medicine people placed children in coming of age ceremonies with supervised seclusion in the forest, desert and mountains around them. This ritual design took children out of the idyll of infancy into the domain of responsibility. Joining the cadre of young warriors to defend the village was a major instrument in shaping young adolescents to be responsible. With ceremonial symbols explained and internalized, the young ones were taught the dances and chants of transformation as they experienced a time of marvels. Their growing minds could make sense of the fabric of the society that they were a part of.

Their ritual experiences in the wilderness, in sweat lodges, medicine wheel ceremonies and sacred journeys outstripped all that they had known before and they emerged as new and stronger individuals. There were rarely any mistaken identities arising, as people knew who they were through the exacting ritual tradition. Instead of being confused, their experience of the terrain around them in seclusion and prayer existed as knots of understanding that stretched across the abyss of ignorance. The symbolic naming, the puberty rituals, the ceremonial recognitions provided by the medicine people enabled a road for growth to arise in a moral and collective way that served the entire community."

There was a hushed silence when Rising Moon finished her Creation Story. Manny looked at her with sheer admiration and love. He stepped in to further the discussion and answer the questions that arose about their tradition. He intuited correctly that Rising Moon was straining to check in on Sian.

9: The Rape of Sian

Rising Moon and Tom walked quickly to their cabin at the edge of Oasis Hamlet, close to the jungle and waterfall.

As they approached, Tom knew something was dreadfully awry. Sian's plants, placed in gourds on the front steps, were scattered and broken. The door was wide open. Inside were the obvious signs of a struggle. Blood drops were on the floor.

Tom called out to Rising Moon in alarm, as he searched the cabin. "Sian is gone, attacked and abducted."

Rising Moon examined the disorder Tom had discovered. Her tracking instincts came to the fore. She noticed footprints by the front door and at the back window in the room she shared with Catriona. The footprints were male and large, leaving an imprint in the earth to match an army boot. She summoned Marshall immediately.

He examined the foot prints Rising Moon pointed out to him and called out to Chung and Martinez, "Have you seen Johnstone?" They had not, but all could see that the footprints matched the size and weight of their survivalist expert.

Marshall was unusually agitated, "Tom, I had noticed his interest in your wife, but said nothing to you, as I did not expect anything like this. Johnstone felt he should have access to a woman and had expressed this once to Martinez. He has obviously taken your wife and if he does not want to be found, it is very likely he will not be found."

Manny arrived at the cabin as Marshall spoke. He scrutinized the signs and looked directly at Marshall before he replied, "Johnstone has never been tracked by an aboriginal. There are two of us who will find him." He then glanced over to Rising Moon. She quickly went to her room, returning with her bow and a quiver of arrows.

Marshall took instant charge. "Tom, I know you will insist on coming but this is a military operation and you must take orders from me. That applies to you too, Manny and Rising Moon. Is that understood?" It was. Marshall asked Rising Moon to lead the tracking operation as her skills outstripped the training of his unit.

"We do not have any weapons here. They are all in a locked compartment in the lab at Marguerite Bay. Johnstone also lacks a gun, but we know he has an eighteen inch double bladed knife strapped to his right thigh, and he carries three throwing knives with him. Chung does not need weapons and Martinez has a traditional bolas, which is a deadly restraining weapon. You have it with you, Martinez?"

"Always," confirmed Martinez.

Marshall turned towards Tom, "Tom, you must come last and if you are not able to keep up with us you need to return to Oasis and wait. Saving Sian's life cannot rest on sentiment." Tom grimly agreed. Marshall beckoned them, "We must leave now before the trail goes cold. Tom, please alert Cappie and Robert to take care of Oasis while we are gone."

Rising Moon quickly found the heavier footprints where Johnstone carried Sian over his shoulder. Her eyes and senses swept in an arc, looking for evidence of their passage. She noticed tree leaves displaced and slender twigs broken. Sian was marking a path to be followed. Then they lost all signs as their small party arrived before evening at a sheer and extensive ridge overlooking the ocean. There were evident signs it had been scaled but Rising Moon instinctively knew it was a false trail and consulted with Manny. He agreed with her.

They scouted around the edges of a marshy pool stretching the length of the ridge. Manny found a woman's footprint in the mud some two hundred yards away. Sian was walking now and had left a sign of their direction across the marsh.

Marshall knew their own slow progress through the marsh would be highly visible, so they backtracked and slowly advanced along a precipitous ridge that lay hidden inland behind the marsh. From there, through binoculars, they could see in the far distance a small green tarp stretched against an outcrop of the cliff face close to the ocean. The search party split into two, Marshall with Manny, Rising Moon with Martinez, Chung and Tom. A classic pincer movement evolved slowly and meticulously.

Marshall instructed Chung to go unseen around the marsh and approach the green tarp from the east. Martinez had the task to wade undetected across the foul smelling marsh. He stripped down to his shorts and wrapped his bolas around his head. The three tentacles of tough nylon with a heavy ball at each end provided a perfect disguise. From a distance it looked like a clump of floating reeds. His throw had an effective range of thirty feet so he knew to make swift progress across the marsh. Marshall and Manny stealthily crawled along the ocean ridge to position themselves on the cliff above the makeshift camp. Tom and Rising Moon were instructed to stay well back until the rescue was made.

Martinez was the first to spot Johnstone emerging from the tarp. He crept without a sound through the marsh and took the three-strand bolas into his hands once he saw Chung make himself visible.

Johnstone immediately pulled out one of his throwing knives and hurled it with all his strength at Chung some forty feet from him. But he had underestimated Chung's years of astute martial arts training.

Chung concentrated only on the knife speeding his way, then plucked it out of the air and returned it with incredible force to thud into Johnstone's right shoulder.

Then Martinez struck, rising from the swamp with one whirl of the bolas over his head, he whipped it through the air and the weights entwined Johnstone's legs bringing him to the ground. Marshall and Manny quickly abseiled down the cliff face and overpowered Johnstone before he could free himself from the bolas.

Tom and Rising Moon ran directly to the camp hidden against the rock wall and saw Sian gagged and tied to a juniper tree. Tom called her name as he rushed towards her. With a sob he released the gag and untied her. Her clothes were torn and her body had been bruised and cut. He held her up as she spat out that Johnstone had tortured and repeatedly raped her. Marshall and Manny had Johnstone shackled between them.

Johnstone had heard Sian's sobbing revelation and shouted harshly, "There was no rape. She loved it, being fucked by a real man for the first time."

Tom swirled around in anger at the man who harmed his wife. The echo of Johnstone's words scarcely touched the nearby rock face before Rising Moon took one step forward, raised her bow and sent the first arrow through his throat so he could shout no further obscenities. She had understood his vile words about her Mother Sian and seconds later her next arrow penetrated his heart, killing him instantly. He fell to the ground from the grasp that Marshall and Manny had on him. They were astonished and shocked by her swift action, yet no-one rebuked Rising Moon. She stood there, totally calm. She was in command of herself.

It felt as though time stopped, before Manny spoke quietly to Marshall. "In the old days my culture would speak of this as dispatching a mad dog human." Several minutes passed before he spoke again, "Johnstone was one of your soldiers, so I leave it to you and your unit to bury him. For my part I will conduct a ceremony to bless his spirit so it may return in a refined state."

Marshall agreed, still in shock and awe at Rising Moon's decisive action. First, he took off his shirt. He was a tall man well over six feet in height. He handed his shirt to Tom, "Please give this to your wife. It will cover her while you give comfort." Tom thanked him with his eyes and covered his hurt wife who stood trembling next to him.

Rising Moon was there to instantly take Sian into her arms. She examined the bruises and knife cuts and said, "Mother Sian, I will find herbs and plants to heal your wounds. Manny will help me with that. We will also conduct a healing ceremony to heal your wounds inside."

Sian whispered, "My warrior daughter Rising Moon, here you are." She leaned her bruised head on Rising Moon's shoulder, "Thank you my child. I have so much healing ahead of me, but there is something I must tell you"

She trembled while drawing in a scratchy breath. "Eventually I realized that this body is not my body. That is how my mind worked when vilely attacked by Johnstone. I moved my mind away from my body and placed it with those I love; you, Catriona, Tom, our community at Oasis, to the plants, animals, lakes, mountains and the vast ocean. I felt I could outlast his onslaught on my body."

Rising Moon was humbled by Sian's courage. She murmured softly, "That could be my mother Trailing Sky speaking to me from centuries ago."

Sian smiled though her bruised lips, "My dear child, your mother and I are now held in your strong arms?" It was Sian who comforted Rising Moon in that moment, as they both cried together.

Tom silently witnessed the exchange between mother and daughter. His hatred for Johnstone abated somewhat, as he surrendered his raging mind to his wife's wisdom.

Tom held his family close to him and noticed with surprise that Sian was looking directly at him. She had suffered from deteriorating eyesight since landing on the new planet.

"Yes Tom, I can see more clearly now. Perhaps the taser shots to my head by Johnstone re-arranged the neurons in my eye receptors." She smiled tiredly to him, "Can you still love me after this?"

"Sian, my lovely Sian" he gently replied, "I am more in love with you than ever before. I will serve you all my days." He held her in the gentlest embrace.

Marshall was quietly smiling at the utter tenderness between them. He spoke slowly and firmly, "Tom, Sian, I pledge myself totally to this emerging society we are building on this new planet. I am here for the long haul of creating a different lifeway. Johnstone is a sordid reminder of what must not happen again."

He put down the machete he was holding. "I will consult with my men to establish tighter security and protection. They hold the same intent as I. Chung will soon resume his life as a monk and Martinez has spoken to me about his strong commitment to community life, left behind many years ago in Mexico."

His men nodded in agreement as he continued to speak. "Sian's wisdom and strength has deeply registered with all of us. My duty is to protect her from harm and we must ensure she receives the care necessary at this time."

Manny was in a state of total overwhelm at Rising Moon's swift action and could not speak. The only way he could express himself was to stand in front of Rising Moon, who he loved at a depth beyond his thinking mind.

He placed his clenched fist next to his heart as he bowed first of all to Rising Moon and then to Sian. He was followed by Marshall, Chung and Martinez. It was not to anyone's surprise that Tom did the same to deeply honor the two women with this spontaneous gesture.

Rising Moon had the down to earth words, "Marshall, your shirt looks much better on Mother Sian than you, so I guess she can keep it. As for your adoration of us two women, we accept."

For the first time Sian let out a glimmer of a smile. The men were amused and grateful.

Chung in his quiet and skillful manner spoke to Sian. "Mrs. Hagen, you know I am trained in Chinese medicine. The knife cuts on your body were inflicted to cause the most pain without killing you. They have compromised the meridian system throughout your body. If you will permit, I have acupuncture needles that can restore the flow of energy through the meridians. For this treatment do not think of me as a man but as the healing breath of Buddha."

Sian was moved and relieved by his understanding. Marshall and Martinez carried Sian to a sheltered grove of trees, out of sight from Johnstone's hidden camp. They gently laid her down on soft grass covered with a blanket from Marshall's pack. Rising Moon remained with Chung to tend to Sian's wounds. She had instructed the men, including Tom, to keep their distance, as Sian needed feminine energy at this time. She intuited correctly that Chung, as healing breath in Sian's mind, could be included. Manny was sent to gather specific plants to crush into a poultice to prevent infection, then to catch the ingredients for the fish medicine that Rising Moon would prepare. She cleaned the many wounds on Sian's body with the plant poultice while Chung traced the meridian structure with his long thin needles. Rising Moon watched intensely where he inserted the needles on Sian's body.

When he was finished, she spoke, "I understand what you are doing Uncle Chung. Would you teach me how to do this when we return to Oasis?"

Chung smiled at the children's name for him and nodded, remaining quiet as he observed Sian's response to the acupuncture needles. He had earlier asked Marshall to quickly return to the settlement and bring back one of the doctors with sutures, bandages and sedatives. His healing strips could only temporarily close the wounds.

Martinez and Tom rapidly created a camp from the supplies in their packs, taking from Johnstone's station whatever they needed. Marshall made good speed to Oasis, alternately walking and running. He arrived in the middle of the night to find Robert on sentry patrol, holding a large knotted club in his hand. Cappie and Subing were called while Marshall retold the rescue of Sian.

Subing immediately went to her cabin, returning with a small bottle. She spoke to Marshall, "Chung will recognize this and know how to use it to regenerate Sian's body tissue." Subing was horrified at the sadistic torture of her friend.

Joyce had been awakened by her husband Robert. She quickly packed her medical bag with sutures, sedatives, bandages and antibiotics. They were joined by Catriona who was dressed, ready to go with violin case in hand.

"Marshall," she said firmly, "I am coming with you and Joyce."

"But not without this," smiled Cappie. He handed a backpack to Marshall, hastily crammed with nutritious food.

They reached Sian just before dawn. The men instinctively moved into the background. Chung joined them once he briefed Joyce about the two acupuncture treatments he had applied to Sian's body. He was delighted to see Subing's small bottle, relating to Joyce that once the sutures were complete to gently apply the salve on each wound to regenerate body tissue.

The heavy dose of sedation immediately administered by Joyce dulled Sian's pain. She steeled her physician's mind, appalled by the systematic torture of Sian. Clinically she closed the many wounds on Sian's body and gently applied the tissue salve to each stitched wound. She administered an antibiotic to prevent any infection taking root in Sian's battered and cut body. Catriona and Rising Moon followed Joyce's instructions precisely.

"She will sleep for a few hours now," Joyce said to Rising Moon and Catriona. "You two women were fantastic assistants. You can be on my surgical team any time." The three strong women embraced and Joyce went over to Tom to give him the news that the medical gods got to Sian just in time. She was confident of a full recovery, certainly of the body, but knowing clearly that such a vicious assault could bring on the symptoms of Post-Traumatic Stress Disorder.

Tom breathed in slowly and out slowly, ensuring he was calm before speaking.

"Thank you for your skill and wisdom Joyce. With such strong women supporting Sian, we will know what to do to bring about her recovery. Look over there at her two daughters, sitting by her, speaking to her unconscious mind. I will do the same with stories about our life and future that brings happiness and hope to the fore. Maggie and Mary are expert therapists for this kind of trauma and I will consult with them very closely, as will Sian."

Catriona was watching her sleeping mother carefully. Quietly speaking to her, offering thanks for all that she was and would still be. She continued to speak while her mother groaned, cried out, screamed "No, No" and then relapsed into uncanny silence. Tears formed in Catriona's eyes and her blood sister Rising Moon immediately came over to hold her, "Keep talking to her Catriona, I am right here with you."

Sian's eyes opened a few hours later. They heard her gasp, "My two daughters, am I dreaming?"

Rising Moon exclaimed, "No Mother Sian, you are not dreaming, your daughters are here."

Catriona spontaneously clapped her hands, "You are awake and you can now see. Please mother, do not move. You might tear the skin around the sutures that Dr. Joyce put into your wounds. We dare not hug and kiss you, as you are fragile, but I know a different way." She opened her violin case, tuned her instrument and softly played all the favorite pieces that Sian treasured. Rising Moon felt Sian relax and gestured to Catriona for the violin. She played the Gaelic lullaby that Mother Sian had sung to her when they first met on the beach at Marguerite Bay.

Sian actually smiled, murmuring to herself, "My two daughters are here." Tom heard the song of the violin and came over to her side. "Tom, you are here?"

He replied gently, "I could be nowhere else my love. Dr. Joyce and Chung treated you just before dawn and we will stay here until you are strong enough to be moved. Our daughters can help you sit up while I make some tea for you."

"Tom," Sian whispered, "Kiss me on the tip of my nose."

He laughed softly, remembering their first kiss so many years ago. "Sian, you are so magical, a treasure beyond imagination." He turned to his daughters, "Do you girls realize that was how I first met your mother when we were both seventeen?" He kissed Sian ever so gently on the tip of her nose.

Rising Moon was deeply impacted by this. "Father Tom, I will get tea. Carry on with nose kissing and tell me more when I come back."

Joyce was drawn from sleep by the morning music. She smiled to her friend Sian and asked if she could inspect the sutures. They were holding firm though there were signs of infection. Joyce applied the Chinese salve and asked Rising Moon to make more of the plant poultice while she injected Sian with another dose of antibiotic.

"You need to rest here for a few days," she said to Sian. "I will ask Marshall and Martinez to make a sedan chair that can be carried on strong poles resting on their shoulders. You will be like the Queen of Sheba, carried by her soldiers into the palace." Joyce grinned in her down to earth way, "Now that will give our historian something to write about, don't you think?"

The close scrutiny by the two physicians and nutritious fish medicine prepared by Rising Moon slowly brought Sian round, but it was the wonderful stories that Tom told about their life together that nourished her the most. Tom sat close to his sleeping wife and told stories of their teenage romance, about vows expressed on the Eifel Tower in Paris, making love in the snow of the Swiss Alps. Catriona gasped in astonishment at her parents' boldness. Rising Moon drank it all in as she learned more about her adoptive parents. They both sat in wonder when Tom related the story of Sian journeying to the Amazon to receive shamanic training for two years. He described in detail his joy of looking after their baby daughter. Then he told how Sian returned changed, enhanced, yet more deeply in love with him than before.

He told stories of their home in Cumberland in the north of England, of how Catriona was saved in a desperate blizzard when she was a young girl. He described his books and plays, then expounded on his recruitment to the International Space Agency. He declined their offer until they agreed to recruit Sian as the resident mystic seer. Tom turned from Sian with a broad smile on his face and spoke directly to his daughters.

"Yes, I was adamant. Every space mission requires a resident mystic seer, don't you agree?" Catriona clapped her hands in glee, while Rising Moon listened intently to every word Tom spoke. It was quite an education for her and new insight for the men.

There was an intense discussion between Marshall, Tom and Manny that had been put to one side, but now needed to arise. They walked a distance away from the sleeping Sian and her two daughters, so they were beyond earshot. Marshall spoke about Rising Moon's swift action, "Tom, Manny we have to discuss Rising Moon's swift execution of Johnstone. How do we explain this to the community?"

Manny replied with wisdom, "My dear brothers, please remember that Rising Moon comes from an eighteenth century tribal society. Her action was appropriate to her tribal ethics, and would have been so for my culture at that time. The abduction and rape of a woman carried with it a death sentence for that felony."

Tom took in a deep breath and said, "I have been turning this over in my mind. I realize that we do not have an established penal code for our settlement on this planet. Instead we have an ethical code that does not cover this situation. In truth we all felt that Rising Moon's action fit the circumstances." He looked around to Manny and Marshall, who nodded in agreement before he spoke again. "We were overwhelmed by her swift action. I certainly could have easily moved to something like that but I have restraints from my home culture on Planet Earth. Those restraints do not apply to her, as Rising Moon acted in accord with her tribal lore."

Manny said thoughtfully, "I can take the responsibility to inform Rising Moon of the evolution of justice from her time to ours, while at the same time fully resonate with her actions. We were all in accord with her at the moment she sent two arrows into Johnstone. There will be no criticism or judgement, just a narrative about where we are now. She has incredible intelligence and integrity. She will understand." Tom and Marshall agreed with Manny's proposal. Rising Moon understood immediately when Manny conveyed this discussion to her.

A week passed by, then Catriona went ahead of the slow moving sedan chair carried in shifts between Marshall and Tom, then by Manny and Martinez. When she reached Oasis she sought out Igor and Nikolai, James and LongFu as relief porters to bring her mother home. Cappie wisely cautioned the community not to make a stampede to meet Sian and her rescuers. What she needed was space to recover and heal. And that is what she did, taking daily counsel with her fellow therapists, Mary and Maggie. Joyce's children Joan and Ruthie had not heard Cappie's strictures, so they would wander into Sian's large living room to show her the stones and flowers they had found. Their innocence and care opened Sian up every time they visited her, always with something new for her to engage with.

Several weeks later, Sian walked slowly to the dining area to have breakfast with her community. Everyone stopped eating, silent as they welcomed their dear friend and mentor. They stood to acknowledge Sian. She carefully sat down, as her legs were still unsteady despite the daily exercises supervised by Tom.

Sian said, "Please my dear ones enjoy your breakfast with me. I will talk to you after I've had some of Cappie's pineapple pancakes." Unabashed, Joan and Ruthie brought their plates, piled high with pineapple pancakes, and offered to share them with Sian. She gracefully accepted. As breakfast drew to an end, Joyce came over and asked the two young girls to come with her.

"Sian, I will talk to them at our cabin, so you are free to express yourself."

An air of anticipation stole across the entire community. Sian began in a tremulous voice that grew stronger as she spoke. "Dear friends, I am recovering well from my ordeal, thanks to your love and support that I feel tangibly every day." She looked around to her friends. "The torture and sexual assault by Johnstone was not something my counselling practice prepared me for. I struggled greatly with fear and shame at first." The community felt her struggle viscerally, astonished by her surface calm yet very aware of the suffering underneath.

Sian continued after a lengthy pause, "After more suffering than I had ever before encountered, I slipped into an internal space where I knew I was so much more than my body. That was when I started to use my mind."

She took a deep breath as she remembered that breakthrough. "With my mind I placed myself with the people I loved, with memories of happiness and joy. So much of that was with you." Sian looked at the suddenly glowing, beautiful faces of every person there. "I would concentrate on my breath and on you. In my mind I planned and built clinics, irrigation systems, schools, raised healthy crops and animals. I built everything in my mind with you. We created other communities on this new planet. This eased the pressure of pain, panic and abuse in my mind, as I made long lists of everything I am thankful for."

The silence she entered stretched in time. Everyone waited for her to continue speaking. "My mind did not dwell on the violation of my body. It had sprung free in order to protect me and keep me alive. It finally began to settle down after Uncle Chung and Dr. Joyce began to take care of my body. I woke up to the presence of my daughters, Catriona and Rising Moon. At that distant camp my dear husband Tom told wonderful stories of our life that infiltrated my wounded senses. I will never forget that gentle gift."

Sian stopped to gently kiss Tom. They embraced for several minutes before Sian continued to speak. "The care and love I have received enables me to cope with symptoms of Post-Traumatic Stress Disorder. I still wake up with nightmares and scream in pain and rage at why this could have happened to me. Thankfully Mary and Maggie are here for me to turn to them for therapy. They have brought me step by step to allow a genuine compassion to arise for Johnstone. With their guidance I was able to see into his painful upbringing and military scars. Without that compassion I know I cannot heal myself."

Sian's friends and loved ones were spellbound by her courage. They wept with her, yet light shone through their tears because of her courage and determination.

Finally Sian said, "This brings me to this present moment with all of you. We have a magnificent future to build together. Right now you are bolder, stronger and faster than I. So while you are creating wonderful new possibilities I have only one request. Please pause for a moment and hold out your hand to me. I will gladly take your hand in mine, because I am going with you on this splendid adventure on our new planet."

10: Settlements

Soon after Oasis was built at the end of 2085, the astrophysicists and engineers met with Cappie and his flight crew to respond to requests from the engineering team on Jupiter One.

With Seymour Hansen's vast fortune the Jupiter Station had created a manufacturing facility. The engineers were designing a different spacecraft to follow on from PRIME 3 and requested further input.

The scientists gathered to solve the problem of the dense particle field in the high stratosphere of the planet. Liz asked Cappie if he remembered when that field began to impede the progress of PRIME 3 to Planet Horizon.

Cappie placed his captain's recorder on the table. He had the exact co-ordinates of when the particle field violently damaged the spaceship and played the recorder for all to hear. He advised the scientists and engineers that a much smaller spacecraft was necessary with reverse engine properties to slow it down when entering such a dense particle field.

Liz sketched a quick outline of a new design and said, "Thank you Cappie. As well as speed reduction we need to disperse the particle field. I can think of two strategies. One is to use sonic emission. That would be a high-pitched frequency to disperse the particles. The second option is to reverse-magnetize the hull of the spacecraft on entry to the stratosphere so it scatters the density of the particles. Maybe both are needed." Liz paused in thought then said, "I can ask Jupiter One's team to send probes into our high stratosphere and test out the sonic and reverse-magnetic options and see whether the particle field disperses."

One of the astrophysicists, John Tinsley, reminded Tom that years ago they had designed a prototype similar to what Liz was suggesting. He also pointed out the staggering advances in nuclear fusion propulsion since that era. "Our design was never picked up due to lack of funding, but we can update it now that nuclear fusion propulsion has been perfected. A smaller, lighter spaceship would enable the reverse engine function to apply. The spaceship could then slow down when it encounters the particle field and in addition have the capacity to hover above a landing pad with stabilizing arms extending from the hull to the ground. It would then be in a convenient launch position. I know this is feasible. At our end we must find a level rock plateau of considerable size and depth to withstand the blast from the engines."

Tom mused aloud, "The fear the next spacecraft will disintegrate in the high stratosphere is real and has prevented the arrival of more pioneers. We can't grow without them and need the input of new minds, creative difference, new technology, and specialists with new skills. We need this to reinforce our endeavors." He turned attention to his previous project with John Tinsley, "John, do you remember the specs we worked out? The manufacturing facility established at Jupiter Station is state of the art. No expense was spared by Seymour Hansen, so what we only thought of back then is now feasible."

Tom murmured that it was a wonder what billions of dollars could do when directed to the right place and cause. This brought a ripple of laughter from the gathering of scientists. Tom asked Liz if she could draw up a set of schematics for the Jupiter One engineers. Then he hesitated, "I think this new spaceship has to be a stripped down workhorse. All the safety measures certainly, but the smaller space and cargo capacity means that the extra facilities that were on PRIME 3 for the long journey from

Planet Earth are not needed. That time frame has been radically reduced with nuclear fusion engines."

They discussed this back and forwards for the next hour and arrived at a consensus for a workhorse spaceship. Liz got right to work. Cappie had been listening to the scientists with mischief in his smile, pleased that they'd left the flight deck intact. With his Irish humor he said, "I have an equally pressing question. Jupiter One and Mars Stations have well recognized names, but they continually refer to us as the new planet. Don't you think it's time we named this beautiful place that has become our home? And do you know who I think can best deliver a name?" They waited in anticipation. Cappie said, "It's the children and young ones. They are the future. Let's trust their imagination."

The task was given to the young adults and children. They convened over dinner one evening and tossed around different names that no-one picked up on until Ruthie chimed in. She said, "When I am looking forward to something new it is always as if I am reaching for a lovely horizon, just beyond my reach. Why not call our lovely planet 'Horizon.' It was beyond our reach, but here we are."

With congratulatory whoops, they endorsed Ruthie's suggestion and rushed over to where Tom and Sian were sitting with Cappie and Liz. "We've got a name for the planet," smiled Catriona, "and here's young Ruthie to announce it." She lifted Ruthie on to the table where she hammed it up beautifully. Ruthie put her arms in the air and shouted out loud to get everyone's attention, "Ta Da, listen up. You are now on the planet we have named "Horizon" and we are so lucky. Ta Da." She did a cartwheel right off the table into Uncle Chung's arms.

The engineers on Jupiter One took their careful deliberations to heart and furthermore named the new spacecraft as HORIZON ONE. Good news travels fast, especially when it was passed on to Ruthie. John Tinsley with several geologists scouted the terrain for a suitable landing pad and found the perfect locale on a neighboring plateau above Oasis. It had deep, solid, expansive rock right at its center. It was level and the few outcrops of rock on its surface were removed by the laser tools Tom had devised. They wondered what to call the place.

Once again, the children came to their rescue to provide the name: Oasis Interstellar Space Port. HORIZON ONE quickly came into production once probes confirmed the positive data required. The first flight of the new spaceship was eagerly anticipated and carried thirty pioneers in the spring of 2086. It was also packed with highly efficient solar units to provide energy for the different communities. Further flights brought more pioneers and a small helicopter that could be fueled by the solar units. Cappie and most of the Special Forces unit were capable of piloting and servicing this craft, which proved to be a vital cog in the wheel of expanding communities, once they re-constructed the helicopter from the carefully boxed parts.

Marguerite Bay on the five mile beach became the orientation locale. The beauty of this sub-tropical paradise on Planet Horizon enchanted the new pioneers. They had been strictly screened by a selection committee headed up by Seymour Hansen. He was looking for special skills in architecture, science, building and electronics as well as creative difference, community builders and eco-farmers with families. They landed first of all at the Oasis Interstellar Space Port, where they were greeted by families who took them into their homes and introduced them to communal living. Their intensive training began with the delightful trek to Marguerite Bay. Sian and Tom led their new friends along the ridge that overlooked the ocean to the exquisitely maintained camp of Marguerite Bay. The scientists, who worked in shifts at the laboratory stationed there, were delighted with their unusual role of custodians.

They had built six cabins amongst the tents. Behind the low plateau of the encampment the biologists worked closely with eco-farmers to create a small farm with pens and pasture for chickens, goats and sheep, as well as simple irrigation systems to grow plentiful vegetables, rice, maize and a variety of beans. This was replicated in the fertile land between the two alluvial rivers that framed Oasis settlement. Their experiments with the fertilized animal embryos in deep freeze proved successful. So much so that the first border collies and standard poodles were soon trained for herding and hunting. Chung and Robert were expert dog trainers and took a delight in delivering the trained dogs to families that wanted them. Sian had quietly requested a standard poodle and received the gentlest one. It adored her. They actually shared similar traits, which were pointed out by Catriona much to Tom's amusement.

With training supervised by Tom and Sian, the new members of the community played with delight. At the same time they learned the necessary teamwork and ethics to sustain viable communities on Horizon. The teams worked tirelessly in between swimming, soccer, volley ball and walking on the beach. Cappie added his unique mark by organizing the Cooking Team. He would take leave from Oasis for each pioneer orientation to establish the special magic of this team and all that evolved from it; music, philosophy, discussion and dancing. It was a blend of holiday camp and mindful living. Marguerite Bay provided the perfect crucible for orientation to living on Horizon. The post supper discussions drew out unusual talents and skills, especially music. Tom's Shop turned into a temporary bamboo flute factory and Catriona provided music lessons to the new pioneers.

Astronomers amongst the scientists described the new night-time sky and how they were plotting it. There were new constellations of stars to map, totally different to what could be seen from Planet Earth. They pointed out constant meteor showers hitting the dense particle layer, breaking up and descending like fireworks to the surface of Horizon. The days and nights were longer than on earth. Much to their surprise something akin to Aurora Borealis activity was taking place in their sub-tropical location.

The scientists had also noticed severe dust storms far to the north, so they knew there must be an expanse of desert beyond their sub-tropical paradise. They had carefully tracked weather patterns since the lab became operative in the spring of 2085. Their weather expert reported an initial cycle of cooler, wetter weather in autumn and winter, while spring and summer were much hotter, yet still moist and humid. This sub-tropical cycle was an excellent cycle for crop growing and earth regeneration, but this was based on only one year of observation, they noted.

Martinez and Johanna provided an unforgettable moment at the first orientation. Johanna was a botanist at the lab and had named the place as Marguerite's Bay after her good friend who had perished in the hull breach on PRIME 3 spaceship. Martinez, a member of Marshall's unit, was providing security for the first orientation. After supper, before the evening discussion began, Johanna stood up. She had Sian's ordeal in her mind and in her own way took a very brave step. She announced that she remembered the first time she was at Marguerite Bay, named for her friend who died when the first spacecraft exploded.

Johanna said, "I remember how wonderful it was to take dancing lessons on the beach with Luis Martinez over there. I am asking him to dance with me again and to keep on dancing with me." She blushed at her boldness and

Martinez was struck dumb. He stood up and the newcomers cheered him on with enthusiasm. His handsome face held astonishment mixed with relief. He did not know what to say and then it came out in beautiful Spanish.

"Johanna, me encantó bailar contigo a orillas del mar y quisiera seguir bailando - I loved dancing with you Johanna on the beach, and love to dance some more." Whistles and cheers surrounded Luis and Johanna with chants of "Dance Luis, Dance Johanna, Dance." He held out his hand to Johanna, who was nervously flushed by her boldness. They danced on the beach to a song held by Cappie's deep baritone and taken up by Catriona's violin. They were not the only one's waltzing on the beach as the sun went down. Sian and Cappie had quickly transformed the evening's discussion session into dancing lessons on the beach. The joy was collective.

Mary and Maggie were a vital part of this first orientation, outlining the medical and counseling care that was available in their discussion session at the end of the first week. At the end of their orientation, Mary stated calmly that she and Maggie were a lesbian couple and shared a cabin in Oasis. They were clearly supported by the entire community when she spoke to the new pioneers to establish open-ness about sexual preference rather than choose fear and discrimination. Maggie announced that they were considering having a child and felt that Luis Martinez would be an ideal sperm donor. They had already discussed this with Johanna, who was enthusiastic about the opportunity.

Mary said, "Luis is kind, compassionate and has wonderful attributes, all of which would be in his DNA. I once supervised a fertility clinic so can extract and use a sperm donation." She addressed Luis directly, "Dear Luis, would you be willing to do this for Maggie and me? You would be a donor, not a father though we hope you would like to be our first uncle."

Luis was taken aback by the request. He was speechless and looked helplessly in the direction of Johanna, standing next to Maggie. She smiled broadly to her new dancing partner and said, "Luis, this would be a wonderful gift to our two friends and I am all for it, but it is your decision to make."

Luis composed himself, aware of the smiles from the new pioneers. He spoke to Mary and Maggie, "I see this has Johanna's approval, so when the time comes I will be happy to contribute to your family. You just have to educate me." Johanna was the first to embrace him, quickly followed by hugs from their two friends. The new pioneers stood up and offered their applause.

The orientation at Marguerite Bay took three to four weeks to instill the core values the community had shaped. The Oasis settlement had the capacity to be constantly fluid, never staying the same. Robert had previously expressed to Tom and Sian that at some point he and Joyce would like to establish an eco-village much like the one they had established in the Scottish Highlands on Planet Earth. With the influx of newcomers arriving to Oasis, he and Joyce felt that this was a good time to proceed with their dream. They had gathered together five families, all in favor of establishing an eco-village, and had explored the hinterland relentlessly with the help of drone data. They found an ideal location two days inland.

They were ready to leave by the time the orientation finished. Camping for two nights on the way, Robert's brother and his family went ahead to survey the land, ensuring that each twenty acre lot would have fruit trees, forest, arable land and water access. They had talked this over with the council at Oasis at great length, receiving support and co-operation. Cappie suggested that he could use the helicopter to fly in their tools, a solar unit and animals. Robert was grateful and mentioned that James and Ruthie could fly on the last flight with the animals, as they had a gift for calming the creatures needed for farming.

Sian clapped her hands with joy, "James and Ruthie can stay with us until you arrive there. Maybe you can give me a week with them."

Robert laughed and agreed, "The helicopter and children will have to be hosed down after the journey with the animals, but that is not too great a problem. My brother and his family will have started the cabin building by now and Uncle Chung is constructing his meditation hut. It will be a joy to have Chung with us for at least three months. We will leave our cabins in Oasis sparkling clean for the new pioneers and wish them great joy in this adventure."

Sian enquired, "Do you have a name for your eco-village, Robert?"

He pondered her query a moment, "I couldn't really think of anything other than the community we created in the Scottish Highlands on Planet Earth, called 'Crossroads.' The memory of it struck a chord with the adults who had lived there and are here on Horizon. Of course we had to run it past the children and they agreed that adults could sometimes come up with good names." They laughed at that and embraced before the inevitable departure.

The parting with Rising Moon and Manny was not so easy for Catriona. Manny and Rising Moon had extended an invitation for others to join in their venture of living by the Wisdom of the Elders creed. The community remembered Rising Moon's riveting talk about the Creation

Story of her tribe. Their home would be known as Black Elk Village in honor of the legendary Sioux medicine man who prophesized centuries before that the hoops of all nations would coalesce as one combined family. Catriona had known all along that her blood sister would return to the haven they both had created. Part of her wanted to go, but she knew instinctively that her place was with her mother, at least for now.

Tom was elated at the settlement progression and said to Sian and Cappie, "At last we have some movement into different forms of living well. That is creative difference to my mind. Crossroads and Black Elk Village certainly take some of our leaders away, but this makes room for a sharp, intelligent coterie of pioneers with different skills to replace them. We have to be ready for changes to Oasis and Marguerite Bay. Our progression depends on diversity and new talents. The exodus to new locations and the incoming talent create a new and vibrant mosaic."

"I agree," said Cappie. "I had thought that it would be a while before this happened but I share your delight Tom that the sense of adventure is alive and well. We must foster this as best we can. I know that Seymour was looking for different kinds of talent in the new wave of pioneers and I would say that so far his team has delivered well. Don't you think so Sian?"

Sian smiled, "It is moving along as I had hoped and prayed for. I look forward to the emergence of new leadership that will keep things consistent with living well with the environment and with one another."

An unusual conversation took place with Igor's family. Igor solemnly asked his father Nikolai and mother Elena if he and his adopted brothers, George and Andrew, could have their permission to join Manny and Rising

Moon at Black Elk Village. Nikolai listened intently as Igor spoke of his time there with Rising Moon and Catriona, and how they had helped him heal a deep depression. He stated he'd never before felt so whole. Also that George and Andrew loved the simple, earth-based manner of community living based on ceremonial respect. Igor knew in his heart that was where he belonged. Nikolai looked to his wife Elena, who was smiling an almost secret smile.

"My dear Igor, there is something your mother and I must share with you." Nikolai waited until he had their rapt attention. "Elena and I are both descendants of the Doukhobors from Russia. They followed a path of peace and community, much as you describe for Black Elk Village." Nikolai was smiling and reached out for Elena's hand, which he gently held in his huge paw of a hand.

"The Doukhobors created a movement for peace, ethics and community in nineteenth century Russia. They rejected both state militarism and the clergy. In 1895 they sent a strong message of protest by burning three piles of government-issued guns and swords to emphasize their ethics for non-killing and community. This immediately brought state persecution and exile. An initial migration of seven thousand five hundred Doukhobors to Canada soon followed with the help of Tolstoy." Nikolai paused, suddenly overwhelmed at recalling his family history.

Elena picked up his story, "Tolstoy was an incredible philosopher and is regarded to this day as the conscience of humanity. He articulated the beliefs of the Doukhobor Movement in his prolific writings, referring to them as 'people of the twenty fifth century,' which is quite a statement about how they were ahead of their times. They had ethics, values, education and community-living bound up in a new paradigm that re-visits us today with the establishment of Oasis and for the two new settlements to

215

be created at Crossroads and Black Elk Village. We are just hearing about them. Do you remember Sian presenting the vision of settlements on the new planet?" The three young men eagerly assented and drew closer to their parents.

Elena continued, "Our ancestors did not migrate to Canada. They settled with other communities in Georgia and at the same time stayed true to their Doukhobor beliefs. This was passed down from generation to generation and came to rest with Nikolai and me. We chose to make a career as astronauts with the Russian Space Program rather than serve in the military. We are delighted that you are deciding for yourselves exactly the direction that Nikolai and I would choose. The Wisdom of the Elders fits the creed we were born into, love, caring, ecology, community and peace. I speak for both Nikolai and myself. Of course you have our permission, but just know this. Your father and I would feel privileged to join you in this adventure."

George, the youngest boy let out a yell as he launched himself into Nikolai's strong arms. "This is what I want more than anything in the world."

Nikolai said with much happiness, "This adventure as a family makes me feel that I am going home to my ancestors. We are the 'people of the twenty fifth century' after all." Igor was stunned with delight at his parents' words and was slow to respond. Andrew and George had no such restraint, embracing their adopted parents with laughter and gratitude.

A similar conversation was being held between Lan Lan, Bao and their parents Subing and LongFu. The two girls had never forgotten how completely free they felt when they had lived in the tipi with Catriona and Rising Moon. They too felt Rising Moon as their blood sister, yet were bound by more than that. They knew that their mother

Subing resonated with the same experience that had rocked them out of selfish pre-occupations. They would like to try it out, but did not wish to leave their parents behind.

Subing looked to her husband and said softly, "They are correct, my dear LongFu. But I am not going on such an adventure without you."

LongFu looked at his beautiful wife and daughters. He was solemn and restless, turning his objections over in his mind before he spoke. "Subing, when we splashed down in the ocean after ejecting from the spaceship, I was so relieved you were alive that I swore to myself that I would follow you anywhere. I was also terrified that I would never see my daughters alive. And here they are making a request for us to contemplate." He paused as he noticed the tears in the corner of Subing's eye.

"I have many reservations about what our daughters are contemplating, mostly that I may not be able to embrace the newness as well as they can. But for Lan Lan, Bao and for you, I will do my very best. I am ready for this adventure as long as we are together." Lan Lan and Bao were in tears as they melted into their father's arms. Subing held all three close to her.

Rising Moon and Manny came to bid their farewell to Sian and Tom, as they were departing soon for Black Elk Village. Rising Moon and Catriona knew their bond could never be broken. Rising Moon laughed and said that she would so miss borrowing Catriona's violin.

Tom overheard her and asked her to come to his Shop. Once there he presented her with a wooden box. "You can open it Rising Moon," he said gently. She did. In the box lay a beautiful red stained violin with the bow resting on one side. Tom had made it for her. Her mouth dropped open and she could not say a word. Speechless, she looked at Tom in disbelief and burst into tears.

Catriona spoke brusquely, "Come now Rising Moon, my father has been making this for quite a while, always having to hide it when you went to see him at the Shop. Let me wipe your tears." Catriona did this lovingly as she spoke to Rising Moon. "Your violin's timbre is deeper than mine but let us see how our two violins dance with one another. And one other thing you should know. The strings on your bow are made from my long hair as we could not find a horse."

Rising Moon laughed through her tears.

Catriona continued, "So you carry me wherever you go. Let us play together the Mendelsshon piece as our finale, for now anyways."

With tears streaming down her face Rising Moon followed Catriona's lead as they threw out with passion their joined hearts into the cosmos. The entire community heard the ecstasy of the two violins and congregated at Tom's Shop for heartfelt farewells. Their flotilla of small crafts left next day from Marguerite Bay with extra parachute fabric to make more tipis. There were two more couples, with children, that took the step to accompany Rising Moon and Manny to Black Elk Village.

Catriona remained, standing very still on the Five Mile Beach. A solitary figure as their crafts pulled further away. She knew in her heart that one day she would join them.

Rising Moon looked back to her blood sister standing alone on Five Mile Beach. She knew that it was just a matter of time before she and Catriona would re-unite.

11: Jihadists

Several months after the new settlements were established at Crossroads and Black Elk Village, Marshall received an alarming encrypted message from Seymour Hansen on Jupiter One. They both had an algorithmic computer console designed by Liz. Marshall decoded the message and immediately sent an urgent message to Tom and his Special Forces men. When they arrived he read out slowly the communication from Seymour Hansen.

"SERIOUS ALERT – Received notice from Chinese Space Agency. HORIZON ONE was hijacked at the Earth launch facility in China by extremist jihadists. Pilot and Navigator were sleeper members of this jihadist cell. IMPERATIVE YOU CHECK PIONEER COMMUNITY FOR SLEEPERS. Massacre of all staff at launch facility on Earth and destruction of communication systems. Same at Mars Station. Jupiter One Station on lock-down when they arrived. They destroyed all communication systems except for the console built by Liz, which is with me. Fourteen jihadists in total, eight men and six women, heavily armed, well trained and dangerous with intent to take over Horizon. Assembling spacecraft HORIZON TWO with weaponry. Will take 2 weeks. HORIZON ONE was on a scheduled flight to bring a further thirty pioneers to Horizon. All killed at Earth Station. The fourteen terrorists will be tired from unbroken space travel but do not underestimate their intention to kill and take over. Repeat: they will likely have sleepers in your community. HORIZON ONE has wormhole and Horizon co-ordinates logged into its navigation system. The pilot and navigator know where to land and how to get through interstellar space. Prepare well. – Seymour Hansen."

Sian had joined the tense gathering to listen to the communique from Seymour Hansen. Tom looked at her, when Marshall finished speaking, and said, "Sian, with your extrasensory capabilities could you go over each pioneer in your mind who could possibly be a sleeper? We must find the enemy within first of all."

Sian calmly assented and glanced up at the sun beams dancing on the table in front of her. She took in a deep breath and closed her eyes. In her mind's eye she scanned every wave of pioneers, searching for anything that felt out of place. Her friends stayed very quiet until Sian's eyes suddenly opened wide. "There is a couple from Venezuela, who do not feel like a couple at all, always on the edge of community co-operation, like a masquerade. That was the feeling I had when I first met them."

She looked intensely at Marshall and Tom, "I strongly feel they are not alone, so we must be very skillful how we find that out. The man's name is Miguel, a skilled engineer and irrigation specialist from Venzuela. His wife is Rebecca, a nurse. I remember Maggie also speaking to me about how strange this woman felt in the clinic. I trust Maggie's intuition."

Marshall and Martinez checked first that Miguel and Rebecca were not at home before searching their cabin. They lived next to Maggie and Mary. Meticulously they went over the simple contents of their cabin and found a grey metal case underneath their bed. Martinez forced the locked case open to reveal a cache of sophisticated light weight weapons; grenade launchers, laser weapons and hand guns. They wondered how the weapons had been smuggled on board the spaceship and carefully removed the weapons. They replaced the metal case under the bed, waiting inside for the couple's return. Chung was outside, weeding the plants at Maggie's adjacent cabin. His hoe was the only weapon he needed. Miguel and Rebecca entered their cabin just before supper time to find their own weapons pointed at their heads. Their hands and legs were tightly bound.

Martinez conducted the questions, which he asked in English. "Why do you have grenade launchers and weapons in your quarters?"

"Do you really come from Venezuela, or are you from somewhere else?"

Miguel stared at him with contempt before stating, "You do not know who you are dealing with. We were born into jihadism, just as our ancestors were born into jihadism. Like them we entered *Shahadah* with vengeance in our hearts. This Islamic declaration of faith is to avenge the injustice of your people against ours. Our uprising has a long term goal and will continue for as many centuries as it takes to eliminate your evil culture. Whether on Planet Earth or here on this new planet, Jihadism will prevail and conquer. *La ilaha illa Allah* There is no God but Allah."

Martinez calmly pointed out that the people in Oasis were international and had not participated in any injustice towards their people. Miguel ignored Martinez's presence such was his assurance in arrogance. He carelessly spoke rapidly to Rebecca in Arabic, not realizing that Martinez was fluent in three Middle East languages. They inadvertently revealed a further two sleepers. Martinez remained calm and continued to ask questions in English.

"Are there other members of your cell in the Oasis community?"

"What were you intending to do with these weapons?"

Miguel had already spoken to Rebecca about a rendezvous with a jihadist Dutch couple, Joel and his wife Agnes. Miguel again spoke in Arabic to Rebecca, indicating that Joel would know something was up as he was destined to meet him before supper to receive instructions. The couple studiously ignored Martinez and Marshall. Martinez continued with his questions in English to see if any other sleepers may be identified. He asked if they'd suffered any discrimination while in Oasis and had they not enjoyed the process of building a community. Miguel glared and spat at him. Martinez carefully wiped the spittle from his face with a piece of cloth.

He smiled at both of his captives and spoke in fluent Arabic, "*Asalaamu Alikum* Peace Be Upon You. Thank you for leading us to your partners. You will stay here under house arrest. The gentleman with the hoe outside does know how to use it as a weapon. We will be paying a visit to Joel and Agnes and they too will be placed under house arrest, *Inshallah* God Willing."

Miguel was furious and he tried to stand and head butt Martinez but a swift elbow from Marshall to his temple felled him on the spot. Martinez intimated to Rebecca not to follow her partner's intent and alerted Marshall about where Joel and Agnes had their home.

Their cabin was empty and while Marshall searched for, and found, a similar cache of weapons, Tom and Cappie with hand gun and automatic rifle apprehended Joel and Agnes in the dining room and brought them back to their cabin. They had their hands bound behind their backs and their ankles lashed together.

The interrogation was by Marshall. "We know your jihadist cell has hi-jacked the HORIZON ONE spacecraft that is due here in ten days. They massacred all personnel at the Earth and Mars Stations." He stopped to ensure that he was in command of his emotions. He looked at both of them, still shocked that these two Dutch agronomists, who had worked so hard to establish the irrigation system at Oasis, intended to harm them.

"Was it your intention to kill your fellow pioneers when the spaceship landed here?"

"We do not have any fellow pioneers," sneered Joel. "You are unbelievers and will die when we take over. Those that wish to convert to *Sharia* Law will live a different life than they do now."

Marshall inquired, "Why do you think anyone will convert to your twisted vision of Islam? You persist with an outdated ideology that is not welcome to most Muslims, let alone the pioneers here." Joel's face flushed and he began a tirade about western unbelievers and the ultimate supremacy of jihadism. Marshall interrupted the flow of obscenity by pointing out the considerable non-western component of pioneers around them.

Tom had sat observing while Marshall questioned the young Dutch couple. After listening to their well-rehearsed script he quietly entered the conversation. *"Allahu Akbar* God is Great. We are on this new planet in the late part of the Twenty First Century. You present a distorted version of Islam that has no foundation in the teachings of the Prophet Mohammed." His quiet voice immediately got their attention, and he continued:

"You reflect a dichotomy of *Darul Islam,* living inside Muslim countries as opposed to *Darul Harb,* which refers to territories of war dominated by non-Muslims. This artifice is not found in the formative principles of Islam. The basis of your call to arms by present jihadist leaders is stuck in a past that does not exist, and certainly does not belong in the future." The silence of evening songbirds did not last long.

"How dare you insult our beliefs," Agnes exploded.

Tom quietly observed the young woman and wondered where her sweet demeanor had vanished to. He remembered her, seemingly happy, when he worked alongside her building the irrigation system at Oasis. But something deeper and dangerous about her was carefully hidden. In a measured tone and logic Tom pointed out that she and her partner were ignorant about the beliefs that had led them to their readiness to kill neighbors.

He continued, "In the present era *Darul Islam* and *Darul Harb* are spiritually bankrupt, replaced in modern Islam by the term *Darul Aman* where secular laws in countries like Canada are seen as similar to core principles of Islam. This reality has been totally distorted by your jihadist perspective."

Joel and Agnes were shocked by Tom's words, as he continued speaking. "The emergence of *Darul Aman* provided direction for Muslims to co-exist with non-Muslims. It is a charter supported throughout the Qur'an where Muslims are free to practice their faith and at the same time obey the laws of the land. He quoted instances of this from the Qur'an (2.177) "It is not righteousness to turn your face towards East or West, but rather righteousness is… to fulfill the contracts which you make."

Joel screamed in rage at him, "Do not quote my faith to me, you bastard."

Tom responded, "It would seem that you know less than I about the contents of the Qur'an." He allowed a minute to pass by before continuing. "You are ignorant, out of date and not intelligent about the Prophet's teachings. It is hard for me to understand such persistence with a flawed ideology."

His serene composure enraged Joel, who tried to stand up and lash out at him, but succeeded only on falling on the cabin floor. Tom spoke directly to the fallen prisoner in the same calm manner, "Instead of creating modern solutions to keep your faith and the laws of the country you are in, jihadism placed you in a mediaeval context that is irrelevant. You are locked into ancient stereotypes that were useless in the Middle Ages and totally obsolete in present time."

Tom paused for a moment before driving the stake in, "What mental pathologies did you have before jihad? What teachers did you study with to learn the noble and wise teachings of the Prophet Mohammed? *Allahu Akbar*"

Any composure that Joel had maintained quickly vanished with these goads. His anger rose as he began to swear and curse at Tom, promising death and torture to every pioneer he could get his hands on. He stopped only when his long and vicious outburst exhausted him, as sub-tropical darkness began to envelop the cabin.

Tom retained his steely calm, "Nobody here at Oasis has been unkind to you. No-one has discriminated against you. You are free to express your faith as you please providing you abide by community rules. This example of conduct is upheld in the Qur'an. Yet you are prepared to open fire on us when your comrades arrive here on HORIZON ONE."

He paused to allow this to sink in to the prisoners. "Do you not remember the vision expressed by Sian at a community council you both were present at? She said,

"We wish to establish community here that takes care of the environment, bound by caring and sharing for one another just as we care for the ecology of this new planet." You have been embraced by this ethic ever since you arrived on this new planet."

Agnes shouted at him, "Shut up your filthy mouth. How dare a piece of shit like you speak the name of our Prophet? You will be the first one I shoot."

Tom realized he had successfully rattled their self-assurance and permitted a broad smile in their direction before addressing them once more, "Thank you both for revealing so much. Your ignorance and pathology are evident. I will return tomorrow to provide further lessons on the teachings of the Prophet Mohammed."

Marshall did his best to prevent a smile from appearing on his face, for he realized that Tom was not finished speaking to the Dutch couple. "Before I leave you, realize that breaking the contract of being here at Oasis is *haram,* absolutely forbidden by core Islamic principles. You have transgressed Islamic Law. But rest assured, you will not be executed or harmed, which is what your misguided version of *Shariah* Law would do." Tom said. "The Oasis community will find a solution for you and your two comrades to thrive on territory you can call your own. As a community we will greet your deadly intent with generosity and opportunity. The rest will be up to you. I take my leave. *Asalaamu Akbar.*"

Marshall left the cabin with Tom, as two Special Forces soldiers took guard of the prisoners. "Tom," Marshall exclaimed as soon as they were out of earshot, "That was masterful. Where did you learn so much about Islam?"

Tom smiled, "My university studies were in astrophysics and religion, which is probably why I avoided both and became an author and playwright in my early career." He then grimaced as he took a long breath in between his teeth and let out his frustration on the out breath. "These two were easy to crack as they were not brought up in the jihadist culture of Miguel and Rebecca, who in fact come from the tribal area of Northern Syria. They were sent to Venezuela to obtain credentials to infiltrate the PRIME 3 mission. The home grown jihadists are well organized and highly trained. They could not be broken down so easily as the Dutch pair. But it is clear that we needed much better screening for the first coterie of pioneers. Thank goodness Seymour has tightened things up since the PRIME 3 episode."

Both couples were placed under house arrest and the ripples of disbelief, anger and betrayal traveled quickly through the Oasis community. Cappie was directed to use the community helicopter to bring Manny, LongFu, and Robert from the other two settlements. Tom and Marshall called the community together that same evening to explain what was unfolding.

There was heated discussion about deadly retaliation upon the four jihadist sleepers amongst them but Sian cautioned restraint. "Dear ones, this is not the route to take. We'll defend ourselves against the jihadist attack emanating from the arrival of HORIZON ONE, but the four people under house arrest will not be executed." She paused to allow her heartfelt words to sink in to everyone's mind.

Johanna in exasperation shouted back, "They were going to execute as many of us on the ground as they could. They cannot get away with that betrayal and potential violence."

Sian spoke directly to her friend, "Johanna, I feel despair at the betrayal just as you do. I understand the deadly fear that four members of our community were willing to murder us when the spacecraft arrives. I resent this deeply, just as everyone here does, but we must distinguish ourselves from their hate. The jihadists on board HORIZON ONE have massacred personnel at the Earth and Mars Stations. They also killed thirty pioneers destined to join us. You heard that from Tom reading out the encrypted message from Jupiter One."

She took a deep breath as what she was about to say pained her deeply, "The jihadists onboard do not know that their comrades, planted in our midst, are under house arrest. We must formulate a strategic plan to defeat them. There is no reasoning with them that will work. I wish there was a way, as that suits my preference, but the wave of massacres following the jihadists on board HORIZON ONE rules out that possibility. That must be clear to everyone. For the four jihadists under arrest in Oasis, I propose that we find a place for them to live on their own, far away from us and without their weapons. We have worked alongside them and though they mean us harm we must be compassionate. They can thrive in their own way if they choose to."

Liz was in agreement and said, "From the drone data we have examined, there is a large island some two hundred kilometers from here. There is water and land that looks fertile with varieties of tropical fruit bearing trees. We can take them there, still bound and under arrest, and leave them with rations and tools. That is a first consideration for all of us to endorse. What matters next is how to defeat the spaceship jihadists."

Johanna asked to speak. She brushed back her long blonde hair and spoke in a hesitant voice, "I have seen at first hand the devastating power of the laser tools that Tom

228

created. We have four laser tools. Can they be connected together as one device and placed on the spaceship landing rock and ignited when HORIZON ONE loaded with jihadists comes to settle down?"

Liz was quick to reply: "Yes, I can do that and relay it to an electronic detonating devise some distance away." Tom's grimness never left his face as he agreed to this.

Marshall brought military order to the proceedings. "Thank you Johanna, that will be our first greeting and we need to set it up with precision. We have sophisticated laser weapons taken from the captives. The grenade launchers are top of the line weapons. Once the hatch of the spacecraft opens, Martinez and I will fire each grenade launcher in a sequence of mere seconds between each grenade. We have four grenades and know how to use them. Additional Special Forces with sniper rifles will be the second sphere of attack. Radiating out from the landing spot, we must dig a circle of deep pits with sharpened stakes pointing upwards. The pits will be concealed by a frame covered in vines and branches. If any jihadist gets beyond the pits, in addition to the snipers we have thirty archers, thanks to Rising Moon's training. Set further back will be a triage area for anyone who is wounded, as we must expect casualties. The jihadists will be heavily armed and never forget that they are highly trained and deadly in their intent to kill us."

Marshall looked around at the intense faces of his friends, "Our singular advantage is the element of surprise and the fact that their backup on the ground is no longer a danger to us. Is this all clear to everyone?" It was.

Marshall outlined his plan. "I will need teams to dig the pits and place strong sharpened stakes in them, Chung will supervise that. Martinez and I will be first in line with the grenade launchers at the landing pad, so we will build defensive rock walls in front of us. Manny when he arrives will be in charge of the sniper unit. Maggie, Mary and the nurses can prepare a triage area. The archers will be in daily target practice, Liz and Catriona are in charge of that." There was a deep silent hush once Marshall stopped barking out his orders. His military mind was fully engaged. He imparted to the entire community the gravity of what they were facing and they took from him a steely determination to prepare for combat.

Tom and Sian stood before their beloved community. They could see the determination in the faces of their friends. No-one was going to take away what they had built on Planet Horizon. Tom spoke slowly to them, "This forthcoming battle marks the end of our innocence. But with the loss of innocence comes further wisdom, rather than hate." Everyone, including Sian, nodded in silence.

Tom said, "The jihadists have massacred people on their way here. We have ten days to prepare. Marshall's strategy is sound and we must perfect it right down to seconds of timing. Sian and Liz are correct about how to treat the threat from within. The four sleepers amongst us will be treated fairly, as we supply them with supplies and a new beginning. Our determination to endure is not to cultivate hate as that will erode all of our integrity." He paused to allow his words to sink in. "We are defending one another so that once this is over we can go about building community with eyes wide open rather than half shut. We have work to do and much to organize."

He gazed at the sky for a moment. "Cappie has taken the helicopter to Black Elk Village and to Crossroads Eco-Village. Soon we will have Manny, LongFu and Robert with us. We come together to defend what we have built. Rising Moon wanted to come back also, but she is eight months pregnant with her first child, a daughter to be named after Catriona. She is concentrating on us, particularly the archers she trained. I know they will do her proud. Now sleep if you can. Know that we are being severely tested. And we are equal to it. Good night to you, my dear friends."

They prepared well and trained meticulously over the next ten days, waiting for the imminent battle. Then to everyone's surprise the battle was over in minutes.

Tom had felt moments of utter dismay that there was no escape from fractious fanaticism. Their former Planet Earth had been destroyed by greed, disorder and fanaticism. The frequent news from Jupiter One Station was one of further deterioration and ongoing conflict world-wide driven by fanatics seeking possession of scarce resources. That survival reality had now caught up with them.

These thoughts flashed through Tom's mind as he waited intensely for the jihadist pilot to reverse the spacecraft engines for HORIZON ONE to slowly come closer to the solid rock at the Oasis landing. It hovered ten feet above the ground. The support legs were extended to stabilize the spaceship on the sculpted plane of hard rock that served as a landing pad on the plateau above Oasis Hamlet. Tom's signal detonated the four lasers, creating an explosion that ripped through the rear of the spacecraft. With the four lasers exploding underneath the engines, the spacecraft toppled slowly to the left of the landing pad.

The pioneers had prepared well for the jihadist intention to take over their new home, Planet Horizon. The space hatch opened and heavily armed jihadists rushed out shooting their high powered laser weapons in all directions. Before they could move down the ladder they were met by carefully fired grenades from weapons held by Martinez and Marshall. They fired four grenades at intervals and decimated the armed force intent on killing them. Each grenade exploded, scattering titanium shrapnel with deadly effect inside the confined space of HORIZON ONE.

Six armed terrorists managed to break through the grenade barrage and reached the edge of the landing pad only to stumble into deep concealed pits with sharpened poles upon which they impaled themselves. Manny was spotting the fallen jihadists through binoculars and shouted out that there were two left. The pilot and navigator took their time before stepping out of the open hatch with their hands in the air. Through his binoculars Manny could see they were wearing suicide vests. On Manny's instruction the snipers swiftly took them down. One of the vests exploded and accounted for the sure death of both of them.

It was such a relief that not a single pioneer was killed, though a stray bullet from a falling jihadist had caught Marshall in the shoulder. His flesh wound was the only casualty. The archers had dispatched two jihadists who managed to crawl out of the death pits. All eight men and six women jihadists on board HORIZON ONE were dead.

Marshall insisted on a de-briefing, yet it turned into a retrospective examination of why they were on Planet Horizon and whether their communal values had been compromised. Sian and Tom talked about the battle when the community gathered in the communal dining area. There was a clear sky overhead and a fresh breeze coming from the ocean, a rebuke to the violence they had just participated in. The consensus was that their actions this day were to preserve the vision they strongly adhered to. There was a fierce feeling that evening from the manner they had prepared for battle and how they stood and fought together. Yet there was genuine compassion on the next day, as the four sleeper jihadists were led to the helicopter by Manny and Martinez. The four had to take a long walk, shuffling between two lines of pioneers who had once thought of them as friends. There was no hate, cursing or shouting at them, just a silent regret. The four prisoners screamed and yelled expletives in English and Arabic, which slowly came to a stop. No-one reacted to their abusive language. The jihadists painfully shuffled along, their ankles bound as well as their minds. Manny was in the cockpit next to Cappie with a gun pointing at the first two securely bound jihadists, Miguel and Rebecca. Martinez was in the hold behind Joel and Agnes, armed with a side arm. Cappie instructed that their unwelcome guests be gagged for the duration of the flight.

It was an uneventful journey. On arriving at the large island, Cappie set the helicopter down next to a fresh water lake with a copse of fruit bearing tres nearby. Each prisoner was placed bound and gagged fifty yards apart. Cappie looked at them for a long lingering moment and said, "You will find a way to release one another. There is water close by. In the pack placed by the lake, there is food supplied by the community to see you through the next few days. At this spot tomorrow I will drop rations and tools." Then he surprised them with an expression he had learned from Tom. *"Asalaamu Alikum Wa Rahmatu-lah Wa Barakatuh."* The prisoners looked at him with total astonishment. He had said to them, "May the Peace and Mercy of Allah be upon you." The long return to Oasis was eerily silent as Cappie, Manny and Martinez reflected on the last ten days that had endangered the way of life they were creating on Horizon.

One week later Marshall took the precautionary measure of sending a drone over the island where the jihadists had been left. He was shocked to see on the live stream of data that one woman had been hung from a tree by the lake. The bodies of two others lay inert next to the tree. The final body was located close by. When he grimly reported this to the community, there was no rejoicing at the implosion by the sleeper jihadists, just the realization that they had acted in good faith with their enemies. There was a further helicopter ride to bury the four bodies. Tom recited the appropriate Islamic verses for burial as Cappie and Marshall observed silence.

Manny was staying with Tom and Sian at their cabin and was eager to get home to Rising Moon. He had one other passenger going with him. Catriona wished to travel there to be present at the birth of her namesake and insisted that there was room. Cappie had agreed to take her there.

With a note of anxiety Sian asked, "Are you coming back Catriona? I do know how much you love it there."

Catriona embraced her mother very gently, aware of her alarm. "Mother, the time will come when I will join Manny and Rising Moon, but that is not yet. I will stay with Rising Moon until after the baby is born and then return home." Sian was relieved. She would not impede Catriona from leaving, but longed for her to stay a little longer, as she had many skills to impart to her daughter.

They were all in the comfort of the large living room of Tom and Sian's cabin, open to the evening sounds and bird calls. Tom opened a conversation with Manny that both knew must take place. Tom briefly related to Sian and Catriona the ceremonial experience in the Hopi Sacred Kiva to transfer the energy of plants and animals from Earth to Horizon. He went directly to the point of the conversation, "Manny, your grandmother said to me, before the Four Sacred Keepers entered the kiva, that you would tell me what happened inside. Also that you would know when to speak to me about it. I think that time has come."

Manny smiled fondly to his good friend and agreed that this was the time.

Tom placed his question, "Your grandmother had me sit in a chair above the North Stone of the medicine wheel. Undergrgound in the sacred kiva, she was located at the North Stone and there was a reason for being right above her that I cannot fathom."

Manny was very calm and in no hurry to speak. He unrolled his medicine bundle, taking out the stem and bowl of his ceremonial pipe, placing tobacco in the bowl. "Tom, let us smoke the sacred pipe together before I relate what my grandmother wished you to know." He chanted softly and then smudged his friends and their daughter with sage from his medicine bundle. They followed him in the protocols of smoking the sacred pipe.

They sat in a circle as Manny carefully prepared to speak to Tom. "Remember Tom that my grandmother was the Keeper of the Sky People and sat at the North stone of the medicine wheel. You were right above her so she could track and find the new planet. There was also the Keeper of the animals at the East stone. The Keeper of corn, plants and trees, an elderly woman elder, sat at the South stone. The Keeper of the Earth was located at the West stone to direct the strong energy of new beginnings to this planet."

Manny stopped and took another long draw of tobacco from the pipe. "I was there to keep the central portal open, but I believe now that it was to simply be a witness. The portal at the middle of the medicine wheel was kept open by the Sky People, who knew that the Four Sacred Keepers would be joining them once the ceremony was complete. I saw each one of them smile peacefully and place their hands on their chest before dying, as they joined the stream of energy traveling though the portal to the new planet. My grandmother spoke to me before it was her time to expire. She said to tell you that it was done. The new planet was fully seeded. And furthermore to let you know that at your own point of dying, you and Sian would become part of the sacred stream of the Sky People. Then she smiled to me, clasped her hands on her chest and died peacefully."

Manny stopped to regain his emotions before continuing, "These are the words for you Tom, from my grandmother. I believe Sian already has a sense of this, though you can scarce believe it for yourself." The silence stretched in a comfortable realization of what was intimated.

Catriona spoke for her parents, "Blessings to you Manny. Rising Moon and I often talked about the Sky People and I know my parents are cut from the same cloth. I do not think it a coincidence that Oasis has a Buddhist monk in residence and is always hanging around with my father. So I think your training has started father.' With that she clapped her hands with her special glee.

Tom smiled at her tease and quietly thanked Manny. "I have never forgotten your grandmother and have felt her extraordinary presence many times on this new Planet Horizon. I will follow through on her words to the best of my ability."

Sian at last spoke. She was enchanted by Manny and the insight of her daughter Catriona. "I am deeply humbled by your grandmother, Manny. I have a strong notion of where I go after this life but was in dread that Tom would not choose to go in the same direction. This prophecy from your Hopi grandmother has given me confidence that we will travel together and that gives me a new and vital intention for the life I will live here on Horizon."

12: Catriona and Igor

Catriona smiled quietly to herself as the solar driven helicopter drew her closer to Black Elk Village.

She spotted the large island where she and Rising Moon had rescued five of their friends and took them back to their tipi haven by the river. Excitement grew in her breast as Cappie did a wide sweep over the high bluff that first welcomed Rising Moon to the planet.

The helicopter hovered above the lakeside beach where Catriona had landed in such desolation. Cappie took the helicopter slowly along the river and over the settlement. She was elated at seeing five tipis in the village. She could see three tipis on one side of the river, with two more across the bridge that she and Rising Moon had built. She clapped her hands in joy and let out a shout of delight. Manny laughed with her. He knew the bond between Rising Moon and Catriona was very deep, and saw that this was her rightful place, but had the wisdom to say nothing of what he intimated.

Cappie set the helicopter down on Flat Rock Meadow, close to the village. The Black Elk Village community was gathered there. Cappie was on leave from Oasis, as his flight crew had insisted he stay for a while. Nikolai, Elena, Subing and Longfu were tightly bound friends not only from space flights but from the time they saved Elena's life when their escape crafts splashed down in the ocean. To have Captain Murphy with them was a special joy. Their children had been filled with stories of Cappie finding the worm hole between galaxies and other space adventures. Their families embraced Cappie, who was delighted to see how well Andrew and George had blended with Nikolai's family. Catriona sought out her blood sister Rising Moon. There she was, standing at the back of the crowd. Rising Moon's deep dark eyes were glistening with joy at the sight of Catriona. In moments they were reconciled in a loving embrace, breathing in their mutual happiness to see one another.

The two new families who had ventured to Black Elk Village were standing shyly to one side. Like a whirlwind Catriona hugged them all and brought them into her happiness. Joan and Philip with their two children, Annie and Joseph, were a boon to the community. Philip was an expert in permaculture and irrigation, while Joan brought nursing and mid-wife skills with her. They were pioneers from the Yukon in Canada. Manny's sister Elizabeth was also there with her husband Danny. Both were trained paramedics and like Manny, were steeped in the lore of the Hopi. They had two teenage boys, Zac and Henry, who had learned flute and violin from Catriona while at Oasis. Catriona looked around the community and did not see Igor. She asked where he was.

Rising Moon said, "He is hunting to the west of here and should be back before nightfall."

Then she looked knowingly into Catriona's eyes. "You will see a new Igor from the boy you remember. He has grown to be a skillful leader in our community. His explorations have created careful maps of our entire region. He even found a herd of wild horses close to the mountains. He is our eyes and ears, especially after his first spirit quest. His attention and gentleness to the animals is a lesson to all of us." Then Rising Moon smiled, "He is a better hunter than me. Manny and I are very proud of him."

The community had prepared a splendid supper from what they grew and harvested from the land and lakes. They sat together around one fire pit while Manny and Cappie told the story of the battle with jihadists and how they dealt with the four sleepers in the Oasis community.

Nikolai was very thoughtful on hearing this. He said, "I am no stranger to extremism and have seen enough to anticipate that without a target for their beliefs the four jihadist sleepers exiled to the island would implode amongst themselves. And that is what they did is in not?"

Cappie pondered for a while, stroking his white beard, "You are right Nikolai. The jihadist implosion and deaths on the island recalls to my mind a classic book from the last century, written by William Golding. It was called *Lord of the Flies*, a gruesome story of military schoolboys stranded on an island and how they descended into mutual self-destruction and savagery." Nikolai and LongFu nodded in agreement.

LongFu was a highly literate man and said, "I remember this book also. It described the dark side of humanity and provided a parody of the savagery underlying civilization." He stopped speaking for several minutes before continuing, "I believe that without values and ethics similar to what we have established here and elsewhere on Horizon, there is not a way to stop the conflagration of fire that enveloped the boys on that island. The basic training at Marguerite Bay for everyone establishes common values, without militarism, without clergy insisting on this way or that way, just a living design to bring the best out in everyone."

Subing was delighted at her husband's eloquence. Igor was not the only one who had changed and grown.

During the feast and exchange of news, conveyed mostly by the young adults, Igor quietly arrived. Catriona spotted him immediately and felt instantly overwhelmed by his presence. He joined them with scarce a sound from his footsteps. She noticed that he seemed taller, his frame more muscular, and he walked with the grace of a mountain lion. Igor smiled to his friend Catriona, who gasped helplessly as he stood in front of her. His eyes were clear and steady though she could also see steel at the core. She was stunned by the softness and confidence in his brown eyes. He had picked a bouquet of tropical orchids and bound their stems with a flowering vine. He offered them to Catriona. She accepted, carefully examining each flower including the vines. It felt like the greatest gift she had ever received. Everyone was immediately struck by the open feelings of these two young people. Rising Moon noticed the blush on Catriona's cheeks as she received Igor's gift. She leaned over to whisper to Manny, and they both smiled in the direction of Igor and Catriona.

Rising Moon said, "What beautiful flowers Igor. Catriona cannot see anything else at this moment."

Catriona laughed. "I know you're there my blood sister. Just give me a moment to drink in this magnificent gift from Igor." Smiling, she looked into Igor's gentle eyes.

The spell of wonder was interrupted by Rising Moon, as at that moment, her water broke. Their tipi was long readied for this birth. With Manny's support she walked slowly there and was accompanied inside by mid-wife Joan, followed by Catriona and Elena. They were joined by Elizabeth who chanted Hopi blessings for this birth. Manny sat outside the tipi and prayed for Rising Moon and the new child. He became very aware of the presence of his Hopi grandmother and of Rising Moon's mother.

It was an easy birth for Rising Moon and before Manny knew it, Catriona stepped out of the tipi, holding her namesake in a soft antelope skin and placed the newborn in his arms. He was overwhelmed with joy and wonder. Catriona had to prompt him to hold her up and announce her name. Inside the tipi, moments earlier, Rising Moon told Catriona to remind Manny about what he had to do, as he would become lost in the eyes of his child. Manny smiled to his daughter and held her up to the sky announcing that this child's name is "Catriona Grace Fredericks" and that he would serve her all his days. The community cheered and clapped, celebrating the first child to be born in Black Elk Village.

Catriona spoke urgently to Manny, "I have to take little Catriona back to Rising Moon so she can nurse her."

Nikolai and LongFu chuckled as Manny did as requested, remembering how they had felt at holding their first born child. The interrupted feast continued with storytelling that knit the community together. Nikolai told tales of his Doukhobor heritage and how children were treasured, educated and cared for. Cappie was surprised by the once reticent LongFu who continued with accounts of his adventures with twin baby girls. Subing smiled and confirmed that her husband was the major force and influence of their infancy.

LongFu finished his stories by calling over to Manny, "My friend, your baby has the best uncles and aunties in the world." Lan Lan and Bao pulled out their bamboo flutes and played a composite of Chinese and aboriginal melodies.

Cappie was having the time of his life with the families of his former flight crew. Lan Lan asked him if he would like to come and live with them in Black Elk

Village. The two young women had grown very fond of him, especially when he taught them some of his cooking secrets. Cappie smiled, "That is a lovely thought and I assure you I will visit as often as I can." He paused and glanced at their parents. "My job at Oasis Hamlet is very fulfilling for me. The cooking team there is the engine that drives things in the direction of a caring community. It heads all of us in a direction so that something like *Lord of the Flies* does not happen. Every pioneer who comes to Planet Horizon goes through an orientation at Oasis, so that a mutual set of values can be grasped by all. It is put into practice in different ways that keeps the ethics of community living intact."

He saw that he had the intense attention of Lan Lan and Bao. "I so admire your parents for supporting your desire to live in Black Elk Village, to take on a different way of living. Very different to what you were used to on Planet Earth." Then he broke off and stood up as Rising Moon stepped out of the tipi with her child sleeping in her arms. She was radiant and happy. She slowly walked round the gathering, introducing everyone to her sleeping baby then stood before them.

"My baby has met her community. I am so happy to have you as all my relations. I call on my parents and the Creator to bless this child Catriona Grace Fredericks and this community." She turned to Manny and whispered to him, "The Sky People are here Manny. All the Keepers from the sacred kiva along with my mother and father are here. I feel their presence, don't you?" Manny was grinning from ear to ear and no answer was required.

For the next two days the adorable new baby held Catriona's attention. Rising Moon chided her gently that someone else was waiting for her attention.

"You mean Igor?" was Catriona's testy reply.

Rising Moon smiled, "He has been patiently waiting for you."

Catriona spoke too quickly: "Yes, but have I been waiting for him?"

Rising Moon saw through her evasion, "My sister, I know you better than you think. I can still see the expression on your face when Igor placed the jungle orchids in your hands. Time stopped for you, did it not?"

Catriona had no reply. She knew her sister was right.

"Just enjoy your time here with him," Rising Moon continued. "Go fishing, play music, do not bristle at him Catriona. Igor is a magnificent man and you know it, which is why you are afraid of your feelings."

Catriona stopped her thoughts, breathing deeply in and out, as her mother had taught her, before she replied: "You are right Rising Moon. I was caught off guard. Igor has matured so far beyond what I knew and I was reluctant to give him any chance to come close to me." She smiled to her sister, "I think it is time to open that door."

They both giggled and hugged like young girls.

Catriona was not equipped to resist Igor's quiet confidence. He did not romance her or speak of love. He told her stories of his expeditions, often alone, and how he memorized rivers, forests and mountains and made precise maps. She felt the excitement of his sighting a herd of wild horses in a long valley that led to the nearest mountain range.

"I will have a horse here for you the next time you come to Black Elk Village," said Igor in a matter of fact manner.

Catriona borrowed Rising Moon's violin and played music when they went fishing and enjoyed a lunch by the beach where she had first met Rising Moon. She told Igor the story and he laughed out loud at how ferocious Rising Moon must have appeared. They walked, talked, sat under the drift of the two moons that lit up every night sky. Yet both knew what was happening within their hearts.

Igor asked her a surprising question, "When you were a child what was your bedroom like?"

Catriona smiled as fond recollections arose in her mind. "I had the most marvelous bedroom. It was more of a music room than a bedroom, full of musical instruments. My mother was a music teacher for the entire region and children without instruments came to practice with me in my bedroom."

She giggled and clapped her hands, "I had all these stuffed animals and would place them next to instruments and then move them around. My elephant would be on the clarinet on a Monday. He would switch with dolphin's drums on a Wednesday, then on to the monkey's keyboard on a Friday. Same for Teddy, Tinker Bell and Piggy." Igor started to laugh as Catriona continued speaking. "My father was such a goof. He would knock on the door and ask if he was to be Elephant, Tinker Bell or Bear and then come in and play their instruments." Igor was rolling over with laughter by this time.

Catriona continued speaking, "My bedroom had a large bay window and my father would sit there with whatever stuffed animal I assigned to him. Often my mother would come in and conduct the entire ensemble. I have not thought about this delight for a long time. I remember it as a time of utter happiness and joy." Catriona's face was lit up with the memories and she turned to him, "What about you Igor?"

Igor pondered whether to reveal too much, then decided to do so. "I remember how I clung to my bedroom as a child. It was my sanctuary. My parents were often under police scrutiny for their beliefs, so to compensate they created a very safe place for me."

He slowly gathered himself, "Let me just stand for a moment in the doorway of my childhood bedroom." Igor closed his eyes to allow the memories to return. "I see the corner where books, paintings and wooden stools are piled up in disarray. My father's carved toys are on a bookshelf until I find a niche for them on the floor. My bed has two levels, one for me to sleep upon and the other for my stuffed animals to talk to before sleeping. Our conversations turned into drawings and stories with my mother. It was a comfortable bed with large pillows and green-checkered blankets. I had a telescope, set up by my father, next to the window and I would fly in my mind to galaxies with my favorite animals."

Then he paused, "Perhaps it was too much of a sanctuary, as I did not like to leave this house. Though I had to when my parents entered the Space Agency in Moscow. I did not want to leave my safe bedroom behind but my father was very smart. He cleared it out and painted it in colors I hated. I begged him and my mother to let me see it one last time."

There was a tremor of emotion in Igor's voice and Catriona stayed very still waiting for him to continue. "On that last visit to my bedroom, mother pointed to the empty window where my telescope once focused on the sky. I felt the loss, stripped down in an empty space once resonant with discovery. I stood in front of the window and felt my mother's gentle hands on my shoulder and still remember her saying, 'There is nothing to hold you back, Igor. Your dream is still inside. Now step into freedom.' In that empty bedroom my mother's wisdom drew me to a new place. She smiled as I looked for the telescope. Nothing was there. My treasures were boxed and sent on to Moscow. This was their way to move me on from fear rather than cling to childhood safety. My mother held my hand and stared at where the telescope was not."

Catriona reached over and gently held Igor's hand, "And here you now are, my magnificent Igor." He raised her hand to his lips and gently kissed her fingers.

Catriona returned to Oasis with Cappie the next day. She felt that she had just grown up after meeting Igor again. Once home, her mother Sian asked about the baby, village, community, Manny and Rising Moon. Catriona gave her a full account. Then Sian pointedly asked Catriona about Igor. She noticed the sparkle in her daughter's eye.

"He is a magnificent man, mother, and I believe I have fallen in love."

Sian smiled wisely, "He will come for you Catriona, mark my words, which means we have much work to do about what I wish to pass on to you."

Catriona looked up at the serious tone of Sian's voice, "Yes mother, I am ready for that. It's about your time with the shamans of the Amazon in South America is it not?"

Sian nodded and said, "That is correct my daughter. You heard many times your father and I talk about the two years I spent training with wise shamans. They taught me how to "see" and "anticipate" at a totally different level. I have used that discernment to identify energies for healing, but there is much more to it than that. If you wish we can begin immediately before Igor comes and carries you off over his shoulder. I expect that to happen in about three months." Catriona did not express any indignation, just laughed along with her mother.

Her training began in earnest. Sian taught Catriona complex breathing techniques that would untangle her discursive mind from everyday thoughts of body survival. The process took Catriona beyond the limitations of ego, so she could discern reality with startling insight. With the Amazon shamans, Sian had frequently used *ayahuasca*, a hallucinogen, which distorted her senses somewhat. She eventually relied on breathing techniques learned in India, a form from *Asparsa Yoga*. She referred to it as dead man's yoga. She explained the three stages of breath control to Catriona, beginning with yogic breathing: In-breath holding fullness, Out-breath holding emptiness. She guided Catriona to cultivate a slow count of twelve for the Holding Fullness and Holding Emptiness portions. It was then followed by several minutes of short explosive breaths, after which the death breaths began. These were long in-breaths and retention of breath for a slow count of twelve, followed by the out-breath and holding the emptiness for as long as is possible.

She explained, "Catriona, the yogic breathing produces an initial calm. The short explosive breaths will produce a sort of portal you feel yourself going through. You may feel light headed and dizzy. The death breaths are the key following this build-up." She looked at her daughter, "Are you ready to try this?"

Catriona nodded and listened carefully to her mother's instructions.

Sian guided Catriona, "With the death breaths, on the in-breath and retention just feel stable, on a particular plateau of experience. On the out-breath and holding emptiness for as long as you can, your limbs and body will shake and tremble with periods of profuse sweating and extreme cold particularly in the hands and feet. Then on the last gasp of holding emptiness, take an in-breath. The trembling and shaking will stop, and you begin to experience a deep clarity that feels like being hyper lucid. The next out-breath and the holding of emptiness for as long as you can, will again produce trembling and shaking throughout the body, extreme sensations of heat and cold but from a different level of experience. On the last gasp of holding emptiness after the out-breath, the in-breath produces a feeling of cognitive calm but at a different plane of your consciousness. When doing the death breaths over a period of time, you will take steps to different plateaus of cognition."

Catriona was taking in the procedure and at Sian's prompt, after a full week of training, was able to articulate what was happening. After practicing the breathing sequence Catriona reported, "I am feeling a different and expansive "space" after the death breaths."

Sian smiled, "You are a fast learner, my child. What is happening is that your mind is being convinced that this is the last breath your body will experience. In actual fact it is not the case, but the trick is to move the mind into the perception that this is so. Then the energy devoted to the survival of the body can be switched into connections with energies and archetypal material that enhance your discernment. What else do you discern?"

Catriona gathered her thoughts, "I felt that I could communicate and receive across a wide spectrum of mystical realms and tap into healing and transforming energies. I cannot really find the words."

Sian looked with admiration at her talented daughter. "Once we have mastered this together there are a few other things I would like to bring to your attention."

Catriona was eager to learn Sian's gifts. She was also relieved that the small choir and orchestra she had created were placed in Tom's skillful hands. He was delighted to take on the task of music maestro for the Oasis ensemble, as all the instruments had been made in his Shop. He understood the urgency of Catriona's training and looked forward to the daily excitement of working with the young musicians of Oasis.

Three months later, Catriona awoke early. It was not the morning chorus of bird calls or the murmur of the waterfall close by that awakened her. It was a presence outside the cabin. She stepped through the door and with a gasp saw George, Igor's youngest brother, standing at the bottom of the steps to the cabin.

"George" she exclaimed, "What are you doing here?" She rushed down and enveloped young George in her arms.

"Igor sent me," George blurted out. "We came by land from Black Elk Village to Marguerite Bay. It took us three weeks to get to Marguerite Bay. He was sent on a spirit quest for true love by Rising Moon and I was to accompany him. That was my spirit quest." George said proudly.

Catriona exclaimed to him how great that was. George blushed shyly at the praise and said, "Igor is building a tipi at Marguerite Bay as that is where he wants to marry you. Oh yes there is something more, he wants Mrs. Sian to do the wedding ceremony."

By this time, Sian and Tom were standing in the doorway, awakened by George's voice. They welcomed him. This was the moment Sian had anticipated. She said, "Come in young George and have some breakfast with us. We obviously have quite a day ahead of us." She turned towards Catriona, "I have something for you dear child. But come and make a big breakfast for this spirit-quester. He must be starving."

He certainly was, as he tucked into a mammoth breakfast of pancakes and fruit. While he was eating and telling Tom the story of their trek, Sian was carefully gathering her surprise for Catriona. It was the golden wedding dress made for Liz by Subing. "Catriona, I have adjusted the wedding dress to fit you perfectly. You must try it on."

But before that could happen George with his mouth full of pancake burst out, "Wait up Catriona, I forgot something that Igor told me to say." He chewed and swallowed his mouthful of pancake. "He has made two wedding rings from some soft rock he found, and asked me to give this necklace to you that he also made." George dug into his pockets and pulled out an exquisite amber and quartz necklace. "Subing and her girls picked the colors that would match the golden wedding dress that Liz wore. Is that right?"

Tom chuckled at the young boy's earnestness.

Catriona was in tears as she hugged George tightly.

He, however, was not finished. "Oh yes, there is something else. If you accept the necklace and wish to marry my brother Igor, I am to tell Cappie, because he will tell everyone else in Oasis to come. That's everything I think. Can I have another pancake please?"

Tom laughingly came over to George, "Well done George. Everything is in hand. Here is another pancake for

250

you. Did you know that the Oasis choir and orchestra have been secretly rehearsing for this wedding?"

With his mouth full again, George muttered, "Yeah, we have been preparing something special to celebrate the wedding back at Black Elk Village. That will take place when we go home. I hope we do not have to walk there as it is such a long way. Can we get a ride in Cappie's helicopter?"

Tom laughed and assured George that he'd see to it.

"Subing made trousers and shirts for Igor and me," said George. "We had to be careful that our wedding clothes did not get dirty on the journey." With his belly full, George left to find Cappie to spread the good news.

Catriona tried on the wedding gown and it was a perfect fit. The golden silk dress fit her slender form perfectly with a slim train at the back. Catriona was thrilled, "Mother, bring this with you. I must go straight away to Marguerite Bay." She smiled a dazzling smile as she kissed her mother and father and was gone to the trail that led from Oasis to Marguerite Bay.

The exquisite ocean sparkled, the interior mountain range danced and the well-trodden trail hurried her on. She hardly felt the earth beneath her running feet. She sang all the way from Oasis Hamlet to Marguerite Bay. Her heart was pounding. And there was Igor. He had completed the tipi, using blue parachute fabric stored at the lab. The scientists had helped with the construction. They all cheered as Catriona ran past them and was enveloped in Igor's strong arms.

"I guess that means yes," he said.

Catriona kissed him on the lips and buried her entire body in his embrace, "Of course," she whispered and then giggled, "I see your humor has improved." Catriona had his exquisite necklace in her hand. "Please place this round my neck dear Igor."

He did so with utter tenderness and there stood the dazzling love of his life. "Your mother is happy to conduct the wedding ceremony?" Igor asked.

Catriona's smile said everything. Igor took her inside the tipi he had built. Hannah and John Tinsley, who were on duty at the lab, had helped with the cedar bough floor. The sacred fire at the center was burning and the wedding tipi had taken on a sacred aura.

Catriona gazed at the beauty and asked, "Do we say our wedding vows beforehand?"

Igor responded, "If that is your wish. Do you want me to speak first?"

Catriona nodded, as she had a surprise prepared for this wonderful man she was to marry. Hannah organized the lab scientists to place the benches and tables around the tipi, as the Oasis community began to arrive for the wedding at Five Mile Beach. Tom and Sian had anticipated the wedding so were semi-prepared though a great deal of impromptu organization came into play at the last minute.

Catriona reached out to hug her parents. Sian held the silk wedding gown to her body after politely asking the men to leave the space. Catriona emerged holding her mother's hand. She was stunningly beautiful with her long auburn red hair swept to one side. The elegant golden dress made by Subing fit her graceful form perfectly. It fell to her feet like a flower kissing the earth and George was holding the slim train at the back.

Igor's pants and tunic of soft buckskin were also made by Subing. George had taken good care that they were kept clean and the two brothers looked very handsome. Rising Moon had embroidered her tribal motif into the necklines. George was ready for the occasion. He carried the rings and had listened carefully to Sian's directions for the ceremony. Sian then called the wedding party forward, Igor and Catriona with George and Liz in attendance. Everyone took in a sharp breath at their sheer beauty. Before the ceremony began, Tom conducted the Oasis choir and orchestra to resounding effect. Then everyone fell quiet, only the ocean waves murmured. Sian asked Igor to express his vows. He looked round at all his friends and then gazed on the rapture of Catriona's face.

In a quiet yet strong voice he began to speak. "The rivers, mountains and jungles of Horizon have taught me to treasure every living being I encounter. They prepared me to treasure and honor Catriona and know that my heart and hers beat as one eternal love song." There were many smiles among those gathered, especially his friends from the first spaceship journey. "Catriona is the treasure I vow to honor every moment of my life. Because of her I am more of a human being and I pledge my life to this exquisite flower who wishes to grow with me. The strings of our hearts are entwined through all time and space."

Igor paused and gathered himself to recite the poem that had just entered his mind.

"An endless horizon of happiness is all I have dearest Catriona.

I see you, stars dancing in your eyes, beautifully serene,

Giving promises, sharing vows made magnificent by friends drawn from the universe.

You know True Love, my Catriona

And have brought me there to love beyond measure.

You nurture my soul, sustaining two pilgrims as one True Love

An endless horizon of happiness is all I have dear Catriona."

Then it was Catriona's turn to speak her vows. Only she did not speak, she sang them. Catriona closed her eyes, breathing in her darling Igor, Marguerite Bay and everyone she loved. Then she began to sing.

My Precious One, listen to the song of my heart.

Peace and Joy fills our life as we commit to each other

Rainbows sparkle and dance guiding our way.

See the stars Precious One, as they shine in the darkness.

Hear the wind Precious One, as it whispers your name.

Feel the warmth of the fire, as it glows in the darkness.

Feel the calm Precious One in the still of the night.

Close your eyes Precious One feel the freedom within

Gratitude fills our hearts for all that has been.

Dance with me Precious One in the wonder of Life.

On the wings of Brother Eagle let your spirit fly high.

Close your eyes Precious One feel our hearts beat as one.

Feel my love Precious One, as I kiss you good night.

Her last beautiful note rested on the ocean as a whisper. It was carried by the soft wind caressing the shoreline. Igor was struck dumb by Catriona's voice. Tears poured down his face as he bowed his head to the source of his life standing beside him. There was not a dry eye in the community. Catriona's song touched every single heart with memories of joy and happiness.

Sian had to take a deep breath of composure to continue the ceremony. She spoke to Igor and Catriona, thanking them from her heart for consolidating their friendship in such deep love. George presented the rings at the right time and received a thumbs-up from Tom. The ceremony was soon over. Sian pronounced Igor and Catriona as husband and wife. Before they could resist, Liz and Johanna abetted by Sian herself picked Catriona up and raced her into the ocean. Tom, Luis and Marshall did the same for Igor. The blessings of the ocean for this marriage. There was complete, dizzy joy. The children shrieked with delight at the soaking wet wedding party and joined them in the waves to sing their well-rehearsed songs.

Cappie had pulled together his cooking team and like magic a wedding feast was made available for all. A small bonfire was lit, stories of past weddings were told and dancing filled the beach, as Catriona's prodigies played the violin and flute. This was a wedding no one would ever forget. John Barclay, the official historian, wrote it up for posterity in the Oasis archives, just as it all unfolded. In the early hours of the next morning the community bade the newlyweds good night. The now dry children's choir sang one last song that Tom had recently taught them. Luis and Marshall had taken a bed and blankets from one of the Marguerite Bay cabins, placing it inside the tipi, where Liz and Johanna festooned it with jungle flowers. They built up the sacred fire at the center, then left.

Catriona and Igor were still dancing on the beach to their own music, surrounded by the soft silence of the wind along the shoreline. When all was quiet, Igor lifted Catriona in his arms and carried her to their bridal bed in the tipi. They gently bonded with sublime love making. They enjoyed Marguerite Bay's beauty for the following week before Cappie flew them back to Black Elk Village.

The community at Black Elk Village had been very busy preparing for their return. Nikolai, LongFu and Manny had built a tipi for Igor and Catriona, which was placed on the mound across the river, some way beyond Nikolai's. They had one parachute left of the same blue colour as that used by Igor in Marguerite Bay. The women wove a beautiful floor of sweet scented cedar boughs. To Manny's astonishment, Rising Moon displayed her carpentry skills. She made elegant shelves, table, tool racks and bed frame in front of his startled eyes.

Rising Moon looked up at him with a grin, "Manny, you are doing just fine looking after our daughter. It was Catriona who showed me how to do this and she left the tools knowing that I would need them. I will teach Catriona Grace to do it one day." Manny was constantly surprised by Rising Moon and whispered to his daughter that they were both so lucky. Rising Moon heard him and stopped her work to come over and embrace them. They also rebuilt the community *inipi,* their sweat lodge. Rising Moon had insisted on this to celebrate Igor and Catriona's marriage with a special *inipi* ceremony to welcome them anew to the community. On their arrival with Cappie, Catriona and Igor were warmly embraced by each person in the village. George somewhat shyly received the same welcome home. Nikolai asked his captain to stay for the *inipi* ceremony that would take place later that same evening. Cappie needed no further prompt and communicated to Liz at Oasis that he would return one day later than planned.

In preparation Manny had previously taken the older boys along the river to gather the grandfather stones for the fire pit. He also showed them how to bend the long willow branches they had collected into a dome held together with vines. This was the frame for the *inipi*. It had an entrance at the West to celebrate new beginnings. Once the frame was complete they carefully covered it with parachute fabric and animal skins. Inside the sweat lodge no light could penetrate other than that given off from the red hot stones.

The entire community entered one by one through the West door, crawling in on their hands and knees with respect for their planet, announcing their names as they entered the womb of Planet Horizon's earth. The only exceptions were baby Catriona and Lan Lan, who asked if she could take care of the baby while Rising Moon was in the *inipi*. Heated rocks were carefully placed in the fire pit inside the sweat lodge. LongFu and Andrew were the fire keepers for this occasion. Manny had his ceremonial pipe, with a stone bowl and beautifully carved stem that entered it smoothly.

He passed it to Nikolai, father of the groom, to lead the ceremony for Igor and Catriona. Nikolai received sweet-grass, herbs, and finally tobacco from the women. He tamped the tobacco into Manny's pipe with the quill of an eagle feather. Then he listened to Rising Moon's chants to the four directions, to the earth of Horizon and to the

Creator, before lighting the pipe with dry grass in flame from the rocks. The pipe was passed from person to person. When directed by Manny, Nikolai said his own prayers of gratitude and respect. The symbolic threads of the pipe ceremony enveloped them easily as they settled into a deep, quiet stillness where time and space seemed to stop.

Manny placed medicines and herbs on each rock. Then he poured water over the glowing grandfather stones in the fire pit inside the sweat lodge. As the heat increased they offered their prayers of thanksgiving and celebration to the Creator and the earth of Planet Horizon. They celebrated their vision for creating Black Elk Village. Manny and Rising Moon skilfully used herbs and medicines to purify and strengthen their bodies and minds. The four rounds of prayer and healing had much humour. The women's round of prayer was full of blatant, bold advice to the newly-weds. They were direct and ribald and earned a great deal of laughter. The men's round was more playful. In this *inipi* ceremony Manny held a round for the children. Their prayers and commitment to Black Elk Village had an intensity that took the adults by surprise.

The community felt no boundaries between generations and genders as they moved into the sublime state of one mind. The ceremony closed with the fire keepers, Lan Lan and Catriona Grace also joining in. The West door was left open, so there was no boundary between inside and outside. Igor spoke his wedding vows once more and waited for Catriona to sing. She did so and stunned everyone into a deep and comfortable silence. When she finished her wedding song to Igor, no one moved. Not a word was said. They all stayed there happily until the heat of the rocks died down.

The peaceful silence was broken by Catriona Grace demanding to be fed.

13: Musings on the Future of Humanity

In the later part of the twenty first century the rabid desolation of Planet Earth was writ large in the regular communications between Planet Horizon and Seymour Hansen on Jupiter One. Seymour reported that the reaction to crises across Planet Earth did not anticipate adaptation or forward thinking. The velocity of Climate Change made the planet increasingly unsustainable for humanity despite the various accords signed by the international community. Democracies such as the United States of America were at the mercy of the powerful carbon-combustion cabal and were rarely permitted to do anything constructive about Climate Change. And so the democracies disintegrated into devastation and anarchy.

China's autocratic and highly centralized government was the only state that could take monumental measures but was riven with internal conflicts. Chinese leaders evacuated the coastal areas and built inland cities to relocate hundreds of millions of people to higher ground but were unable to maintain social order. Their autocratic edicts were resisted by many sectors of the population, even by the army. No other nation had such a command culture as China and it broke down in the face of massive opposition and the accumulating impact of radical Climate Change. This outcome in China was predicted in 2014 when Naomi Oreskes and Erik Conway wrote a provocative sci-fi fiction essay titled "The Collapse of Western Civilization." Their radical view from the future was largely ignored and dismissed as speculative fiction. That was a big mistake, as the International Space Agency

Headquarters in China became compromised and was relocated to Jupiter One.

The steady evolution of settlements on Planet Horizon provided a different trajectory during the darkest time Planet Earth had ever experienced. The success of the Crossroads Village spun off two similar settlements. Oasis expanded to encompass several hamlets within its orbit. The Black Elk Village consolidated two more camps. The regular flow of pioneers to Horizon from Planet Earth embraced the required orientation to create commonly understood ethics. Crossroads Eco-Village became an additional orientation center to Marguerite Bay. Johanna and Luis facilitated a similar program there, while Tom and Sian continued at Marguerite Bay. On Planet Horizon there was a steady move to currency, financial agencies and markets for the proliferation of settlements. Seymour Hansen had built his vast financial empire by exploiting every loophole in the global financial structure on Earth. He knew precisely the regulations required to prevent Capital morphing into overwhelming greed and power. His team drew up protocols of strict regulations to prevent the predatory speculative options that had created disintegration on Planet Earth.

To accommodate the influx of three thousand pioneers, Seymour and the Oasis Council had long deliberations about creating eco-towns on Horizon. This led to the establishment of the first one, inland on a more temperate series of interconnecting plateaus. Self-sufficient neighborhoods of elegant architecture and easy access were established as the foundation stone of the town. A public transport system was planned without personal vehicles. The eco-town was engineered to be ecologically friendly and socially inclusive and all neighborhoods contained community gardens and permaculture zones.

Each sector had a council that contributed one person to the town council. Marshall was voted in as the first mayor. He, Liz and their young family were ready for the challenge. Seymour's wisdom and wealth were part of the design. He established a series of small independent companies to provide a manufacturing and business sector to connect to the markets already established by the three eco-villages. Green tech industries were a priority. His loyal assistants were in charge of the companies and all financial links back to him were severed. They abided by the set of financial regulations crucial to the new venture of expanding communities on Planet Horizon. Education, medical care, music and recreation were a responsibility supported by the companies. No company was permitted to get too big and the emphasis throughout was on preserving ecology. Business operations ploughed thirty per cent of profits into a communal fund for the eco-town in addition to taxes. The energy source was a lattice of sophisticated solar units and one company was established to furnish this. The search for carbon based fuels was forbidden.

Five years after Catriona's wedding, Seymour intimated to Tom and Sian that he wished to spend his remaining years on Horizon. He had transformed the Jupiter One Station into a mega city with manufacturing, research and communication sectors. He had initiated orientations for pioneers passing through, based on the model sculpted by Sian and Tom on Horizon. Their friendship had strengthened over the years, as Seymour had leaned on their wisdom and compassion to overcome the tragedy of losing his family to the massacre by a vicious militia. He felt that his time on Jupiter One was complete and now seventy-five years old, though still brisk in demeanor and thought, he wished to be part of the growth of Horizon.

It was no surprise for Tom to see Seymour Hansen disembark from one of the regular spaceship runs to Oasis. He was tall, with receding grey hair and a slight stoop to his shoulders. The granite glint in his eyes had softened. He smiled and warmly embraced Tom and Sian, when he stood on Horizon for the first time, taking in the breeze from the ocean and listening to the sounds of the forest close by. He could at last experience a pristine beauty that had long disappeared on Planet Earth. He breathed in a sigh of relief to be with his good friends. He reminded them both of the first time he had met them, ten years ago in 2080 on the UN steps in Geneva. That it was Sian who had the grace to embrace him gently on that occasion. They smiled at the fond memory.

What surprised Tom, but not Sian, was that he did not wish to establish himself with the business sector of the eco-town. His choice was Oasis. He sat on their comfortable verandah, overlooking the waterfall and forest, feeling totally at ease. He expressed faith in his capable assistants, who were glad to be assigned to the eco-town. With a broad smile, Seymour said to Tom and Sian in his deep voice, "I have enjoyed following closely the impact of Oasis, even going so far as to introduce some of your orientation protocols to Jupiter One Station."

Seymour looked strained as he said, "Ever since I lost my family to eco-militias I have been looking for a better way to live. I found part of it on Jupiter One, as my business fortune transformed into options that served settlements here on Horizon." He stopped talking, stood up and warmly shook the hand of Cappie who had just arrived to visit him. "My dear Cappie," his voice boomed like a foghorn, "My forte is cooking, as Tom well knows. I would love to be part of your cooking team, as I understand that is the vital cog for creating community."

Cappie chuckled at the welcome and replied "You would be most welcome Seymour, but you do realize there is much more than the cooking team driving the engine."

Seymour nodded in agreement. "Yes, of course. There is much to discuss, perhaps you can bring me up to date on what you have so skillfully created on Horizon." Sian looked over to Tom with a confirming smile. Both received a broad wink from Cappie.

Seymour said, "I also want to do the full orientation at Marguerite Bay and live my life at Oasis. I hope Master Chung is still in residence as I have been studying Buddhism." His deep booming voice dropped a few levels as he revealed his spiritual yearning.

Tom interjected softly, intuiting where Seymour was searching, "Chung is here at Oasis, but does not care for the term Master, though that describes him well. I will take you to his retreat hut tomorrow. He has made quite a difference to Oasis with teachings on the daily practice of mindfulness. He trains the children and women in martial arts. That is his way to show it is not necessary to be Buddhist to be alert and mindful." Tom reflected for a moment, "What I admire most about him is that every year he keeps his promise to a little girl, Ruthie at Crossroads Village, and spends three months there taking his mindfulness to that community."

There was a comfortable silence until they heard an intense tone to Cappie's voice when he started to speak. "There is something else I would like to propose now that Seymour has joined us." He took his time to locate the best words, "We have been hard at work over the years establishing settlements along the lines of a design we all approved of. I think it is time we came to a stop and deliberate on what it is we have created. How did we do it?

263

How did we prevent the loss of generosity? My proposal is that we usher in a philosophical musing based on our collective experience."

"Cappie!" exclaimed Sian, "I have been thinking exactly that. What a great suggestion. How about we structure our musings in an open discussion with the community? I can ask our historian to record it so the discussion can go to other settlements and bring forward their views. That would be better than Martin Luther nailing a Manifesto to the door. What do you think?"

She looked around at her friends gathered on the verandah, while the jungle and river framed them in the evening light. They were smiling their consent. Sian continued, "I would like to talk about Climate Change, but from a particular perspective. Do you remember the encyclical brought out in 2015 by Pope Francis? I have long treasured that brilliant and brave speech from earlier this century. I could present his considerations to the community."

Sian's offering sparked a fiery flash in Cappie's eyes.

"Wonderful suggestion Sian," said Cappie. "Our historian has all the fancy equipment to make a virtual record. I feel that something brilliant could emerge" They all agreed and asked Cappie to continue speaking. Sian reached out and fondly touched him on the shoulder. Seymour leaned forward to take everything in.

Cappie said, "My navigator Nikolai and his wife Elena grew up in the culture of Tolstoy and introduced me to his writings. I can speak to the choices we made for Horizon in terms of community responsibility and during the jihadist battle. Somehow we have been able to maintain a generosity and sense of integrity that was lost on Planet

Earth when things drastically deteriorated. That has been on my mind in recent months."

"How insightful Cappie," Seymour spoke quietly. "I am in a good place to discuss the economic travesty on Planet Earth and how to avoid it. I can also examine the rants of George Orwell and Pirsig about civilization." Then he laughed out loud. The echo traveled along the neighboring river. He looked over to Tom, "There is another rant I remember from our friend Tom at the UN in Geneva ten years ago. That really stung me personally, yet inspired the first step to finance the space mission to this planet."

Tom grinned at the reminder and said, "Go easy on me Seymour."

Sian stifled her laughter and Cappie slapped his hand on his thigh at Tom's momentary discomfort.

Sian's practical nature added to the emerging consensus, "We must bring John Barclay, our historian, into the conversation so he can anticipate how to record this overdue deliberation, virtual reality or hologram." She thought pensively for a moment, "We have been talking about these issues for years, but not in any consistent way as we winged it with respect to our vision for Horizon. I like the idea of hearing Robert and Joyce's views at Crossroads and also the thoughtful friends at Black Elk Village. This recording could turn into an heirloom for Planet Horizon. I am so excited, someone squeeze me please."

Tom smiled and obliged, while Cappie left to find John Barclay with a request that the scientists address their work at the Marguerite Bay laboratory.

The philosophical musings discussed that evening caused a buzz in Oasis and throughout the neighboring hamlets. Maggie volunteered to be the MC, leaving Mary to talk briefly about the clinics and health care they had established.

A week later on one sultry day, cooling down in the afternoon under a hot sub-tropical sun, their deliberations were ushered in. Everyone was there in the elegant open-air dining place.

John Barclay readied his equipment. He recorded the surroundings, with a scenic take of the late afternoon sky, over to the ocean waves beyond the ridge, capturing the elegance of the cabins, the lush jungle vegetation and curious birds.

Then he focused on the community as they gathered, zeroing in on their faces.

Maggie smiled a warm welcome to the community and introduced John Tinsley, convener of the science team.

John was a short, skinny man with a mane of unruly hair and nicknamed as the 'mad professor.' He eloquently outlined the scientific mandate centered on the laboratory at Marguerite Bay, emphasizing that everything went beyond all expectations.

He said, "My greatest surprise was how science became an inclusive part of the community. One of the first things we did was to create a Young Scientist's Club along with mentorship programs for interested adults. It was like a small university, which soon overflowed into the school established in Oasis. Some of us even became unexpected school teachers." There were many smiles from parents and children.

266

John continued speaking after running his fingers through his wild hair, "Perhaps our most significant step was the success of the fertilized embryos of animal species in deep freeze. The biologists were able to bring to maturity sheep, goats and hens with a seventy per cent success rate. The two breeds of dogs were more robust and I can see quite a few border collies and standard poodles in our midst." Sian's poodle, named Lily, let out a delicate burp to show her approval. Everyone laughed.

John added, "We had no idea of the impact of space travel on these specimens. The team of biologists had to quickly adapt their usual protocols to unusual conditions. They did a fantastic job as the results of their work now populate the three eco-villages and the animal pens at Marguerite Bay."

Mary stood up with a question. She was very intense, "Were any of the fertilized deep frozen embryos human?"

John stopped for a moment before answering, even his hair settled down at the question.

"I am glad you asked that question Mary. Yes, there were. The Planet Earth director of the Space Agency insisted on this in case our population should be depleted by unforeseen circumstances."

A ripple of surprise went through the community. "The other scientists and I were uncomfortable with this edict. We felt it was wrong, too much like a Frankenstein horror movie. As a group we discussed the issue with the leaders of Oasis Council. There was total consensus that such a project was not in accord with our ethics. It was not a direction we could take." There was loud applause from the listeners.

John said, "As scientists we never felt separate from the community. We felt strongly that what we saw evolving at Oasis and Marguerite Bay did not require such biological intrusion. So the human embryos were destroyed. The biologists were happy to deliver dogs, sheep, goats and hens." That brought a smile of relief to Mary's face. She thanked John and sat down.

John said, "Our engineers and astrophysicists helped to design smaller spaceships and worked on strategies to navigate the dense particle field in the upper stratosphere of Horizon. We made significant adjustments to spaceship design so that travel here is safer. Now for something else, let us have a cheer for the botanists."

The community responded in unison with whistles and cheers as the botanists stood up and took a bow.

"I am not a botanist, but sometimes I wish I was," said John. "What could be more exciting than creating orchards of fruit saplings to join the abundance of tropical fruit trees already here on Horizon? It was botanists who found a copse of coffee bushes near the Crossroads Village. I think they saved Tom's life as Crossroads regularly send sacks of coffee beans, which we process. Tom needs his 'java' and so do we."

Tom stood up and took a bow, waving his coffee mug in his hand and gestured for John to continue.

John spoke about the astronomers. "Thanks to the prompts from our young scientists, the astronomers are charting the beautiful night sky above us and the movement of Horizon's two moons. Look over there." He pointed to the east where the first moon was just beginning to show, "That one is named Rose and the other one that will appear in about an hour's time the children named as Apollo.

Having two moons every night is something that excites us as much as the children."

He glanced round the young members of the Science Club sitting in the front and gave them a smile before speaking directly to them, "Some of you have worked with the drone team which has been mapping the vicinity we live in. We occupy only a tiny part of this planet and the drones provide a birds-eye view of the incredible terrain around us. So far we have not discovered any signs of habitation other than animals, birds, rivers, ocean and forests. But perhaps we can consider all these items as part of our extended family. That is the philosophy we learned from Rising Moon and Manny. I would call it Elder Wisdom Science."

John beamed a huge smile to the youngsters, "The scientists are sitting alongside you, so talk to them about what they are up to. But before that conversation takes place I would like to point out the two most surprising things for us scientists." The audience waited in anticipation. John said, "As you know the scientists rotate in shifts at Marguerite Bay and part of our work is to be custodians of the place as well as lab rats." That brought out quite a laugh. "We absolutely love taking care of that paradise next to the ocean on Five Mile Beach, and know that it greatly benefits the wider community. But what we love the most is that the children invited the musicians amongst us to join their choir and orchestra."

The children yelled out their approval. John smiled and finally said, "There is much more I can tell you, but let us have five minutes of Ask a Scientist."

Mary thanked John and invited him to enjoy the applause. She added, "John has not mentioned the enormous assistance the lab has given to the clinic established in Oasis. The scientists created medicines from local plants so we can treat the sub-tropical infections that arise. Have your five minute conversations with a scientist before our next speaker is up."

Five minutes later Maggie introduced Seymour as the benefactor who made settlement on Horizon possible. Spontaneously, every one stood up in gratitude. Seymour was taken aback by their gesture. He felt a few tears well up behind his glasses.

He took a moment to regain his composure and bowed gracefully. "Thank you." His booming voice mellowed to softness as he said, "All of you kept my imagination and hopes alive.' He took a sip from his cup of water. "I would like to tell you the story of events that brought us to this beautiful planet."

The pioneers were riveted as Seymour continued to speak. "Our species is pretty good at creating problems, which we usually solve in one way or another. But in the recent Industrial Growth Civilization on Planet Earth things ran away from our problem solving capabilities. Ecological short sightedness and corporate greed blocked scientific common sense. It is such a breath of fresh air to hear John speak about the inclusiveness of science on Horizon. Thank you John." Applause came from the audience.

Seymour said, "Human nature became defined by symptoms of greed, corruption, fraud and corporate control. This overlooked the history of aboriginal cultures who knew how to share, endure and conserve their ecology. They had an inherent view of long term sustainability characterized by planning seven generations into the future. I am so happy to learn that such Wisdom of the Elders has been implemented in Black Elk Village by Rising Moon and Manny."

There were many fond smiles at hearing the names of two of their leaders.

"However, the global economy did not accept any of these proven historical strategies of thriving. It evolved to gross financial manipulation and a state of accepting no limits. Powerful corporations morphed into an out of control monster that failed to sustain the well-being of human society and Planet Earth. Sustainability was not in their vocabulary and people became disconnected from one another and from Nature. The truth, as you all know from being here, is that Nature is the matriarch of all creatures and that includes us."

One of the children put up her hand and asked, "Does that include Oliver, my dog?" Seymour smiled, "Of course it does. Perhaps you and Oliver can take me for a walk with your parents after this and we can talk more." He remarked, "Let me continue before I take off with Oliver. " The young girl giggled.

"Citizens of Planet Earth became dazzled by technological power and relied on someone else's definition of economy and society. That someone else was something else, the carbon fuel cabal, and it did not have their best interests at heart." He waited for that thought to sink in. "So what happened over the past hundred years to bring about all this tragedy to Planet Earth? I will simplify the events so the younger children can follow the logic."

He took another drink of water from his cup. "What evolved during the Industrial Growth Civilization was a complex web of powerful corporate and government interests that became known as the carbon fuel cabal. It was not just energy industries in oil and gas. It extended into the manufacturing and servicing sectors. Also into mining, pharmaceuticals, high tech and other large scale corporations. All of which were swallowed up by corrupt financial institutions which ran the marketing and advertising sectors. And that included the bank I was once President of." His confession, given with a grim smile, was well received.

"This collective power extended through the media and was successful in making science and ecological concerns into public enemy number one. The extensive regulatory agencies of this cabal had a bottom line for profits only. It was so influential that it stopped nations doing anything constructive about climate change. This powerful, intermeshed cabal circumvented the Climate Change accords agreed upon by the international community. So effectively did they discredit scientists blowing the whistle about climate change that the necessity of taking early precautions rarely took place. Billionaire members of the cabal financed effective campaigns to create denial of climate change, paying rogue scientists huge amounts of money to lie to the general public. The cabal was in charge globally, yet clearly knew what was happening. But they chose continuing profits while gas and oil extraction continued at an exponential rate."

They all waited for Seymour to carry on speaking. "How do I know all this and how can you believe what I am saying?" He looked sternly at his audience before speaking again. "I was once a prime member of this cabal, yet I still chose to listen to scientists and took careful notice of what was happening to the global economy and ecology. I eventually quit!"

Seymour was stopped by thunderous applause.

"I quit. But taking out my billions of dollars did not affect the carbon fuel cabal in the least little bit. It had become so big, entrenched and interlocked with other powerful agencies that it seemed to have a mind of its own, beyond anyone's control."

This slowly sank into the minds of the listeners.

"I divested my large fortune from fossil fuels and placed it into solar, wind and wave power. And when Tom spoke at the UN in Geneva in 2080 to an audience of the power holders, I was there to hear him."

He beckoned to Tom to stand up and take a bow.

"Tom delivered the greatest speech on Climate Change I have ever heard. He surpassed the historical rants of other strong voices and rattled my cage vigorously. So I bankrolled the space project that brought us all here."

Everyone stood up to give Seymour and Tom a standing ovation.

Seymour had one more thing to say, "Mark my final words very carefully. The carbon fuel cabal is our primary teacher. We now know ahead of time what will keep us connected while we take care of nature. The new eco-town in the interior is shaped by what we have learned. We know what to avoid and know how to do it in this new beginning for humanity." There was another standing ovation as Tom walked over to embrace his friend with an affectionate hug.

Once the celebration died down, Maggie called on Sian to speak. With quiet elegance Sian stood before the community and revealed an unusual spark of stand-up comedy.

She said, "You are familiar with Tom's famous speech at the United Nations in Geneva. I think we should start calling it "The Rant that Rattled Seymour Hansen.""

Tom and Seymour laughed at her mischief and wondered what was coming next.

"I do not need to go into the causes of Climate Change, as that has been laid out in Tom's UN speech and by Seymour's address to us. Instead, I want to go back in time to 2015 and bring to your attention the human consequences presented so clearly by Pope Francis in his encyclical on Climate Change – *Laudato Si'*. And then to impress upon you the importance of applying his directions here on Horizon."

She looked around at the eager faces, especially the children who were hanging on to every word she spoke. "In addition to being Pope, Francis also had a brilliant scientific mind. He offered precise scientific analysis about the intertwined cascade of factors that ushered in runaway climate change. The cascade effect was not well understood. Once a series of tipping points interconnect and reinforce one another it draws in further tipping points with a trajectory that cannot be reversed. The conversation after the international Climate Change accords should have been about adaptation rather than trying to reverse the process. I will not take too much time with this as I am anxious to hear Cappie speak. So let me reduce this 2015 encyclical down to what we need to take in for ourselves, right now on this new planet."

She concentrated on what she would say next and noticed the color of the flowers that had been placed in front of her. A deep purple orchid surrounded by white ones. She breathed them in.

"Pope Francis was clear in 2015 that the way of life on Planet Earth no longer worked. His conclusion, drawn up seventy five years ago, was that Climate Change imperiled humanity's existence. He stated that desolation

274

was inevitable unless we radically change how we live. His encyclical is full of concern for the poor, destitute and the most vulnerable. He launched a direct attack on the way the world operates by criticizing the acceleration and distraction of economic dynasties that over-rode all other concerns. His advice to us from the past is to change our ways. I summarize them as:

- Get rid of individualism and greed.

- Hold dear our connections as human beings.

- Reject self-centeredness and self-absorption.

- Truly care for our brothers, sisters and Nature.

Sian stopped talking and remained silent for several minutes, feeling the wisdom from the past entering present day life on Horizon. Then she said, "I am quoting different phrases from the encyclical, but want you to see the parallels it has with this beautiful planet. It is a sacred duty in my mind that we create and foster a caring, sharing community and apply that in equal measure to the environment we are blessed with. I may be preaching to the choir, as we have this as our basic ethic for being here." There was a collective chuckle from the audience.

Sian said, "Pope Francis was realistic about the powers-that-be of his times. Listen to this quote: 'The most we can expect from our leaders is superficial rhetoric, sporadic acts of philanthropy and perfunctory expressions of concern.' His realism extended to rich countries that cultivated a throwaway consumer culture. He chastised politicians and business moguls alike for putting profit before the common good. We heard from Seymour a moment ago just what happened over the past hundred years. The carbon fuel cabal was able to obstruct every anticipatory step that would alleviate the distress of the poor and vulnerable."

She glanced again at the beauty of the orchids, wondering who had picked them. It must have been Tom she thought. She began to speak again. "Pope Francis provided a powerful call in 2015 to protect Planet Earth. This was a moral and ethical imperative, for without it we would all certainly die. He also rebuked the slowness of action, the timid lack of prevention that denied climate science the opportunity to redress matters. He was not unaware of the power structure in the Industrial Growth Civilization and how deeply it was entrenched across the planet. His was an advocacy of environmentalism for the poor first of all."

The children were absorbing every single word Sian uttered.

"What I want to strongly impress upon all of you is that Planet Earth was a sacred gift. Just as Planet Horizon is a sacred gift. It is up to all of us to take care of and be good stewards of this planet that has so graciously received us. Rising Moon and Manny are exactly on the same wavelength as Pope Francis, to see the earth as sacred and worthy of our respect. There is so much else in the Pope's 2015 encyclical. I have selected only those threads that reflect on how we choose to live on Horizon. Let us live well and walk with a sense of integrity on the face of Horizon."

She knelt down and picked out the purple orchid and held it to her bosom. There was a deep and lovely reception of everything she had said.

Cappie walked slowly from the back of the crowd and made his way to where Maggie and Sian were standing. He was smiling to the community, young and old, all of whom adored him.

He had provided inspiration, steadiness and fun in his prime capacity as master chef of the cooking team. These values had permeated through the other teams, as Cappie circulated within the different work groups in Oasis.

"You look like Father Christmas," shouted a young fan, "Your hair is white and so is your beard and you are chubby."

Cappie laughed along with everyone. He placed his notes on the table in front of him and took in the faces of those gathered there. "I am just waiting for the red suit to be delivered," he said. That brought much laughter, which quickly fell quiet as Cappie began to address them. "I will talk to you about a Russian thinker I greatly admire. What he had to say impacts the direction we have established here on Horizon."

Tom and Sian exchanged knowing looks. They anticipated what was coming and Cappie certainly delivered.

"Lev – or Leo – Tolstoy was a Russian philosopher. I learned about him in the Space Academy from my navigator and his wife. You remember Nikolai and Elena?"

There were many heads nodding in the audience.

"They grew up in Russia with the culture Tolstoy advocated. They know much more than I, so look forward to them speaking on this recording when it goes to Black Elk Village." He provided a brief history. "Tolstoy died at the age of 82 in the year 1910. During his lifetime he was widely acclaimed as 'The Conscience of Humanity.' That persists right up to present time, almost two centuries later.

277

The core values he expressed are in sync with the 2015 encyclical from Pope Francis. Tolstoy was convinced that the cultivation of love was humanity's bottom line to create enduring ethics that would thrive. He created a universal unity from the proliferation of world religions and ethical ideas. What emerged was a brilliant tapestry, a clear direction to be responsible, loving and caring. This is not idealistic but totally down to earth.'

He stopped and took a cup of water from Maggie. He thanked her and took a drink.

"Now what does this direction look like and how relevant is it to what we have done on Horizon?" There was another pregnant pause, "Tolstoy framed his writings within a reference to Christianity, but his views are best described as a humanist spirituality, without archaic church structures and without oppressive state militarism. His refreshing solution was to create the conditions for people to be authentic and responsible. This began with a co-operative style of community that encouraged personal example as the driving force. Look around you at your parents and their friends for a moment."

This was addressed to the children.

Cappie waited for them to glance around. "You are looking at the people who made Tolstoy's dream come true."

There were some tender hugs exchanged between the generations.

"You have all experienced the strong work ethic we have on this planet. That is one basic way of bringing a sense of responsibility alive. In the clinic and school at Oasis there are no hired cleaners, everyone takes care and responsibility. The doctors, therapists, teachers, children

278

and parents do the work to maintain cleanliness and effectiveness. The same ethic runs through all the teams and we get the chance to move from one team to another. So we become skillful in irrigation, permaculture, building and of course cooking."

A loud cheer went up for that statement.

"You heard from John Tinsley that the scientists take turns to maintain Marguerite Bay for our use and recreation. And they love doing so. We just use our imagination to co-operate and invent ways to make things move smoothly. Do not forget that we sing and play music together. This is essential. I offer a big thanks to Tom. His wood working Shop makes a constant supply of musical instruments. The teaching of the choir and orchestra with the children always includes most of us. This is our spirit of co-operation, the willingness to share and be supportive. We learn how to cross the bridges of misunderstanding and are fortunate to have many wise mentors amongst us, starting with Sian and the healers. I ask Sian and her gang to take a bow, please stand up for us." They did so. Sian, Maggie and Mary played it up with pirouettes and were warmly applauded.

"So we are all Tolstoy's children," Cappie exclaimed with a loud voice. "What do we derive from this statement? It does not arise out of nothing. It takes wisdom and deliberate choices so everyone can feel a sense of belonging and become grounded in a steady, caring community. That is a huge achievement. Think of it this way, we have to maintain a delicate balance between high tech, space ships, sophisticated communications and the heartfelt sense of belonging. That strong direction was evident amongst us during the battle with jihadists. We stood together to protect all that I have described from being destroyed. Difficult decisions had to be made."

The grim memory of the helicopter ride with the four sleeper jihadists and their subsequent implosion loomed suddenly in his mind. Cappie's voice was intense, "We knew we would die if there was no defense to combat the jihadist cell, which hijacked a spaceship and was intent in taking over Horizon. None of us would be alive without the carefully designed strategy to combat them. The four sleepers in our midst were treated with compassion and provided with an opportunity to create a lifeway on a distant island. It did not work for them, as they imploded amongst themselves when the target of their ideology, namely us, was beyond their reach. We always have to consider the quality of our decisions, especially the difficult ones. I have to say that the evening discussions after our silent meals are a wonderful forum for reflection."

He dug into his shirt pocket to pull out a card he had written on, "I have a Tolstoy quote on the back of this card. I carried it with me on every space mission. Will you allow me to read it out?" Everyone consented and listened intently as Cappie pulled out his well-thumbed card. He read out loud in his deep baritone, *"Just as one candle lights another and can light thousands of other candles, so one heart illuminates another heart and can illuminate thousands of other hearts."*

There was a profound pause, as they felt the words resonate with the fluttering dance of the early evening breeze. Cappie was quiet for several minutes and softly said, "I believe firmly that is what we have created on Planet Horizon. Just think about the searing love stories in our midst that illuminated our hearts; Liz and Marshall, Maggie and Mary, Johanna and Luis, Rising Moon and Manny, Igor and Catriona just to mention a few. Recall the joy of the orientations at Marguerite Bay and Crossroads Village. Note the willingness of our young people to make the stretch to an eco-town. The way we have chosen to live makes this illumination of the heart tangible."

There was a silence stretching into infinity, full of unsaid words.

Cappie slipped his card back into his shirt pocket and said, "Does this sound familiar to you? Does it resonate with your experience on Planet Horizon?" Cappie waited for his questions to sink in, "Pope Francis's beautiful prose and Tolstoy's philosophy carried an ancient knowledge of interconnectedness so we could become good mentors for all our relations, to people and to Nature. They provide a vision of community that Tolstoy, centuries earlier, outlined for the 'People of the Twenty Fifth Century.' They championed a better way to live and provided directions to be the loving heart of the Earth and Cosmos. That is us, a community beyond its time."

Cappie suddenly smiled to his audience, "Please my friends take in the guidelines I have offered to you this evening. Make it so in your everyday lives. Thank you for listening to me."

The children jumped up and down with a special glee. They knew what was coming next, yet had been sworn to secrecy. Cappie was not quite finished. He said, "Now for my final surprise." Cappie did a little jig much to the delight of the children. "Rising Moon taught the children how to do a circle dance when she was last here. It includes the entire community. I have covertly arranged for the children's choir, with flutes and drums, to lead this dance and celebrate all that we have created on Horizon."

The choir organized themselves under the moonbeams flooding over them from the two moons, Rose and Apollo.

The children were at the front and they held hands with one another. They began to chant the delicate rhythm of the circle dance just as Rising Moon had taught them.

The drums and flutes picked up the cadence for the children to then grasp the hands of their parents, friends and neighbors.

They were all happily drawn in as they moved, dancing and singing around the tables and benches, along the trimmed pathways of Oasis, over to the ridge that protected them from the ocean, to the trail that lead to Marguerite Bay and then back to the benches and tables.

Tears flowed down Tom's face as he took the whole vista into sight.

He linked his arms with Seymour and Cappie who were deeply moved. "We did it my friends. We did it Sian. We did it!" he exclaimed as he stood up readying himself to join the children's dance.

Sian gently kissed Tom on the tip of his nose, "No Tom, we did not do it. They did it."

She gestured to include the entire circle of dancing people. "Just look at how the children are leading, while parents and neighbors follow them with pride. We just provided direction. These wonderful beings shaped it into a reality that is tangible and enduring. My prayer is that their directions will be followed by future generations."

She smiled gently to Tom, Seymour, John and Cappie – her best friends in the new world, "Now, let us join in the dance."

About The Author

Ian Prattis is an award winning author of fourteen books. Recent awards include Gold for fiction at the 2015 Florida Book Festival (*Redemption*), 2015 Quill Award from Focus on Women Magazine (*Trailing Sky Six Feathers*) and Silver for Conservation from the 2014 Living Now Literary Awards (*Failsafe: Saving the Earth From Ourselves*).

Julia Ann Charpentier says of Ian Prattis: "His admirable command of language brings to every scene a striking visual clarity." Of his Gold for *Redemption* Anita Rizvi calls it "a riveting novel chronicling one man's journey through the stages of innocence, darkness, destruction and transformation." She goes on to say, "What is so exquisite is the tenderness and honesty with which the author deals with the human condition . . . he refuses to sanitize experience. He depicts the stations of a personal Calvary that ultimately leads to Redemption." His poetry, memoirs, fiction, articles, blogs and podcasts appear in a wide range of venues.

Born on October 16, 1942, in Great Britain, Ian grew up in Corby, a tough steel town populated by Scots in the heartland of England's countryside. Cultural interface was an early and continuing influence. Ian was an outstanding athlete and scholar at school, graduating with distinctions in all subjects.

He did not stay to collect graduating honours, as at seventeen years old he travelled to Sarawak, Borneo, with Voluntary Service Overseas (1960 – 62), Britain's Peace Corps. He loved the immersion in the myriad cultures of

Sarawak and was greatly amused by the British colonial mentality, which he did not share. He worked in a variety of youth programs as a community development officer and also explored the headwaters of Sarawak's major rivers, with expeditions into Indonesian Borneo.

Returning to Great Britain after Sarawak was an uneasy transition. He did, however, manage to stumble through an undergraduate degree in anthropology at University College, London (1962 – 65), before continuing with graduate studies at Balliol College, Oxford (1965 – 67). At Oxford, academics took a back seat to the judo dojo, rugby field, bridge table, and the founding of irreverent societies at Balliol.

Yet, by the time he pursued doctoral studies at the University of British Columbia (1967 – 70), his brain had switched on. He renewed his passion for other cultures, placing his research on North West Coast fishing communities within a mathematical, experimental domain that the discipline of anthropology was not ready for. Being at the edge of new endeavours was natural to him, and continues to be so.

He has been a Professor of Anthropology and Religion at Carleton University since 1970 and has worked with diverse groups all over the world and has a passion for doing anthropology. "It's better than having a real job," he says, "everything changes and the only limits are imagination and self-discipline." His career trajectory has curved through mathematical models, development studies, hermeneutics, poetics and symbolic anthropology, to new science and consciousness studies. The intent was always to expand, then cross, existing boundaries; to renew the freshness of the anthropological endeavour, and make the discipline relevant to the individuals and cultures it touches.

He studied Tibetan Buddhism with Lama Tarchin in the early 1980s, Christian meditation with the Benedictines, and was trained by Native American medicine people and shamans in their healing practices.

He also studied the Vedic tradition of Siddha Samadhi Yoga, and taught this tradition of meditation in India. He was ordained as a teacher and initiator, the first westerner to receive this privilege, and is acknowledged in India as a guru. Since meeting Thich Nhat Hanh, the Vietnamese Zen Buddhist Master, he found a way to take his experiences to much deeper levels. He received the Lamp of Wisdom from Master Hanh in 2003 as a Zen Dharma teacher.

Later in life he lived in a hermitage in Kingsmere, Quebec, in the middle of Gatineau Park forest when his pet wolf was alive. He now lives in the west end of Ottawa with his wife Carolyn, with the Pine Gate Meditation Hall in their basement. He edits an online Buddhist Journal and is the resident Zen teacher of the Pine Gate Mindfulness Community in Ottawa, which began in 1997.

At the outbreak of the Iraq war he founded Friends for Peace Canada a coalition of meditation, peace, activist and environmental groups to work for peace, planetary care and social justice.

Since retiring from Carleton University in 2007 he has authored four books on dharma, two on the environment, a novel and a legend/autobiographical combo and enjoys the freedom to create at his own pace. He received the 2011 Ottawa Earth Day Environment Award at the Museum of Nature.

He has yet to discern the ordinary meaning of retirement!

Manor House
905-638-2193
www.manor-house.ca

Ian Prattis / *New Planet, New World*

Manor House
905-638-2193
www.manor-house.ca

Manor House
905-638-2193
www.manor-house.ca